Y0-AWG-320

DEADLY HIGHWAY

DEADLY HIGHWAY

Super Highway Beta 1.0

J. Stewart Willis

Copyright © 2018 by J. Stewart Willis.

Library of Congress Control Number:		2018901384
ISBN:	Hardcover	978-1-5434-8225-6
	Softcover	978-1-5434-8226-3
	eBook	978-1-5434-8227-0

All rights reserved. No part of this book may be reproduced or transmitted in any form or by any means, electronic or mechanical, including photocopying, recording, or by any information storage and retrieval system, without permission in writing from the copyright owner.

This is a work of fiction. Names, characters, places and incidents either are the product of the author's imagination or are used fictitiously, and any resemblance to any actual persons, living or dead, events, or locales is entirely coincidental.

Any people depicted in stock imagery provided by Thinkstock are models, and such images are being used for illustrative purposes only.
Certain stock imagery © Thinkstock.

Print information available on the last page.

Rev. date: 01/30/2018

To order additional copies of this book, contact:
Xlibris
1-888-795-4274
www.Xlibris.com
Orders@Xlibris.com
767330

To Michelle and Jim for their love and uncompromising support.

CONTENTS

PROLOGUE

Lieutenant Colonel Charlie Hendricks got out of his vehicle and walked over to the wreck of a Humvee. He looked in the driver's compartment and saw blood puddled and drying black on the seat and the floor. In his mind, he pictured the explosion, the vehicle thrown to the side, the explosion compressing brains inside skulls, men thrown against the Humvee's twisted frame, jagged metal penetrating human flesh, minutes of pain for those still conscious, hands grabbing them and carrying them to helicopters, the feeling of agony as they listened to the beat of the chopper blades, medics giving them shots, waking up on a medevac plane headed for Germany and the horror of convalescence.

Charlie stared. He didn't have to be there, but he had to see. When the call had come, he'd jumped in a Humvee and joined one of his lieutenants in a convoy of a wrecker, a flatbed, a backhoe, a grader, a truckload of gravel, and an infantry squad in a personnel carrier as they proceeded out of Kabul to the east on the Nangarhar Highway. The lieutenant could have handled things by himself just fine. Just recover the wrecked vehicle and patch the road. All routine. But Charlie couldn't stay at his desk. This was where an engineer's action was, and he had to be there.

Charlie had one month left on his tour. Orders for his next assignment at the Pentagon were already cut. His promotion to bird colonel was coming up. He'd wait until then and retire. The writing was on the wall. His promotion would come a year after that of some of his contemporaries, the men who were still in the running to become general officers. There was no use hanging on, although Charlie knew he would miss the army.

Charlie leaned down and picked up a piece of shrapnel, twisted and sharp-edged. He shook his head. Flying through the air, burning hot, it could have taken off a man's arm. Charlie would take it back to the office and put it on his desk with the three scraps of shrapnel that were already there. He would contemplate them at quiet times and think about what they represented.

They were ugly, ugly, ugly—visceral—and fascinating.

CHAPTER ONE

How the hell did I end up in this job? Charlie Hendricks thought to himself as he got off the Blue Line and headed for his office in Rosslyn. He crossed his building's grand foyer and joined a packed elevator, his thoughts continuing. *I did it because I was scared. Twenty-two years in the army and not a single early promotion. Two tours in Iraq and one in Afghanistan, but nowhere.* He thought of the airfields and roads he'd built and repaired, of the dredging he had managed in New York Harbor when he'd worked for the New York District. He had tons of experience, but no future in the army. He hadn't wanted to put in thirty years, be forced to retire, and have to look for a job when he was in his fifties. He had thought that he would do better at forty-four.

He arrived at work just before eight on Monday morning. He sat down at his desk and turned on his computer. He then got back up and went to get a cup of coffee. He thanked goodness that Eddie Bixby had gotten there early and started the coffeepot. With his coffee in hand, Charlie returned to his desk and sat down. "Thanks, Eddie. I really need this coffee. You're a good man."

As Charlie started to pull up fedbizops.gov, Eddie Bixby looked up from his computer. "Hey, Charlie, it's finally here!"

Charlie Hendricks got up from his desk and hurried to look over Bixby's shoulder. "It's about time. This could make us for years. Almost as good as a new fighter or bomber."

"You think we should go tell Davies now?"

"No. We need to know what we're talking about. Download the solicitation, print out a couple of copies, and let's at least scan it before we go to the big wheels."

"That will take a little while. I bet there are hundreds of pages."

"We still need to do it. Need to separate the meat from the boilerplate. I'll go make sure the printer has plenty of paper."

"Okay. I'll start the download."

Charlie filled the paper trays. "Okay, the printer is ready."

Charlie returned to his desk and studied the solicitation on his computer screen. Finally, he heard the printer begin to grind away. He thought to himself, *Hallelujah. Maybe this is the answer to my prayers.*

He and Bixby were in an office on the tenth floor of an office building in Rosslyn, Virginia. It would have been an impressive location if the office had windows. Unfortunately, it was an inside office. The big wheels had the windows with a view overlooking Theodore Roosevelt Island with the Kennedy Center and Watergate in the distance, across the Potomac River. He and Bixby were part of the Government Relations Office of the Bedford-Ewings International Corporation, a fancy name for the lobbying office. However, Hendricks and Bixby did no lobbying. Their job was to track business opportunities offered by the federal government. That meant spending time reading through government documentation on the Internet. It wasn't the interesting job Charlie had wanted.

Despite having retired from the army at the age of forty-four, Charlie had still found that the job market was tight. He had used the military network, contacting retired officers in various companies in the Washington area. One of the people he had contacted was Brigadier General Sidney Davies, who was deputy here in government relations. Davies had warned him that the company primarily used electrical engineers, mechanical engineers, software developers, and logisticians. Davies had thought Charlie might work into general management or maybe logistics and got him an offer of a job starting in the Government Relations Office. In short time, Charlie had realized it was grunt work, nothing challenging, but he had to start somewhere, and here he was. He hated it.

The paper that was being printed was a solicitation from the Department of Transportation for the initial phase of the replacement of the Interstate Highway System. That sounded like civil engineering to Charlie, but he knew he wouldn't be building anything. B-E International didn't do that. The company took on the management

2

of contracts. It was called system engineering. To bid on a contract of the size of the replacement of the Interstate Highway System, B-E would put together a team of companies with different areas of expertise and integrate their work to accomplish whatever had to be done. Although B-E wouldn't be building anything, Charlie was sure the system engineering aspect would require civil engineering experience in dealing with whatever company did the construction. He was going to jump on the opportunity as soon as he could.

Bixby pulled the papers from the printer and handed a pile to Charlie, who divided them into sections and put clips on each. He would refine the sections later when he better understood how the solicitation had been assembled by the DOT.

He watched Bixby return to his desk and begin his own assembly process.

Charlie had little in common with Bixby. They sometimes ate lunch together, but no friendship had developed. The guy was nice enough, but he had been in this office for three years and would probably still be at the same desk when he retired. Bixby was glad to have a job that didn't demand too much, just an overall perspective of what the company could do. He had been around long enough to have a good feel for that.

The truth about working at B-E International was that Charlie would probably never make good friends there. He'd have associates. He would even like a lot of them and enjoy lunch with them, but when the day was done, he and they would go home to widely dispersed locations in the Washington area, or he would go to the Pentagon and play handball with guys he had known in the army, where the handball players were a group who knew one another. His friends would come from the neighborhood where he lived, probably friends that his wife made.

Charlie lived in Springfield. Bixby lived in Warrenton. There was no way they could share a thing.

Charlie and his wife, Linda, had bought the house more than twelve years earlier when he was assigned to Fort Belvoir. Its cost had strained their finances. They had lived there for two years doing almost nothing outside the home. They had no money to spare. It had been a real sacrifice to buy the house, but it had worked as planned. Linda stayed there while Charlie spent tours in Iraq and Afghanistan, and they lived there when he returned from Afghanistan and was assigned to the Pentagon. The home had provided stability that many never found in the military. They still had friends in Springfield from ten years ago, and Charlie's two boys had the remarkable experience of a number of years in the same school system.

Charlie studied the solicitation. It was going to be run out of the offices of the US Department of Transportation on New Jersey Avenue in Southeast Washington. That seemed a little out of place to Charlie. He wondered why the department wasn't on Independence Avenue or some other more imposing place. He figured Metro must have some way to get there. As he read more, he found they were going to set up an annex in Savannah. *Goodness,* he thought to himself. *That might be a nice place to live.* It would get him and his family away from the hubbub of Washington, D.C. He decided that, if B-E won the contract, he'd have to look into Savannah some more.

CHAPTER TWO

Gunnar Davidson swiveled in his desk chair and stared out the window of his office in the Bedford-Ewing International Building in Fair Oaks, Virginia. He admired the view into the thick woods behind the building beyond where the grass was carefully mowed up to the edge of the trees. The underbrush had been cleared from under the trees for fifty feet or so into the woods, which gave an almost unreal sparseness to the view. He thought that it must be European in appearance, perhaps German.

Davidson's nerves were on edge. He was excited about the solicitation from the Department of Transportation. He was going to be briefed on it at nine this morning, but he had already read it. The briefing was a formality to get things going.

Davidson had been a Virginia State senator from Southeast Virginia, a territory of naval bases and shipyards. When Frank Bladyslaw had run for the Presidency, Davidson had been a leader of his candidacy in Virginia and had received his reward for his efforts, having been nominated and approved as Under Secretary of the Navy for Research and Development. It was a plush job, but it had only lasted four years, as Bladyslaw, the nation's first Polish President, had not been reelected. It had been long enough, however, for Davidson to get to know the Washington world and to make contacts throughout the city. That was enough to sell himself to B-E and become the vice president of its Washington-area operations.

In Washington, B-E had numerous contracts for software development and support, various logistics contracts, and others for the packaging of specialized communications systems. Their clients were in the Department of Defense, the State Department, the Department of Energy, and NASA. B-E, which had its headquarters and most of its operations in Los Angeles, owned two buildings in Fair Lakes and rented space in seven other buildings in Northern

Virginia and one in Maryland. That was Davidson's kingdom. It seemed large, but by the standards of the operations on the West Coast, it was small. The West Coast had an organization that included areas of expertise from which necessary personnel could be drawn to fill needs as required. They were called laboratories, although they did little research. The Washington operations were not big enough to do that. When Davidson's operations won a contract, the expertise needed had to be drawn from other contract work and then the vacancies created had to be backfilled. Sometimes he had to ask the West Coast for the managers he needed. That didn't make him happy. If a manager was willing to transfer from California to Washington, Davidson wondered what the motive might be. Maybe he or she wasn't making it on the West Coast.

Davidson already had his mind made up as to who would manage the Interstate Replacement Program, or the Super Highway as industry had begun to call it. The manager would be James W. Wade who had been part of the Washington operations for several years. Wade was already a project manager for a program they were running for the Department of Defense. Taking him off that project would not make the DOD happy, but the problem would settle down in time. He would tell the DOD contracting officer that he was bringing in a skilled manager from the West Coast. Davidson prayed that the new manager would play the part and do well.

Looking out the window calmed Davidson's nerves. It was peaceful. He remembered his view from the Pentagon, with roads full of cars going everywhere at an unnerving pace. He was glad to be gone from there. His current salary was three times as much as he had earned as a senior bureaucrat, and he now had a golden parachute. Further, he no longer had to waste time testifying before Congress. His office was bigger, too. And his commute was shorter. He was becoming happy with the job. But as a new manager, he needed a feather in his cap. The replacement of the Interstate Highway System was going to provide the prestige that was needed.

Davidson had been afraid that the West Coast would try to run the contract from out there. He had made a major effort to ensure it would be in his territory, traveling often to Los Angeles and working management aggressively to emphasize the need to be in the backyard of the Department of Transportation, since the project would be run from there and the initial work was going to be on the East Coast. He had won, and the work was about to begin.

There was a knock on the door of Davidson's office. Ralph Evenson, Davidson's deputy, stuck his head in. "Are you ready? The briefing team is here from Government Relations and can begin any time."

Davidson rose and headed for the door. He carried nothing. It was all in his head He and Evenson entered the conference room, where James W. Wade, Sid Davies, a man named Danny Fortiano, and two other men were waiting. They sat down and faced a large screen that had been pulled down from the ceiling. Davies rose. "Sir, as you know, we have received the much-anticipated solicitation from the Department of the Transportation for the construction of what will be the prototype of the highway that will replace the Interstate Highway System, a new system often referred to as the 'Super Highway.' The formal title of the solicitation is the Interstate Highway Upgrade Test Bed Design, Construction, and Implementation Project. In software parlance, it would be a beta version of both hardware and software. I would like to introduce you to a new member of my office, Charles Hendricks, who has prepared a briefing, which he will now present. Eddie Bixby, whom I believe you know, will be working the slides from a laptop."

Hendricks, with a laser pointer in his hand, stood as Davies sat back down. Bixby flashed the title slide up on the screen. Before Hendricks could say anything, Davidson spoke up. "Welcome, Hendricks. Do you go by Charles or Charlie?"

"Charlie, sir."

"Okay, Charlie. I just want you and Bixby to flip through the slides when I tell you to. I can read just fine. If I have questions, I'll ask. Go ahead to the next slide."

Hendricks stood with his hands crossed in front of himself, feeling something of a fool, as Bixby flashed through the slides.

Davidson asked no questions.

When the slides had all been flashed on the screen, Davidson leaned back in his chair. "As you all realize, this contract is big. Whatever company wins the contract has the potential to make billions over many years. This solicitation is just the first step. This is a fly-off. We're to develop a concept for the new highway and propose it. Based on all the proposals submitted, the concepts of two companies will be selected, and the two winners will be asked to make proposals for the actual construction of a twenty-mile stretch of the new highway parallel to Interstate 95 in Georgia. Success to that point has the potential to lead to major contract work in the future. Every major company in the States will be bidding on this. We're going to need to put together a systems engineering proposal and will need to team with a major construction company and a power company. Hopefully, any software and electronics can be developed in-house, although we may need help from the West Coast."

He turned to Wade. "Jim, I want you to lead this. I hope you're well rested from your trip to Hawaii."

Wade turned slightly red. As did all the B-E managers, he made frequent trips to the West Coast and to projects the company was overseeing. His United Airlines miles added up and enabled him to take periodic golfing trips to Hawaii. It was one of the undiscussed perks of being on a government contract.

Davidson continued. "Finding a respectable construction company is going to be tough. The international ones like Bechtel are going to want this for themselves. You need to put together a team quickly. We have three months to get a proposal ready. I'd like concepts on my desk in four weeks. If you have trouble obtaining partners, let me know, and I'll help. Any questions?" He glanced quickly around the room. "Thank you, gentlemen."

Davidson stood and left the room with Evenson in his wake.

Wade sat, looking a little stunned. He felt the burden of what had been assigned him. It was the problem with being successful. You got the tough ones—the ones that required success.

He looked around and sighed. He looked up. Hendricks was standing by him. "Sir, there's going to be a lot of civil engineering involved in this project. I'm a civil engineer and would appreciate the opportunity to work with you on this."

Wade looked at Davies, who was smiling. "He's a good man, Jim. He talked to me about this before we came over. I was also wondering if you needed a deputy."

Wade looked back and forth between the two. "I guess you're my team."

*   *   *

Eddie and Charlie packed up the projector and the laptop, let the screen wind back into the ceiling, and left the conference room.

As they walked through the lobby, Eddie noted, "So, you're going to leave me?"

Charlie was suddenly concerned about Bixby's feelings. "Hey, it's nothing personal. I'm a civil engineer, and this may be the only opportunity this company offers. I'd like to work in my field."

Eddie realized he had sounded like a whiny little kid. "Hey, I understand. You're not the first. I understand ambition. Just seems like I lose partners before I can break them in."

"I understand, but, to me, this is exciting." Charlie wanted the subject changed.

As they settled into Bixby's car for the drive back to Rosslyn, he asked, "Tell me about this guy, Gunnar Davidson. Seems like he's wound tight and impatient."

Eddie looked around as if someone might be listening in the car. "He's not an engineer, not even technical. He's a politician who got an assignment as a deputy of some kind at the Pentagon when Bradyslaw was president. I think B-E hired him because of his Washington contacts. I think he roars through the slides because he doesn't know enough to ask questions, although he wants it to look like he already understands everything. At least he's smart enough to turn things over to his managers."

Charlie nodded. "Okay, so the manager is this guy Wade?"

"Yeah, Jim Wade. He's been bouncing around for twenty years or so running different projects. He's running a classified one now. Been doing it for a couple of years. I guess he's being pulled off that."

Charlie wondered about that. "He looked a little shell-shocked."

Eddie concurred. "He sure did. I think he was comfortable where he was and would have preferred to stay there. But this is big and very important to Davidson. The proposal is going to put a lot of pressure on everyone, especially Wade."

"Okay, I can see that. I guess I'm jumping into it." Charlie continued to educate himself. "How about this guy Fortiano?"

"Danny Fortiano. Yeah, he's Wade's man. Goes with him everywhere, as if he had something on Wade. Thinks he's a real hotshot. Stevens Tech guy. Spent a few years in the army and got out. He'll run over you if he gets a chance."

Charlie looked over at Eddie. "I appreciate the info and warning."

"Hey, you didn't hear any of it from me."

CHAPTER THREE

Linda Hendricks had waited for this for twenty years. She was settled in Springfield in a home she and her husband had owned for more than twelve years, but she had never felt it was permanent. It had been a haven in the tempestuous life of an army family. Many people wouldn't consider army life as tempestuous, but it had felt like that to her. It had felt like being buffeted in a storm, bouncing from one place to another. Sometimes she had wondered if it was worth it, if living with Charlie was fulfilling her dreams. He loved the army and the adventures it offered. She did not.

Now there was hope. Their house in Springfield had always felt like it belonged to a temporary, passing phase of their lives. Now it was becoming a home. Her husband was out of the army, and her two sons were both in high school, old enough to care for themselves. She was, finally, able to do what she had wanted to do for years. She had gone to work for a caterer. Periodically, over the years, she had worked in temporary catering jobs but had never been able to plan on what tomorrow would bring. Now she had joined a catering firm, Yvonne DuBois Catering, in Washington, where it served the government and diplomatic communities. It was what she wanted to do and was an exciting world. Often she worked late and returned home well after the family had gone to bed. Charlie wasn't always happy about that, but she felt it was her turn. Charlie and the boys could care for themselves.

Linda thought about all this as she drove around the Beltway. She was headed for a planning meeting at Walter Reed (Walter Reed National Military Medical Center) in Bethesda. It was a planning meeting for a fund-raiser for the construction of a building, a hostel for long-term visitors who had loved ones in the hospital. It wasn't a government building and would be built off the installation. Nonetheless, the hospital was interested in the building and felt it needed to provide liaison. As a result, they had volunteered a conference room for the meeting in the main building tower at the hospital.

Linda exited the Beltway onto Rockville Pike toward DC. When she got to the hospital, she turned in and stopped at the gate. She had been given a pass to a parking lot in Building 55 and got directions at the gate. Going to the parking lot, she passed a large complex of buildings. After she parked, she wasn't sure where to go. She knew where the tower was but didn't know how to reach it. She decided to play it safe and walk around the complex to the front door, pulling a rolling suitcase of catering items behind her. It was a long way, and she was glad she had allowed extra time. In the lobby, she asked directions to the conference room and headed for the elevator.

Linda found four people in the conference room ahead of her. They looked at her expectantly. She offered her hand to a man dressed in a naval uniform. "Hi. I'm Linda Hendricks from Yvonne DuBois Catering."

The officer shook her hand. "Hi. I'm Commander David Alspach representing the hospital. Let me introduce you to these other folks." Two women stepped forward. He introduced the younger woman and then the older lady. "This is Jeanie Carville of the Wives of Wounded Warriors Support Group and Betty Gaskins of the Gold Star Mothers. They are the leaders of this effort. And the gentleman in the back is Stephen Davenport from Senator John McDonald's office. This project is of major interest to the senator, and he is lending his support to putting the fund-raiser together."

A handsome man in is late forties or early fifties with hair that was just beginning to gray came around the conference table and took her hand in his. "Hi, I'm Stephen. I'm pleased to meet you. I've worked with Yvonne before but never had the pleasure of meeting you. Are you new?"

"Yes, I just started with the company three weeks ago."

Davenport smiled charmingly. "Well, Yvonne must be impressed with you to send you out to plan an event like this. How about a cup of coffee?"

He turned to a credenza at the side of the room and began filling a cup from a large dispenser. "What do you like in it?"

"Just a little cream. Thank you."

Davenport passed her the cup and picked up his own from the table.

Commander Alspach spoke up. "We're waiting for one more, a representative from the site of the event, the Goshen Towers Ballroom in downtown Bethesda."

Linda had been glad Alspach had said his rank. She had no idea what his sleeve was trying to tell her. She's had trouble in the army, too. When she was young, she had wanted to give rank to people who were not in uniform in accordance with how they looked or how they impressed her. It had been all right to call sergeants captain, but she didn't call anyone sergeant, knowing officers wouldn't appreciate it.

She turned to the ladies. "This is a big project you're taking on. How did you get involved?"

Jeanie Carville spoke for the two. "The hospital has facilities for long-term visitors, but they're in high demand. We want to increase the availability. Betty and I met in the visitors' building here at Walter Reed. My husband is here and will be for some time. Betty, unfortunately, lost her son. We're both the victims of IEDs in Afghanistan. There are men who stay here a long time, and it's hard on the loved ones. We want to make it better."

Linda looked at Betty. "I'm so sorry about your son."

Betty looked down. "I appreciate that. But now, I need to work on the future, to help others."

Linda felt inadequate. "My husband was in the army, both in Iraq and Afghanistan. I feel very fortunate that he wasn't hurt." She was working on her own but somehow felt her past connection to the army made her more a part of what was going on. She hated that. She wanted to leave the army behind.

Linda wondered if she really did feel fortunate. She knew there had been danger in Charlie's assignments, but she had always taken it for granted that he would come home. His assignments had mostly been a nuisance for her, leaving her to take care of all the bills and house maintenance by herself and to raise two boys. She suddenly realized that things could have been a lot worse.

Stephen Davenport put his hand on Betty's shoulder. "These are two brave, determined ladies and are to be much admired. This is a major effort they've undertaken. As I've said, Senator McDonald has thrown his weight behind this, and our office is preparing a mailing list. He's going to ensure this is a first-class event with Washington's major players invited."

The conference room door burst open, and a ruddy-faced man with curly red hair burst in carrying a bundle of scrolled papers. He looked a little flustered, his tie a little loose and his sport coat flapping around him. "Sorry, I'm late. This involved more walking then I had expected."

He put the papers on the table and began unrolling them. "I'm Ben Swaim from Goshen Towers. We appreciate your planning your event for our facility." He turned to Davenport. "And you are?"

Davenport looked a little amused. "I'm Stephen Davenport, representing Senator John McDonald's office, and these ladies are Jeanie Carville and Betty Gaskins who are managing this effort, and the third lady is Linda Hendricks from Yvonne DuBois Caterers." He then motioned to Alspach. "And this is Commander David Alspach from the hospital, who is liaising with the ladies and has been kind enough to provide us this conference room."

Swaim quickly moved around the room shaking hands and then returned to his papers. "I have here the floor plan of our ballroom. I have it laid out with tables for three hundred people and three bars. I'm ready to talk about what we can provide."

Everyone sat at the table and began discussing the event. They spoke of the nature and size of the tables and chairs and of the bars. Swaim provided the information and discussed kitchen facilities available off the ballroom. Linda opened her suitcase and brought out samples of tablecloths, napkins, china, glassware, and silverware. The group discussed it and made their decisions. Based on the items chosen, Linda offered pictures of possible centerpieces, and one was chosen, with the request that some red, white, and blue be added.

Linda was ready for that and offered solutions. Finally, they went over the food and bar requirements and then discussed the labor that would be involved. Swaim and Linda provided costs, and the women decided on a price to ask of the attendees. Davenport increased it by fifty dollars. The women wondered if they could really charge that much, and Davenport said it was no problem. Everyone looked pleased.

As they got up and started out the door, Linda remained behind and started packing her suitcase. Davenport asked if he could help and brought things to her. "Do you have to drag that thing all the way back to your car?"

Linda thought it was a bit of a stupid question, but she wanted to stay pleasant. "I'm afraid so. But I'm used to it."

"Where are you parked?"

"In the parking lot, Building 55, behind this building."

Davenport nodded. "That's a long way. May I help you with the suitcase?"

Alspach smirked and looked away. Linda was a pretty woman. She wore a wedding ring, but still she was pretty. A young man might not think so, but Alspach was in his forties."

Help was what Linda was hoping for. "That would be very kind of you."

Linda and Davenport went down the elevator, and Davenport turned to the rear of the building, leaving Linda standing in the lobby. "Hey, where are you going?"

Davenport looked back. "Through the building. There's no sense in walking around."

Linda was pleased and grinned. "You know your way?"

"Sure. Senator McDonald comes here all the time to visit the injured."

They proceeded through a labyrinth of halls, Linda feeling thoroughly lost. They passed numerous men in wheelchairs, some being pushed by young women and older men. There was even one man lying flat, facedown, on some kind of mobile stretcher. She tried to avoid looking at the injured men. They finally came out a door across from the parking lot. Davenport led the way into the lot, and Linda took over and found her car. "That was wonderful. It cut the time in half, and you did all the work. Thank you. Where are you parked?"

Stephen opened the driver's door of Linda's car, and as she got in, he said, "Oh, my driver's out front. He'll wait for me. It's been a pleasure. Drive safely."

CHAPTER FOUR

In the afternoon, Jim Wade called Davies and Hendricks to come back to Fair Lakes and had them and Danny Fortiano follow him downstairs. They went to the cafeteria because Wade's office was in a classified area where Davies and Hendricks couldn't go. It was awkward, but Wade couldn't find a conference room on short notice. They got coffee and sat at a table well away from everyone else.

Wade looked at Davies and Charlie. "Look, I appreciate you two offering to help. Have you ever put together a proposal before?"

Both said no.

"I thought so. Well, Danny has some experience and will help. We need to put together a team with some experienced guys, plus some good design people. I know a few I'd like to get on our team and will start working on getting them today. Their bosses may not want to let them go, even if it is only for three months. I'll also pull some typists away. The projects won't like it, but I'll tell them it's what Davidson wants. He didn't say that, but he'll back me up. Sid, do you have anyone in your office who might help, typing or otherwise?"

"Might pull a typist for a while, but that's about all. The office is already losing the two of us."

"Okay. I'll start squeezing heads. I'll get us a large conference room on the first floor. Give me your phone numbers, and I'll have Daphne, my secretary, phone you and let you know where it is. We'll plan to hold a kickoff meeting tomorrow with whomever I have at that time, say at ten o'clock. You have any problems with that time?"

"No."

"Good. Okay, in preparation, I want you guys to put together a list of power companies in the Southeast, everything from GE to the utilities. I also want a list of construction companies, a level or two below Bechtel, but still ones that have done major work, especially on roads. Get a list of what they've done. If they have worked in or have offices in the Southeast, that would be good. But if they are big enough, that's not mandatory. You think you can do that?"

Davies and Hendricks said they could. Wade nodded. "Okay, let's get things on the road."

CHAPTER FIVE

Danny Fortiano rolled his Mercedes E-Class sedan into the underground parking lot of his highrise apartment building in Ballston, Virginia. The building wasn't as tall as some of the newer high-rise buildings in Arlington, farther in toward DC, but it was older, with larger apartments and a view of the chaos of Glebe Road and North Fairfax Drive. He could stand for twenty minutes at a time at the window of his fifth-floor apartment admiring the commotion. And his wife loved the mall within walking distance. As far as Danny was concerned, it was the perfect place for a couple with no children.

He took the elevator up to his apartment, unlocked the door, and entered. "Bella, are you home?"

Belinda "Bella" Fortiano shouted back, "In the den, going over bills."

Fortiano went to the kitchen, took out two glasses, and poured wine—white for Bella and red for himself. He carried the glasses to the den, set the glass of white wine by Bella on the desk, and settled into his leather lounge chair. "Where do you want to go for dinner?"

"I don't know. Let me think about it." She picked up her glass and sipped. "Heard you guys are going after a new contract."

Danny nodded. "You must have talked to Wade's wife today."

"Yeah, Bonnie rode the Metro into town, and we had lunch. It was time I didn't have, but we need to keep the boss's wife happy."

"I agree. After seeing her, you may know more about what's happening at work than I do. I've been moved to a new job. As you said, it's working on a proposal for a new project. I went to a meeting with Jim this morning in Davidson's conference room. Jim's leading the proposal and has asked me to work on it with him. He's scheduled a kickoff meeting at ten tomorrow morning. I'll meet with him at eight thirty and get into the mix early."

"That's good, but you know Jim's going to take care of you."

"Yeah, but I'm tired of managing activities for him. I want to step up so that I'm in a position to run a program of my own."

Bella swiveled in her chair and thought, *Stick with Wade, Danny. It's far safer.*

She had a full figure and as she swung around, Danny admired it as usual. "You look great, babe."

Bella smiled. She liked to be told that, although, now in her midthirties, she was beginning to worry some about her weight. Eating out as much as she did was becoming a problem, and salads were so boring. "I think we'll eat in tonight. Do you mind a salad?"

"I don't mind if I can broil a steak to go with it."

Danny wasn't a cook, and neither was Bella. At least he could broil a steak, and he kept them on hand for such situations.

"So, what else did Bonnie have to say?" he asked.

"Oh, she had just gotten back from one of Jim's golfing trips to Hawaii, brown as a berry. Talked all about it. She shops and basks on the beach while Jim plays his game. Since her children have left the nest, she seems content with that kind of life."

"Hell, if you want to get brown, we can go as soon as things have settled down on this new proposal. Right now is not a good time to go if I'm going to make a move. But after that, we'll go get you toasted."

It was an easy statement to make. Bella had brought money to the marriage. She had also brought the aggressive and pushy attitude of her father, Bobby Conway of the Washington law firm of Conway and Harrington. With the money and her job came the apartment, the two Mercedes automobiles, and the extra parking space they paid for the second car in the apartment garage. Bella had wanted to live on Connecticut Avenue. It was one of the few things about which she and Danny hadn't agreed. They had settled on a neutral location between his job and hers on K Street, where she helped manage a firm that organized conferences and conventions. Her salary was more than Danny's, but she was careful not to rub it in. She knew that someday he might be making more.

Danny couldn't imagine Bella being comfortable with the life Bonnie Wade lived. She had too much energy. She worked in an exciting business in Washington and loved to entertain. She had a whole set of high-flying friends. She included some of the Bedford-Ewing people in her parties, often including the Wades, who were always impressed.

Bella and Danny finished their wine and made their dinner. While they ate, Danny asked what Bonnie was working on.

"We're setting up a boat show at the convention center. It's the annual event we've had the last two years. Good job. We need to keep it. It's two weekends from now. You need to plan on being alone."

After dinner, they went to the bedroom. Danny turned on the television and propped the pillows up on his side of the bed. He lay down and spread his legs. Bonnie climbed in and lay down between his legs with her back to him. He put his hands on her hips, and she rubbed the muscles in his legs. She let his hands go where they wished. It was Danny's daily entertainment. She leaned back and turned her head to kiss him. "I love you, babe."

"I love you more."

Bella leaned back and thought about Jim Wade and the condom in the plastic bag in her freezer, stashed well away from Danny's steaks. She loved to remind Jim Wade about it and watch him sweat. She smiled. Danny was going to be okay.

CHAPTER SIX

The conference room was set up with a lot of small, Formica-topped tables and uncomfortablelooking straight chairs with metal frames and tan, plastic seats. It looked like a schoolroom, but then it was temporary. The proposal team would move to its own rented offices soon.

Jim Wade stood in the front of the room as the various people he had pulled from other BE programs filed in and found themselves seats. When everyone was settled, he addressed the group. "As you all have probably heard, the Department of Transportation has put out a solicitation for the development of the design for a highway system to replace the existing Interstate Highway System. This is Solicitation Number DTIS12717B00001, benignly titled 'Interstate Highway Upgrade Test Bed Design, Construction, and Implementation Project.' It is a contract for design that will result in a fly-off. Two companies will be selected based on their proposed designs. Those companies will then, in the next phase, price and bid on the construction and implementation of a twenty-mile stretch of the new design to be built parallel to Interstate 95 in Georgia. Each of you has on the table before you a copy of this solicitation, which I expect you to read in the next couple of days. We will then settle into more detailed discussions of what each of you is to do."

Wade then turned to a large pad of briefing paper displayed on a stand in the front of the room. He flipped over the first page. "Please excuse the antiquated briefing system, but we only received this solicitation yesterday, and I've spent the time since then trying to put together a staff and organization. As you can see on this chart, I've put Sid Davies in charge of the overall development of our proposal. The most critical part of the proposal is the design. I've asked Danny Fortiano to be in charge of this element. Lionel Haverford will be in charge of logistics considerations. Of immediate importance will be a requirement in his area to ensure that any offthe-shelf equipment included in the design will be available and available in sufficient quantities to complete the construction phase. We don't want a design that depends on existing equipment that can't be supplied when we need it. This is plainly going to be a proposal that will involve a team of companies. Matt Somers will be in charge of systems engineering. His job will be to ensure the design can be supported by the different entities on a schedule that meets our goals. Beverly Byrnes will be our software guru. She is to participate in the design and address the software requirements. As always in modern systems, this is critical. Often the software takes longer to develop and test than the assembly and construction element. We'll need to develop and polish the software during the construction phase so that everything works at the end of the job."

He turned to Byrnes, "Beverly, this is critical. You and Matt need to work together to ensure this can all come together in a constructive way. There is no use proposing a design that we can't deliver."

"Finally, I've asked Dave Swenson to manage the process of actually putting together the proposal documentation. He has a lot of experience but will require cooperation from all of you."

"Now, I've asked Charlie Hendricks to go over the highlights of the proposal using the slides he presented to Gunnar Davidson yesterday morning. This was a package of slides he developed based on a three hundred-page solicitation. It was prepared in one day. Please realize that something done in such a short time may have errors due to misunderstandings or missing elements. As you read the solicitation, please note any changes you believe should made. A package of these slides is included in the back of the solicitation package."

Wade turned to Charlie. "Please go over your slides."

Charlie stood. "Thank you. I'll go through these slides fairly quickly. If you have any questions or want to go back, please ask. As Mr. Wade said, these slides were put together quickly, and I've done my best to translate the solicitation into twenty slides."

With that caveat, Charlie began his presentation, using a handheld slide control and a laser pointer. "The construction of the new twenty-mile section of the highway is to be completed in twenty months. It is to be sustainable, as built, for twenty years. On the highway, all vehicles will travel at eighty miles an hour. Its design is to address all existing vehicles that have been built in the previous ten years and is to move them with no hands-on by the drivers. It has to consider how to address breakdowns and flat tires. Its design is required to be able to handle the entrance to and exit from the system at the rate of twenty vehicles a minute at each entrance and exit. It is to enable a pleasant view of the landscape as the vehicles pass along its route. And, for trucks, it needs to be able to automatically move into and out of weighing stations."

Finally, Charlie noted that the team would have three months less two days to submit the design proposal, with delivery on 20 January of next year.

Jim Wade stood and thanked Charlie. "Clearly, this is a demanding task. The reward, should we win, is enormous. Within the next few days, we'll have a work schedule put together." He turned to Danny. "Davidson wants design concepts on his desk in four weeks. That means we're already behind schedule in getting partners. I want you, Davies, and Hendricks to make contact with potential partners and make recommendations to me in two days. Get our lawyers geared up to prepare contracts. I'd like a list of possible partners by noon Friday. I'd like a team of partners working here by next Thursday. I know that's fast, but we don't haven much time.

That will give us less than two and a half weeks to develop concepts for Davidson."

He looked around the room. "Does anyone have any questions? I'm available to answer them at any time. This room is available at all times. When you are working on this project, use the charge number listed in the cover letter to the package of documents on your desk. I've asked David Swenson to be here all day. He can provide a link to me and arrange to get work you need typed over to the typing pool. I know you all have other projects you're working on. You need to do what you can for them and pass off work to other people. You can move in and out of here as you need to."

He paused a moment. "If there are no questions, please get to work."

CHAPTER SEVEN

Sid Davies, Danny Fortiano, and Charlie stayed behind in the room. Charlie introduced himself to Danny, who had made no effort to initiate an introduction. Charlie tried to make conversation. "I'm glad to meet some of the people here. I've kind of been off away from the action down in Rosslyn. Where do you work here?"

Fortiano looked hard at Charlie. "I'm a manager in the classified program on the third floor."

"Oh," Charlie said. "That must be Wade's current program. It looks like he has a lot of faith in you."

Fortiano shuffled some papers on his desk and said with a kind of indifference, "He and I have been together for a while. He's learned he can depend on me."

Charlie felt like Danny was being condescending. "So, you're a team."

Fortiano gave Charlie a cold look. "You might say that."

Charlie decided to change the subject and looked at Davies, who seemed to be trying to look like he wasn't listening to the conversation. "So, what do we do next? I have the list of possible contractors that Wade asked for, but he didn't address them today. I put them together yesterday afternoon."

Davies took the list from Charlie. "That's because he gave us the job of making contacts.

Did you make extra copies?"

"Yes."

Charlie passed two more copies to Davies, who gave one to Fortiano, who took the paper, glared at Charlie, and commented, "Looks like you're hustling to get ahead, Hendricks."

Hendricks felt chagrined. "I thought it was what Wade asked us to do yesterday."

Davies ignored the banter and glanced at the contractor lists. "It looks like Charlie made separate lists of power companies and construction companies. We don't have any phones in this room to work these people, and we can't go to Fortiano's office in the SCIF," he added, referencing the Sensitive Compartmentalized Information Facility, "since Charlie and I aren't cleared for that project. So let's go back to our own offices.

"Danny, will you work the power companies—find out if any are interested and arrange for them to meet us here as soon as possible? Schedule them at different times. If you schedule a time, let me know so we don't double book."

He turned to Charlie. "We'll go back to Rosslyn and work the construction companies. I'll get you to make the initial contact. I'll follow up on those that show interest, and we'll get them scheduled. Before you do that, though, go by facilities and get three or four telephone lines and a copy machine put in this room. We need to be able to work from here."

Charlie felt a little lost. "Okay. Where are facilities?" He was immediately sorry he had said it. He felt Danny giving him a *you-dumb-fuck* look.

Davies almost ignored Charlie. "Look on the directory in the front entranceway. They're in this building."

"Will do," Charlie responded, feeling like the new guy he was.

He resented that Danny would make calls and make schedules, while he was given a twostep process of making contact and then passing it off to Davies.

Who the hell was Danny Fortiano anyway? The guy looked six or seven years younger than Charlie but was plainly his superior. That would take some getting accustomed to.

CHAPTER EIGHT

Charlie returned home at about six. He had worked the phone all afternoon. He had three companies interested in partnering on the Super Highway and had a formalized list ready to give Davies in the morning. In his phoning efforts, it had become obvious early on that he didn't have the horsepower needed to talk to the people who could make the decisions that were needed. He didn't even have a title. All he could say was that he was working on a proposal for the Super Highway and that he was responsible for making contacts with companies that might work as partners on the project. That didn't carry much weight.

To get home from Rosslyn, Charlie normally took the Metro Blue Line, the same one he had ridden to and from the Pentagon when he was in the army. It was still convenient in that he could stop at the Pentagon to play handball if he wished and jump back on the Metro to go home. He would end up at the end of the line, the Franconia-Springfield Station, where he left his car in the parking lot.

Sometimes, the Metro didn't work for where he needed to go. For the last two days, he had driven his car so that he could cover both Rosslyn and Fair Lakes. As he had driven home, he realized he would be driving for a while. Fair Lakes didn't fit the Metro. He wondered where the project offices would be if they won the contract. B-E rented space as needed. The team would probably be in Northern Virginia, hopefully close to the Metro so they could get to the Department of Transportation without using cars. That would be the smart thing. Time would tell.

As he pulled into his driveway, he was happy to see Linda's car already parked there. He felt like they were passing in the night. She often worked late, sometimes coming home after he and the boys were already in bed. It made him feel uncomfortable knowing she was out there so late. And last night, he had worked late developing the list of potential vendors.

As Charlie entered the house, he heard the sound of the television coming from the family room. He hung his coat in the hallway closet. It was late October, just past the beginning of the federal fiscal year. Usually, his suit coat was enough, but it had been cold this morning, almost a frost, so he had worn an outer coat. As he hung it in the closet, he realized that winter was on its way.

He entered the family room and found Linda and his younger son, Ed, sitting on the sofa and watching the news. His older son, Ralph, wasn't there. "Hi, everybody. Where's Ralph?"

Ed looked up. "Isn't home from football practice yet."

Charlie really knew that already. Ralph had been coming home late since August. "He's putting in long days. Hope he thinks it's worth it."

It went through Charlie's mind that Ralph was warming the bench. They had been to three home games so far this fall, and Ralph had yet to play.

Charlie leaned over the back of the sofa and kissed Linda on the cheek.

As she turned her head back from Charlie's kiss, she said, "Hi. No late work tonight?"

Charlie sighed. "No, but I expect there'll be some in the future. I had to work late yesterday making a list of other companies we might want to work with. I have a lot of learning to do about putting together proposals."

"*Putting together proposals*—what does that mean?"

"It means the government has asked for bids for work. The bid is called a proposal. It has to include a description of the work the company making the proposal plans to do and a detailed description of the labor and materials it will require to accomplish the work. This proposal is a little different in that it only requires the development of a design concept to meet the government's needs. If we win the design phase, we'll next do the proposal for costs and labor in a second phase."

Ed looked interested. "You mean you have to do that all by yourself?"

Charlie smiled at Ed's interest. "No. I'll work with a team, to include partners from other companies. I'm working on identifying those companies now."

Linda pulled her attention away from the television. "I hope that doesn't mean a lot of late work. I have to work late. I hate to think of the boys being home by themselves."

Ed protested. "Oh, Mom, it's no big deal. Ralph and I can handle things just fine. We're not kids anymore."

"Still, I don't like the idea."

Ed looked at Charlie again. "So, what are you guys designing?"

Charlie was pleased to talk. "It's going to by the highway that will replace the Interstate Highway System."

"You mean like levitating cars whipping along at two hundred miles an hour, riding on magnetic fields."

Charlie smiled. "I don't think we're quite there yet. But I suspect it will involve computer control of the travel, perhaps some new way to provide the power to move the vehicles."

Linda showed some mild interest. "You mean we won't have to go to the gas station anymore?"

"No, this would only affect the interstate. You would still need gasoline for driving around town. Besides, what we do has to use the existing automobiles. Further, the new system will take years to build. You can't jump instantly into the future. It would be too much of a fiscal impact, and people still have to get around when they aren't on the new highway."

Ed looked disappointed. "Sounds like I'll be an old man before I see this completed."

"Believe me, son, you're going to see a lot of changes in your lifetime. When I was born, we didn't have computers. We only had color television for a few years, and it wasn't very good. We didn't have movies on DVDs. In fact, we didn't have digital music, and our cameras used film you had to send off for processing. Believe me, life changes fast."

Linda moaned. "We still have to cook dinner. Guess I'd better get up and thaw something."

Charlie smiled. "Now, there's a process that has really changed in my lifetime. We didn't have microwaves when I was young." He turned to Linda. "While you do that, I'll go change my clothes."

After changing, Charlie joined Linda in the kitchen and asked, as she defrosted pork chops in the microwave, "So, how was your day?"

"Pretty much routine, putting together plans for functions, arranging cooks and servers, ordering food and flowers, stuff like that. You're not really interested."

Charlie tried not to be annoyed by the comment. "Sure, I'm interested. A lot of these functions you do sound very exciting. You've talked about some of the people you cater for. Celebrities, politicians, big-time lawyers, athletes, all kinds of interesting people."

"Well, I have to admit it's fun. The other day was especially interesting. I had a planning meeting at Walter Reed for a fund-raiser for a new hostel or hotel for people visiting patients in the hospital, an effort that has the interest of Senator John McDonald. It was instigated and is being managed by two women, a Gold Star Mother whose son recently died at Walter Reed and another woman whose husband is currently there."

"Yeah, what happened to them?"

"They were injured by IEDs."

"Oh, that's bad. I've seen what IEDs can do. It's awful. So how is the husband?"

Linda hesitated. "I didn't ask. It seemed awkward to do so."

"Well, the woman may need a place to stay. He could be there a long time. Hard as hell on a woman."

Linda was sober. "When you were away I didn't think about it happening. Somehow, it was too distant a thought. I didn't believe it could happen to us."

"Well, it could have. I worried about you the whole time I was away. But that's the past now. Now, all I have to worry about is driving on the beltway."

Linda was curious. "But you ride the Metro."

"With this proposal, I'm working in Rosslyn and Fair Oaks. Don't know where I'll be on a given day. And I don't know what the future will bring."

"Sounds like you're going to save gas on the new highway, but we're both going to burn it in the meantime."

"Yeah, saving gas in a metropolitan area is like saving paper in the digital era."

While they were talking, Linda put the dinner together—pork chops, apple butter, and salad, pretty simple.

Car lights whipped across the kitchen. Charlie noted, "Ralph's home," and shouted, "Ed, help me set the table."

Ralph burst in the door, "Mom, where are your car keys? I need to pull your car farther forward. I'm still sticking out in the road."

Linda made a face. "I'll do better. My purse is on the hall table. Let me get the keys for you." Linda hated anyone going through her purse. It was her private territory.

They sat at the table. Charlie asked Ralph. "So, how was football practice?"

Ralph groaned. "Sometimes I feel like the tackling dummy. I hope I keep growing. Maybe next year will work out. Anyway, Mollie came to watch and waited for me to shower."

Mollie was the daughter of a neighbor, a local attorney.

Charlie asked, "Did you give her a ride home?"

"Of course."

Ralph was comfortable having a girlfriend. Charlie thought, *Ed will never be. How did they turn out so different?*

Linda spoke up. "Don't get serious. You're too young. Heck, I had dates in high school with lots of different guys. It's part of fun."

Ralph looked down. Enough had been discussed. "I'll keep that in mind, but it's nice to know you have a date with a pretty girl for the dances."

With that, the table became quiet. Pretty much everything had been said for the evening.

Later, Charlie and Linda would watch television, and the boys would do homework.

CHAPTER NINE

Sid Davies studied Charlie's list of proposed construction partners. "Looks like you have two southern companies, big road builders out of Atlanta, and one company, Futral-Partners, that's national but more into other forms of construction, like buildings, dams, and such. How did they sound over the phone?"

"As you said, Futral is more into construction other than roads, but they've worked highway projects, usually subcontracting parts to other companies. They were definitely interested and offer more for a future that would involve other areas of the country. The other two companies were also interested. They do construction in the sense of roads, bridges, and overpasses, often subbing some of that. Both said they were confident they could manage any construction we needed, but might do some subcontracting, depending on the design. Frankly, it's inevitable there is going to be subcontracting. It's the way construction is done. Only they don't call what they do 'systems engineering.' The issue is that the more companies that are involved, the more difficult it is to meet schedules. I don't know how to avoid it."

"Okay, let me give Futral-Partners a shot. It's no Bechtel, but hopefully it's available and interested. I'll use the others as fallbacks. If we use them, I suspect they'll have to be replaced if we end up building elsewhere."

Davies turned toward his phone and then looked back. "Oh, thank you, Charlie. I appreciate the work."

Charlie decided he had been dismissed and left Davies' office.

*   *   *

That afternoon, Davies met with Jim Wade in the proposal room.

"I've set up appointments with potential construction firms for next week, Futral-Partners for Monday and a road construction firm out of Atlanta, Madison-Atwalder Construction, on Tuesday. I did the latter because, evidently, Futral-Partners has already been contacted by some other companies. Any of these companies is going to do a lot of subcontracting, which always introduces extra profit taking. I'd like to keep that to a minimum, but it's always a problem with managing a major program. Nobody has the skills within their companies to do the whole thing."

Wade agreed. "Clearly, if we want Futral-Partners, we're going to have to compete, so we have to offer something. The issue is having a company with a national reputation, which may appeal to the government and provides continuity around the country if we win this thing. But, as you say, they'll subcontract, maybe even to this Madison-Atwalder Company you mentioned. I'd like to be there when you meet with them."

Davies was relieved. He had been planning to ask Wade to participate. "That would be great. I'd like you to sit in on all the meetings." He handed Wade a paper. "Here's the schedule Danny Fortiano has set up for meeting with power companies, Georgia Power, which has also been contacted by others, and Florida-Southern. I'd like to get partners on board by early next week. We don't know if these guys can react that fast or not. We haven't much time."

* * *

Wade prepared a status report for Gunnar Davidson and had his administrative assistant, Daphne O'Leary, take it up to Davidson's office. He asked if he could call upon Davidson if negotiations got rough.

CHAPTER TEN

Jim Wade had lunch at his country club prior to going home. He wasn't in a terribly good mood. The rest of his foursome had left him immediately after finishing the round, saying they had other things to do. Jim wasn't ready to go home. He hadn't played well and had lost nearly a hundred dollars. The money didn't worry him. It was the losing. He hated it.

He finished his Reuben, drained his beer, and headed for his Lexus. As he drove home, he considered his life. The Hawaii vacation had quickly become a thing of the past. The new proposal had brought him storming back to reality. He had gotten to the point in life where he had a nice contract going that would have fit him for several years. Then, right out of the blue, he had been given this new thing. It's what he got for pushing during his entire career to move up in the company.

Then, Gunnar Davidson had been pulled in to head the Washington offices, and Wade had been cut off from an opportunity to move up. At fifty-four years-of-age, his future seemed to have run into a roadblock. He couldn't go to the West Coast. That part of the company was incestuous and closed to outsiders from other parts of the country. Now, with his future limited, he had been dumped into this new proposal. If he won, it might get him a good bonus. If he lost, he would have to carry the millstone of failure. It was not a happy situation.

As he pulled into his drive, circling in front of his house, he noticed that Bonnie's car was home. He hoped she would leave him alone. He'd like to get another beer and sit and watch football, not think about a thing.

Bonnie met him at the door. "How did your round of golf go?"

Wade sighed. "Don't ask."

"That bad, huh? Well, maybe this will cheer you up. The Fortianos have asked us over to their apartment for dinner tonight."

Wade felt like he had been kicked. "I don't know. I'm a little tired."

Bonnie bubbled. "Oh, you're just down about the golf. Going out will do you good. I'll drive, and you just plan to have a good time."

"You already said yes?"

"Sure. It'll be fun."

Wade thought about facing Bella. He wished he could ask Bonnie to cut off their relationship with the woman, but knew he couldn't. His night with Bella had been one of the biggest mistakes of his life. He didn't mind working with her husband, giving him breaks. Although Fortiano didn't do a great job, he did well enough to make it easy to carry him along. Wade worried about showing blatant favoritism, but he could work it. He just hated getting together with Bella and seeing that little knowing smile. Unfortunately, she was hard to avoid. Bella worked a friendship with Bonnie very hard. Bonnie liked that Bella came from power in Washington and could show her special things in life. He knew Bonnie would never give that up. Still, he wanted to try. "Hell, Bonnie, he works for me. Socializing with them looks bad."

She replied, "What do you mean? No one at work sees us. What we do together is a different world. You engineers would just lead dull lives if wives didn't get you out."

Wade was frustrated. He'd like a dull life with just golf and a few golfing friends.

"Okay. Let me go change my clothes."

When he came back down to the television room, Bonnie had fixed him a plate of cheese and crackers, and a can of beer was sitting next to a frosted glass.

"Watch a ball game and relax. We don't need to go out until six thirty. You'll have a good time."

* * *

Jim Wade parked in the basement garage of the Fortianos' apartment building in a guest parking space that had been reserved for them. As he and Bonnie walked to the elevator, Wade felt like he was in one of the many office buildings he had visited over the years. He felt there was

36

nothing personal about the place, just another entrance to the anthill of buildings in Northern Virginia. It even seemed worse when the freight elevator opened for them, instead of the passenger elevator. He felt he had to be careful not to catch his clothes on the battered plywood elevator lining and was glad to escape onto the Fortianos' floor.

Bella flung the door open, took Bonnie by her two hands, and kissed her cheek. "It's so wonderful you could come. You look happy, darling, like everything is going well for you." Bonnie smiled slyly. "You know you make me happy, Bella. You always do."

Bella turned to Wade and smiled. "And I'm thrilled to have you here, sweetheart. Haven't seen you in a couple of months, and I've missed you." She put her hands behind his neck and pulled his face to hers, kissing him on the lips. She stood back and looked at him. "Sweet as ever, but you look a little beat, like work is getting to you. We need to cheer you up." She turned to her husband. "Danny, do have you something to cheer Jim up?"

Danny shook Wade's hand and handed him a drink from his left hand. "Cutty Sark, as usual?"

Wade took the drink gratefully as Danny turned and kissed Bonnie on the cheek. "Like that smell, Bonnie. New perfume?"

Bonnie was a little sheepish. "Just a dab."

Danny grinned, wickedly. "A dab will do if applied in the appropriate place."

He took her coat and looked at Wade. "No coat, Jim."

Wade looked up from sipping his drink. "Not that cold, and we were in the car the whole way."

"That's confidence. I always carry a coat in case some idiot runs into me. You never know." Danny turned to the rest of the living room, which they had entered directly from the hallway. "Come on in and have a seat. Bonnie, there's a glass of wine for you, along with munchies on the coffee table."

Bella bopped Danny on the arm. "You don't call them 'munchies,' you bumpkin."

Danny pretended shame. "I know, I know. Please help yourselves to the hors d'oeuvres. Note the parsley artistically arranged on the plate."

He heard Bella sigh.

They all sat, and Danny looked at Bonnie. "Jim tell you about our exciting new proposal?"

"Yes, but I didn't feel the excitement. He kind of sounded like it was a major task and would take a lot of work. I think he was happy where he was."

Wade was concerned that she was giving him a bad image. "No. It is exciting. A major opportunity for the company, and I feel honored and privileged to be asked to manage it. But it will, indeed, take an intense level of work in the near term."

Danny concurred. "Yeah, it will be challenging, but Jim has a good team supporting him we'll pull it off."

Wade wanted to change the subject. "So, Bella, you and Bonnie had lunch together this week. Seems like you're doing it about every other week."

Bella smiled. "Yes, that seems to fit the schedule very well. Wish we had some time to shop, but I'm a working girl. At least we make the necessary connection."

Wade tilted his head inquisitively. "'Necessary connection'? That's a strange way to say it."

Bonnie jumped in, almost defensively. "Yes, we like to pass the gossip on a regular basis."

Danny grinned. "Well, I'd like to be part of that."

Bella twisted her mouth a little. "I pass on all you need to know. It's a private transaction between us girls."

Bonnie wanted the subject changed. "It's so nice of you to prepare dinner for us."

Bella smirked. "It's no problem at all. The restaurant next door does it all the time. They were glad to help. All I had to do was keep it warm in the oven."

She turned back to the men. "Jim, you should be thrilled to get this assignment. It shows the confidence Gunnar has in you."

Wade thought, *Hell, I don't even call him Gunnar.* "Yeah, I keep reminding myself of that. It's kind of like a pat on the back, but the thump is hard. It challenges you and says, 'Make damned sure we succeed.'"

Danny followed. "And that we'll do. I've already got some good partners lined up. I'll finalize that part next week and get the show on the road." Wade thought, *Good thing you're in charge.*

Bella was interested. "What do you mean by partners? I thought you did all this work."

Danny sat back and explained. "Oh, no. We're the managers. We bring in people with the expertise needed in different areas, organize and schedule them, and accomplish complex work. It's what we did in the space program. We're good at it."

"So, who's going to be a partner?

"We'll find out this week. I'm bringing power guys in."

"Power guys?"

"Yeah. Companies that engineer and construct what's required to provide electrical power to the program."

"Oh, that kind of power."

Danny looked self-important. "You think it had to do with bodybuilding? Aren't I beautiful enough as I am."

Bella gave him a dirty look. "Yeah, we're the power couple."

Bonnie wanted things settled down. "Hey, you're a good-looking couple. We know that. Any man would be happy to have a woman like Bella. You're a lucky man, Danny."

Danny stretched and looked pleased. "Yeah, I remind myself of that every night when I come home."

Bella reached out and took Danny's arm. "That's sweet, Danny. Let me feel your muscle."

Danny flexed.

Bonnie was a little embarrassed. Wade was annoyed but didn't want to show it.

Danny looked at Wade. "How's your drink doing?"

"It's fine. I'm driving."

Danny nodded. "Hope you can handle a glass of wine at dinner?"

Wade acknowledged, "Should be able to handle that."

Bella got up. "Guess that means I need to serve dinner."

CHAPTER ELEVEN

On Sunday, Charlie and the boys went to church. Linda was doing a wedding. She said it was bigtime. The couple was getting married in the National Cathedral. David hadn't known anything real happened there. From what he knew, the cathedral was just a place where funerals were held for prominent politicians.

It had been a normal but somewhat lonely weekend for Charlie. Friday night, he and Ed had watched Ralph's football game. Linda had stayed home and worked on the wedding plans. Charlie had told her later it was a bad night to miss. Ralph had gotten to play on special teams when his team kicked off and had been involved in one tackle. It had added a little excitement to the evening.

Saturday, Charlie had worked on the yard. In the morning, Ralph and Ed had mowed it one last time before winter and had then gone off, Ed with a friend to the movies and Ralph with his girlfriend to who knows where. That left Charlie to finish cleaning the yard while still knowing the leaves had to fall and that everything wouldn't be finished until after Thanksgiving.

Charlie would have liked to have spent some time with Linda, but it seemed like she was spending the entire day on the phone, checking that the cake, the flowers, and everything else, on and on were on schedule. She was really sweating her job, trying to impress. It was almost as if she owned the caterer and felt that the company's success depended on her. Charlie wondered what she would be like if she really owned the company.

Sunday afternoon, the boys took off again. Ralph was in love. Charlie thought, *In love for the first time. It's all in the testosterone. I survived, and he will too. I'm sure the girls can handle him, but his self-confidence would build, if they let it.*

Charlie sat down before the television to watch a football game, but his mind wandered from the game to his job. Somehow, he had imagined he could move into management in B-E. That's what he had done in the army. There, he'd had guys working for him. In the engineering district he'd had civilian guys under him who had been there for years. He had done just fine. But in the new job, it had become clear the previous week that he was just a worker bee. He wasn't sure where he stood, but he clearly wasn't managing anything. He did what others told him to do.

It was disillusioning.

He sipped his beer. *So, what do I need to do? I need to get involved, play a role in the design, work with the team players, help to write the proposal.* It was going to be hard. This guy, Danny, clearly was Wade's favorite. At least he acted that way. It wasn't so much what Wade had done but the way Danny just seemed to assume his self-importance. Charlie knew he would have to get along with Danny—that he would have to play it carefully.

CHAPTER TWELVE

Linda was in the kitchen of the ballroom where the wedding reception was taking place. The reception had begun, although the bride and groom were still at the cathedral taking pictures. This was always the awkward gap when the guests were floundering around, some uncertain where they were and others just a little impatient for some action. She made sure the bar was functioning and hors d'oeuvres and glasses of wine were being passed. The dinner preparation was well underway. She prayed it would be served at the planned time. The picture taking and the visiting by the bride and groom before dinner at the reception often held things up. It could be nerveracking for the caterers.

Linda would have loved to have been at the ceremony. She tried to imagine a wedding in the National Cathedral. That would really be big-time—about as exciting as a wedding could be.

She was busy helping replenish the trays of hors d'oeuvres. They could use all the hands they could get.

She heard a voice say, "You're not allowed in the kitchen, sir."

A familiar man's voice said, "It's okay. I'll just be a minute."

Linda turned to see Stephen Davenport headed toward her. "Hello, Stephen. I should have guessed this is the kind of wedding you'd be attending."

"Hi. I heard Yvonne DuBois was catering this and thought you might be here. Just wanted to say hello. I know you're busy. I just enjoyed meeting you the other day."

Linda felt awkward. She didn't want to be rude. She liked the man, but she had work to do. "I appreciate that. Hopefully, we'll cater other events that you'll attend. It's nice to see a familiar face."

"Hey, it's a small world. No doubt I'll see you again. Hope things go well."

Stephen turned to leave, snatching a couple of hors d'oeuvres off Linda's tray. He nibbled on one and shouted, "Delicious!" as he went through the swinging door.

During dinner, as Linda supervised the waiters, she noticed Stephen sitting at a table with several people, one of whom she recognized as Senator McDonald. Stephen was in animated conversation with the others and especially with the pretty blond woman sitting next to him. She felt silly as she suddenly felt a bit of jealousy. Linda scolded herself for her foolishness and tried to distract herself with work. Goodness, she was happily married, and it was ridiculous to feel the way she did.

Still, she could imagine the life Stephen was leading, all the excitement and the beautiful and powerful people he mingled with every day. She could picture herself at the wedding, at the table, dancing with the bridegroom, living another life.

She drove home late that evening, still thinking about it all. She could live that life.

CHAPTER THIRTEEN

On Monday morning, Jim Wade was handling all the meetings with the potential partners.

They had started out in the morning with Georgia Power. It turned out that B-E was the second company that had contacted them. They were meeting with the other company on Wednesday. Wade knew, sadly, that was going to leave them hanging without a power company at least until the following week, with no guarantee an agreement could be made. The team discussed how Georgia Power would be part of the design team, how federal requirements controlled profits, how charges would be handled. There was little that differentiated what B-E offered from what other companies would offer. Georgia Power wanted security for the future—to be the power company for all future work that might come from the contract should BE win it and to be able to do all electrical subcontracting. The company wanted to be responsible for the installation of all sources of electricity and its distribution.

Wade wasn't too thrilled. He wanted more control. They would talk to Florida-Southern Power on Wednesday afternoon. Florida-Southern was a little smaller. Hopefully, it wouldn't make such broad demands.

At one in the afternoon the representatives of Futral-Partners entered the proposal room. Most wore suits and looked a little like lawyers. One man was clearly not. He wore a rough tweed sports coat, a tie that looked like it couldn't be pulled tightly around a seventeen-inch neck, and a pair of shoes that appeared to be fairly new work boots. His face was ruddy and his hair fast graying. He introduced himself as Bernie O'Hara and introduced the others. He was clearly the boss.

Wade was accompanied by Sid Davies, Danny Fortiano, and Matt Somers. Charlie was taking notes.

The little worktables in the room had been pulled into a circle. Everyone sat down, and Wade spoke. "Thank you all for coming. As you know, we're putting together a team to make a proposal for the design of a highway system to replace the current Interstate Highway System. Success will lead, in a second phase, to a competition with one other company on the proposed costs of constructing the system. The winner of both phases will have the potential to win the construction of the whole system, although the government will own the design, and there are no guarantees. We're talking about many millions of dollars, probably billions over many years. We've brought you in because we would like to partner with a construction company with a national footprint. We understand that you will be doing subcontracting to accomplish the construction and perhaps even to participate in the design. You have that experience, and we would like that capability as we proceed with the design task."

O'Hara spoke up. "We've read the solicitation and are certainly interested in being part of the team. As you have probably guessed, we have been contacted by other companies to be part of their teams. I know this is only the design phase, but we want to play a significant role in that design."

Wade responded, "I understand what you want. If you play a significant role now, that will mean you will play a similar role in future work. You understand, of course, that this initial proposal is a gamble. If we don't win, we don't recoup any of the costs associated with the effort, so the bigger part you play, the more you lose."

O'Hara nodded. "We're gambling on the future and would like insurance that we will be a part of the future. We don't just want to be part of the design team; we want to play a major part in developing the specifications for the system and in constructing or subcontracting the construction of the system."

Wade conceded this. "We understand that will be your role. However, you must realize that the actual design we come up with will dictate what work will have to be done, and only then can we refine who will actually do what. We are going to have an electric utility involved as a team member, and they will want their share as well. We can only commit to ensure the construction team has and will have a role in anything that is clearly construction. We at B-E will retain the role of overall system engineer, software developer, and designer of electronics hardware for control of the day-to-day operation of the system. Of course we're talking at a general level now and will refine things as we go."

O'Hara considered what Wade had said. "Of course, we would like things pinned down, but I understand the uncertainties here. The future guarantees are critical."

Wade pressed. "I understand your concern. We're willing to provide guarantees, but we will need your initial flexibility as we develop the design. What we need is a quick commitment. We only have three months to get this proposal done, and we need to get rolling."

O'Hara countered. "I well understand that. We're anxious to get going as well. May I ask why you think you're the company to manage this project?"

Wade was ready. "Because the giants in this industry have so much overhead they are going to have trouble competing, and we have the same system engineering experience they have."

O'Hara settled back in his chair. "Okay. I have my businesspeople and lawyers here with me. I assume you have yours on standby. Let's get together and see what we can work out. If it goes smoothly, you've got a partner." He didn't tell Wade that the other companies wanted too big a part of the pie.

CHAPTER FOURTEEN

The Tuesday following the dinner at the Fortianos, Bonnie and Bella met for lunch at an Italian restaurant in Rosslyn. It was an easy drive for Bonnie at midday, and there was convenient parking behind the restaurant. Bella just had to skip across the river.

They kissed each other's cheeks and sat in a booth where they could talk without being heard.

Bella inquired, "How's it going? Has Jim been as busy as Danny? I hate when they get involved with these things. I never see my man."

Bonnie nodded. "I suspect Jim's not coming home as late as Danny. That's one advantage of being the boss. But he might as well not be home. He's worried to death about this thing. Seems to think his life is hanging in the balance. He's mean and moody."

"At least Danny's not mean. He's so tired when he gets home, he doesn't want to do anything but sleep. It's the first time since we've been married that I can't wake him up. You'd think he's lost interest."

Bonnie studied Bella's tight blouse. "I doubt if he's lost interest. Just a passing episode.

Not something I've had to worry about in a while. I just try to stay out of Jim's way."

Bella smirked. "Yeah, I don't think it's permanent. Just lonely and boring now." Then she became concerned. "Jim doesn't hurt you, does he?"

Bonnie protested, "Oh, heaven's no. He wouldn't have the gumption. He'd worry that people would find out and it would impact his job. He's gotten used to living on a good salary, and he's not going to rock the boat. We haven't got a daddy like you do."

Bella frowned. "Yeah, Daddy takes care of his little girl. Someday I'll be rich, but he's still careful with his money. I shouldn't complain, but Danny and I could be living a lot better. So, is Jim putting pressure on you, being mean and all?"

Bonnie gave Bella a tired look. "It's not pleasant. Fortunately, I have your pills. I take them and stay cool and just listen to him. He's upset about things starting slowly because of negotiations with the other team members, and he's concerned about them doing their job and not trying to hog all the work. He says everyone has their own agenda and feels there's going to be a continuing fight."

Bella was sanguine. "I guess everyone has to go through it to make it big, even corporations. At least you have your pills."

Bonnie considered that. "Yeah. Thank God you helped me with that. I'm not sure I could manage without them. I think I could even use a heavier dose."

Bella was mildly concerned. "I'm glad I can help, but you shouldn't up it much. It's serious stuff. Jim still doesn't know you're taking them?"

"No. He thinks I'm taking Prozac under doctor's orders. He's amazed at the results, but he doesn't really know anything about Prozac or anything else."

Bella smiled condescendingly. "Well, he's an engineer living in the Dark Ages. He still thinks the world can solve all its problems with machines and computers. With a little help, problems can be handled as if they weren't there."

Bonnie became serious. "Yes, let's keep it that way. You made some inferences at dinner at your house the other day that made me nervous. I wish you wouldn't do that."

"Okay, but don't worry. As you said, he thinks it's Prozac."

A waitress finally showed up and took their orders. After she left, Bella observed, "It's a good thing we have something to talk about. Otherwise we might starve to death around here."

Bonnie agreed. "Yeah, it's a nice central location, but there are other places around here we can try. You have any trouble with the traffic? I didn't."

"No. It's the middle of the day. The traffic is light, and the sun is overhead. People driving to Fair Lakes in the morning from where we live have it made. The sun is always behind them. I feel sorry for the schmucks who live to the west of the city."

Bonnie mulled that over. "I guess I never think about that. I only drive in the middle of the day to go shopping. I don't really think much about the problems of commuting."

The women continued to make small talk throughout their lunch, agreed that the meal was not what they had hoped it would be, left a small tip, and headed for the cash register to pay. Bonnie took the check, paid, and handed the change to Bella, with extra cash slipped in to pay for pills.

They went out to Bella's car where Bella took out a small package wrapped with a ribbon. She made it look like a present. Bonnie accepted the package and thanked Bella. "As always, I'm grateful for these. They help me a lot." She leaned close to Bella. "I meant what I said in there. I need more of these. Life is getting tough."

Bella looked serious. "Okay. Maybe we can have lunch soon and I can help you out. But you need to be careful."

Bonnie avowed that it was no problem. "What I'm taking now is only having a little effect."

Bella acceded to Bonnie's request with a pretense of mild concern. "All right, but be careful. Phone me, and we'll get together."

She watched Bonnie walk to her car and smiled to herself. She had both Jim and Bonnie right where she wanted them.

CHAPTER FIFTEEN

Bennie Pelligrini entered the room griping about the bar scene in Alexandria. "The guys and I went out last night going up and down King Street. All the places were serving food and didn't seem like real bars. Don't know where the women were. Wednesday nights in this place are dead."

Andy Wiggins looked up from his desk. "Are you trying to tell me that Miami is livelier than this town?"

"Hell, yes. It's a party town," Pelligrini barked back. "And a hell of a lot warmer too. I get away from my wife and kids for a while, and I need to have fun. I'll try DC next, Georgetown or Adams Morgan, whatever that is."

Pelligrini was from Florida-Southern Power, and Wiggins came from Futral-Partners.

Sidney Davies and Matt Somers had created three teams to develop ideas for the Super Highway. Pelligrini and Wiggins were on Charlie's team. This was the second day of their meetings.

B-E had rented space in an office building in the City of Fairfax. Jim Wade and his secretary had moved into a corner office suite of two rooms. The secretary's name was Daphne O'Leary. Daphne always addressed people with their full names, as in, "Good morning, Charlie Hendricks. What can I do for you today?" Daphne had been Wade's secretary for years and was highly paid as secretaries go. She lived in a high-rise at Bailey's Crossroads. It was rumored that her apartment faced another building and that she generally wandered around the apartment naked. Charlie admitted that she had a pretty good figure, but she was in her early fifties. He guessed a naked woman was a naked woman, no matter what her age, and she probably got the attention she wanted. He wondered how high she set the apartment's thermostat.

Davies, Somers, a B-E software guru named Beverly Byrnes, a logistics expert named Lionel Haverford, and Fortiano all had individual offices with a common office administrator. Charlie wasn't at all sure about that amount of overhead. It seemed like they had six managers for twenty or so workers. If they didn't win the first phase, Charlie figured the labor cost was all coming out of the company's hide. He didn't understand it but decided it was not his worry.

Three rooms had been set up for the "creative teams." Each room had a rectangular table and chairs, an easel with a large pad of paper for listing ideas, and a couple of computer terminals. For everyday work, the team members had desks in cubicles in one large room, the "bull pen" as they all called it. Another room was manned/womanned by three typists and a fellow who did artwork, drawings, illustrations, and the like as required. A separate room was set aside for a CAD system and printers. There was room for expansion, where eventually a team would be brought in to help finalize the proposal. Much of the floor sat empty. It was planned that, if Wade and his team won the first round, they would expand into this area to support the design and all the financial work that would have to be done in the second proposal stage.

As the teams met, their cubicles were being assembled, and computers and routers were being installed. The telephones weren't coming until tomorrow.

Pelligrini was the electrical power guy on Charlie's team. He resented missing the University of Miami and the Dolphins football games and groused about the lousy Redskins games being the only ones shown on TV in DC. He talked about substations, transformers, threephases, and things Charlie didn't realize were still being taught in electrical engineering.

The other two teams also had electrical engineers.

Futral-Partners had sent two civil engineers and one mechanical engineer. The civil engineers had been involved in work hardening government embassies and other buildings and in boring massive tunnels for roads and water distribution. The mechanical engineer,

Andy Wiggins, had mostly been involved in setting up manufacturing plants. None had worked on road construction.

Since Charlie was the only civil engineer on B-E's team, he had the mechanical engineer assigned to his team.

Wiggins was a subdued guy, who seemed to skeptically view Pelligrini as somewhat of a madman who had to be carefully watched. That didn't seem to bother Pelligrini at all.

A software developer named Joannie Bahr was assigned to the team from B-E as its fourth member and a logistics guy named Henry Usher as the fifth. Whereas the engineers and logistics guy wore suits or sports coats, all be it with loose ties and an unbuttoned top shirt button, Joannie Bahr wore jeans, a sports shirt, and Converse sneakers. Charlie was sure that, if it were summer, Bahr would be wearing shorts and sandals. Her male compatriots would be wearing Bermuda shorts. The software folks took pride in being from a different world.

Ostensibly, Charlie was in charge of this creative group, since B-E was the overall manager. However, it did not appear to Charlie that Pelligrini understood he was in a supportive role, and Wiggins remained somewhat mysterious as to what he considered his role to be.

Charlie approached the pad of paper the size of newsprint, took out a black marker, and wrote at the top of the page, "Requirements and Constraints."

Pelligrini piped up, "Why don't we just levitate everything and be done with it?"

Wiggins frowned. "I'd like to see you levitate a 2010 Suburban."

Charlie agreed. "Look, we have to be serious. We're not designing a vehicle. We're stuck with what's on the road today. Let me write down what we have to do. The solicitation says that we have to develop a system that safely takes the control of the vehicle away from the driver and moves traffic at eighty miles an hour." Charlie wrote that down. "It has to be compatible with existing vehicles that have been built in the last ten years. It has to work for all vehicles with four or more wheels, including semis with existing size and load requirements." Charlie turned his back and wrote that down.

Pelligrini interjected, "If it weren't for the safety, we could just turn everyone loose at eighty miles an hour, and we could forget the new design. We'd quickly reduce the population and empty the highways for the survivors to whiz along."

Charlie looked tired. "But safety is a requirement, so let me finish this. The on- and offramps of this highway have to be able to handle twelve thousand vehicles a day, twenty thousand at peak, and the highway is to handle sixty thousand vehicles a day. That means, during rush hour, the on- and off-ramps have to handle about fourteen vehicles a minute. The solicitation says twenty vehicles a minute, which I suspect has a built-in safety factor and is a way to handle variations in the traffic load."

While Charlie wrote that down, Wiggins added, "Yeah and we have to do it using existing bridges and tunnels. Kind of limits the band width."

Charlie wrote that down.

Pelligrini asked, "What happens to my E-ZPass? I don't want to waste it."

Wiggins sighed. "Come on, Bennie. This is years away. That's not part of the solicitation. I'm sure something will be worked out."

Pelligrini protested, "Hey, we need to think about everything."

Charlie wrote E-ZPass at the bottom of the page.

Pelligrini smiled. "See. I've been listened to."

Charlie nodded. "People using this highway may have to pay for it in some way. It may not be an E-ZPass, but something will have to be developed to help speed access up."

Charlie turned back to the pad. "What else?"

Usher spoke up. "Hey, I'm just the logistics guy here, and I'm not sure what my role will be, but I'm curious about the highway. We know it has to basically be the same width as the existing highways, unless we build them wider and somehow funnel things through tunnels and over and under bridges that exist today. But will the existing highways support eighty-mile-perhour traffic?"

Charlie smiled at Usher. "Good question. Some of them already bounce you at sixty. The current highways support sixty-five-, seventy-, or seventy-five-mile-per-hour traffic. Maybe they're designed for a little more than that, but we have to address converting them to the higher speed. There must be data on that. The Germans would probably laugh at eighty." He looked at Wiggins. "There's something for you to do. I bet your company has all kinds of data on highway construction specifications. Also, there's probably Department of Transportation data on that. In reviewing proposals, they have to have something to base their decisions on. Will you see what you can get?"

Bahr spoke up. "Hey, just like Henry, I'm not sure what I'm designing."

Charlie was taken aback. "Are you kidding? This is going to be all about you. How do you think we're going to maintain these vehicles at a constant speed, neatly separated on the highways? And how do you think we're going to move vehicles in and out of traffic without a major pileup? Software is going to be critical, and it's going to have to be reliable as hell. It can't crash. Now, how's that for a challenge?"

Bahr gulped. "What do you mean it can't crash? All software can crash. And how do we take the software down to maintain it?"

Charlie looked at her. "You can't. Any maintenance would have to be done while the software is live, and it can't interfere with the ongoing functions."

Bahr sighed. "That's scary. I'm not sure I want to be involved with that."

Bennie piped up. "Sure you do. That's why you're paid the big bucks."

"Big bucks, hell," retorted Bahr. "Does Beverly Byrnes know what she's getting into?"

Charlie was perplexed. "You're kidding me, right? This is the modern world, the world of software. That's you, Joannie. This is your world. Consider it a challenge."

Bahr pouted. "Yeah, it's my world. Hope I get some help."

Charlie looked around the room. "Okay, now that Joannie doesn't feel left out, are there any more thoughts?"

Pelligrini raised his hand. "You know that comment about funneling the cars through tunnels and the like might not be a bad idea. We'd just speed them up there and squeeze the cars together."

Wiggins looked pleased. "I knew my course in fluid mechanics was good for something. Bernoulli would be proud."

Charlie hunched his shoulders. "Nothing's off the table."

Bahr pondered what had been said. "I wonder if Joe Schmoe has any idea what we might do to him. Who's going to volunteer to be drivers for the beta version of this highway?"

Pelligrini murmured, "Someone else can worry about that. I have enough on my plate. Hope my wife can handle the nightmares."

"Don't worry," Charlie said consolingly. "You're not in this alone."

Wiggins noted, "I'm getting to appreciate the human race more and more. All kinds of people with IQs from 50 to 150 get on these highways today and buzz along at 70 miles-an-hour with damn few accidents. It's truly amazing. Think what a failure of the software might do to hundreds of cars roaring through a tunnel in a mountain at 120 miles-an-hour. It's truly a gruesome thought."

Charlie was growing frustrated. "Come on, guys. Let's be positive. We're going to create a fast, safe, efficient highway system. We have modern technology to help us. And the company will make big dollars. This is an opportunity."

Pelligrini rose from the table. "Right, coach. Let's go get 'em!"

Charlie felt disgusted and wrote on the pad, "Reliable and Safe Software."

He turned to his team. "What else?"

Bahr asked. "Even if we design software, how are we going to make it work with all cars? The older ones don't have software built in or even cruise control. We have to work with what they have."

Wiggins spoke up. "Hell. Of course we'll have to do that. There's already all kinds of technology on self-driving cars. We should be able to build on that. Maybe we'll have to bring on Google as a team member."

Bahr protested, "But they don't make old cars self-driving."

Charlie responded, "Maybe we won't let old cars drive on this system. Maybe they'll have to stick to US 1 or whatever."

Pelligrini considered that. "That should make the auto industry happy. Junk the old cars and buy new."

Usher noted, "Sounds like a logistics solution to me."

Charlie remonstrated. "It's not like the current system is going to be replaced in one year or even ten. By then, the cars you're talking about will be antiques and can be carried on flatbeds. Let's not worry about it."

Wiggins got serious. "You guys are all worrying about driving these cars with software. Maybe we don't need to do that. Maybe we can just carry them along. Seems to me that might be simpler, and then Joannie could sleep better."

Charlie agreed. "That's certainly true. It's certainly something to consider."

Bahr suddenly began to feel left out. "Yeah, and if we had a carrier, we could build software and communications into it and maybe solve the 'old car' problem. The question is how do we communicate with the cars to control what gear they are in? Some of the new cars are incorporating Wi-Fi, but that's coming slowly, so we're back to the 'old car' problem. And how do we communicate with the carriers? The tower systems for the phone companies don't cover all points, and they can only carry so much load. Seems like we have to provide a system for our use that's independent of the phone companies and that we have to provide each carrier with a box of some kind that can communicate with the master controller and the car."

Usher looked interested. "Yeah. We could provide a box initially, but I bet the car companies will incorporate that in future rollouts, at least as an option. Eventually, they'll probably hardwire the box to the car. I see the box as an initial logistics problem that will eventually go away."

Charlie scribbled on the pad and summarized, "Okay, I think we've put out some good thoughts. Let's go off for a couple of days and try to crystallize some real conceptual designs.

We'll meet back here Monday at ten. Is that okay with everyone?"

Pelligrini asked, "Are we allowed to talk to the guys on the other teams?"

Charlie said, "Of course. We're all one project."

"Good," Pelligrini responded. "That will give us something to talk about tonight in Adams Morgan."

CHAPTER SIXTEEN

Jim Wade, Sid Davies, and Danny Fortiano were having lunch at a restaurant in the Fair Oaks Mall. Wade hated eating in his office, although he sometimes had Daphne run down to the café on the first floor to get him a sandwich. He never felt comfortable eating in the corporate cafés. They were far too conspicuous for senior members of the staff. Some companies had dining rooms for the senior staff, but B-E, on the East Coast, doing government contracts, didn't feel such luxuries were appropriate. As a result, Wade went out to lunch at various places from Fairfax to Centreville two or three times a week. He didn't like eating alone, but he felt cornered into inviting Fortiano all too often. He loathed the man—thought he was a cocky, overmuscled idiot. He kicked himself over and over again for having slept with Bella. He had thought he was seducing her, but now he knew it was the other way around. He had always been careful not to get involved with local women. There were enough in California and Hawaii. He had been a damned fool.

Today, he had asked Sid Davies to join them, just so he wouldn't have to deal with Fortiano alone. Davies wasn't much of an engineer. The brigadier general title gave him a veneer that the corporate leadership liked. They moved him around to be a deputy here and there to add spice to the leadership. He was a nice guy, although at times a little self-important. Wade guessed he had gotten that way in the army serving as a deputy division commander, whatever that entailed.

They sat at a corner table having a cocktail before lunch. Wade had a Manhattan. He felt the need of a strong drink to steady his nerves these days. He knew it would leave an odor. He carried breath spray and mints just in case he had to interact with someone important.

Davies and Fortiano each had beers. They wanted to be compatible with Wade.

Davies had a Budweiser. Fortiano had some kind of locally brewed beer. Davies thought it was a little prissy. He thought Fortiano was always a little affected.

Fortiano didn't care what people thought. He wanted to be different. He thought he was different, socially way ahead of these engineers and retired army officers.

They sat cuddling their drinks on the table, occasionally taking a sip.

Fortiano broke the ice. "I've been checking in with some of our creative teams." He didn't say he had spent ten minutes with one group. "This highway design is going to be tough. Everyone wants to be imaginative and create something new and exciting, but they're finding it's hard to make quantum leaps when they're stuck with ten years of automobiles."

Davies hadn't been to any meetings. He didn't feel adequate to participate. He preferred writing reports on what had been done. He liked the socializing at these lunches, but he couldn't understand why Fortiano was always included. Fortiano seemed to be a mediocre manager. Davies couldn't judge him as an engineer. "Yes, I've wondered about that. Seems like if you're going to create something new, you're going to have to drive each car into some kind of capsule that can then take over the motion, but that would be like building a car for a car. Might as well build all new cars to start with."

Wade didn't say anything. His mind was elsewhere.

Fortiano was uncertain about addressing him but finally said, "Jim, have you given any thought to the challenge?"

Wade took a sip of his Manhattan. "Yes. I've given it a lot of thought. This highway is a challenge. I'll be interested in what the creative teams have to say. We're caught in a tight place. We have to come up with something that leaps out of the proposal at you, but we also have to think of the second phase when cost will be the issue. We have to be whiz-bang in the first proposal and circumspect in the second phase. And, guys, my future and probably yours is riding on this. It's exciting to be involved, but failure is going to have consequences. This proposal is one of those things you take on in life that's too big for you to fail at."

Davies considered that. "I understand what you're saying. This is so difficult that you almost hope you don't win, although from the personal viewpoint, you can't afford to lose. This is a gotcha."

Fortiano looked back and forth between the two senior guys at the table. "Hey, we can do this. We need to create something futuristic-looking, something exotic and sexy, even if the innards are just some old stuff. Get some sexy graphics done along with the proposal. Maybe put it out to the media before we submit anything. Get the public excited."

Davies remarked skeptically, "You sound like PR is more important than design. Do you think the Department of Transportation will buy that?"

Fortiano disputed that. "Yeah, I think they will. Hell, the government decision makers are bureaucrats and political appointees. They need to sell this thing as well as we do. Their tech guys will kowtow because they need their jobs."

Wade studied Fortiano. He wondered if Fortiano knew what Bella had on him. Was this guy comfortable with his wife sleeping with another man to get her husband ahead? Or was Fortiano naive and convinced that he really was special? It was hard as hell to tell.

Wade responded and noted, "I'll consider everything from the Yellow Brick Road to bank suction tubes. Let's see what our guys come up with. Then we'll strategize how to sell it."

That sounded good. Wade hoped the creativity was out there in his teams.

Davies wasn't sure. "Well, I'm going to have a cheeseburger to help me think about that. How about you guys?"

They ordered. Wade had a roast beef sandwich. Fortiano had a panini with ham, Gruyère, and apple.

Davies asked, "What the hell is Gruyère?"

Fortiano smiled at Davies's lack of sophistication. "It's a cheese, imported from Switzerland. Really adds to the flavor."

Davies knew he was being put down. "Yeah. I've had it on cheeseburgers. Really gives them panache. You should try it."

Wade tried to ignore what was going on. "Roast beef is fine with me. Goes well with the Manhattan."

The three men pretty much ate in silence. Wade ate little, but ordered a second Manhattan. Davies tried not to roll his eyes, but he noted that Fortiano did.

Davies inquired, "Jim, do you think this is the toughest job you've ever been given?"

Wade thought about it. "Yes. Everything else has mostly been straightforward. Build communications systems, mostly using existing stuff, off-the-shelf stuff, maybe with small modifications or developing software for specific goals, mostly updating stuff that exists. Not much real creativity. Specific requirements with specific end products. This is different. This requires imagination but within limits."

Fortiano leaned back. "But you have us behind you. We're going to come up with something big."

Wade looked over his glasses at Fortiano. "And something sensible that will work in a fiscally responsible way."

With that, Wade picked up the bill and informed everyone how much he owed. For two or three lunches a week, he couldn't pay all the bills. The ground rules had been set long ago.

CHAPTER SEVENTEEN

Linda sat at a small table in her office, going over plans with the florist that Yvonne DuBois regularly used. They were working on a wedding. The bride wanted all white, so they were concentrating on white roses and lilies. They were going to use roses on the dinner tables because some people were allergic to the lilies. The bride's bouquet and the bridal table would have the lilies, in addition to lily arrangements on pillared stands around the periphery of the room. The bridesmaids were to carry white roses. They were looking at the floor layout, deciding how many stands to use. They would get to plans for the church next.

There was a knock at the door, and Linda called, "Yes, come in."

Margie, one of the staff, stuck her head in the door. "There's a phone call for you, Linda."

Linda wanted to finish with the florist. "Will you get a number so I can call back?"

"He said you'd say that. Said it would only take a minute."

"Did he give a name?"

"Stephen Davenport. Has a nice voice."

Oh, shit, thought Linda. *Maybe it's about the fund-raiser.* "Okay, Margie, I'll get it."

Linda excused herself from the florist, saying it would only be a minute. She went to her desk and picked up the phone. "Mr. Davenport?"

"Hi, Linda, and you know it's Stephen."

"Right. I'm sorry. I'm just sitting here with my florist."

"Hey, I'm sorry to interrupt. I'll make it quick. What are you doing for lunch today?"

Linda was a little flustered. "Today?"

"Yeah, in about an hour and a half. I'd like to talk to you some more about the fund-raiser.

Hate to talk in offices. How about me picking you up outside the door of your office building?"

Linda was surprised. "You know where my building is?"

"I do, and I'll be there at noon."

"Okay, I guess that will work. Yeah, I'll see you at noon."

*　*　*

Davenport was waiting, parked illegally, in a gray Mercedes E350.

He opened the door for her as she approached. She smiled and said, "So, where's the chauffeur?"

He smiled back at her as she got in. "Oh, I only use him for official business."

Linda looked up from the seat. "So, this is not official business?"

"Semiofficial," he said as he closed the door and walked around to the driver's side.

Davenport settled in the driver's seat and pulled out into traffic. "I'm a Capitol Hill kind of guy. Do you mind if we go over to the other side of the Capitol, along Pennsylvania Avenue?"

Linda studied him. "No. That sounds fine. I'm always up for a new adventure. Capitol Hill sounds exotic."

Davenport chuckled. "I've never heard it called exotic, but it is where I live."

They circumnavigated the Capitol with ease. It was obvious to Linda that Davenport was in familiar territory.

As they approached the restaurant, Linda commented, "So this is where the power lives."

Davenport smiled. "A little high power and lots of low power, like me."

Linda gave a coy smile as she looked at Davenport. "Sounds like someone's trying to sound less important than he is."

Davenport looked at her. "I'm not trying to impress. My position does have its advantages, but there's a lot of gopher work too. And the real power lives all over the Washington area. It's nice and convenient here. But you still have to watch yourself at night. A guy from work was killed here."

Linda's expression became serious. "Yeah, I heard that. Did you know him?"

"No. But it made a lot of people around here think."

Davenport pulled into a parking space next to a Chinese restaurant. "Do you mind Chinese? They make other things too."

Linda looked at the restaurant. Somehow she had expected something more sophisticated. "No, Chinese is fine."

They settled into a booth, and Linda asked, "So, what's going on with the fund-raiser?"

Davenport seemed somewhat detached as he waved over a waiter. "Oh, I suspect it's going fine."

They ordered, and after the waiter left, Linda returned to the presumed subject of the meeting. "I was worried when you called. I thought there might be a problem."

Davenport focused back on Linda, "Oh, no. I just wanted to check with you and see if everything is all right and if you have any questions. Jeanie and Betty have called to see if everything is all right and to get help on the invitation list. I've told them everything is fine. I assume that's correct."

"Oh, yes. Everything is going fine. Under control." Linda wondered what was going on. *We could have talked about this on the phone.* She tried to think of what to say next. "Jeanie and Betty seem like very nice women. What got them involved?"

"They are nice women. Maybe in a little over their heads, but they are both representing good groups that will support them. We're trying to help them as best we can. They deserve every good thing they can get in life."

Linda guessed she understood, but she felt a need for the details. "As I understand it, they had loved ones in Walter Reed and lived in guest quarters for a while."

"Betty is a widow. She had a son who was wounded in Afghanistan. Sadly, he died about a month after being flown to Bethesda. He never came out of a coma, never said last words to her. Betty spent all that time in visitors' quarters. Jeanie is there with her husband, a young sergeant, eight years in the army. His Humvee was hit by a roadside bomb, an IED. It mangled his arm and tore up his body. Did a lot of damage to his brain. He's been at Walter Reed for three months undergoing all kinds of surgery and therapy. They don't know when he'll be going home. I expect that Jeanie has a tough road ahead of her. Both women want a nice facility for family members, nice and affordable."

Linda sympathized. "That's so sad. It's a reality of war that many of us don't understand." Davenport looked puzzled. "Wasn't your husband in Iraq and Afghanistan?"

Linda was surprised. "How did you know that?"

Davenport became wary and careful. "Your résumé's on the Yvonne DuBois website."

Linda became a little alarmed. "But that doesn't mention my husband's background."

"I'm sorry. I googled him." Davenport looked guilty.

Linda was astounded. "You googled him? Did you do a background check?"

Davenport defended himself. "Look. I work for a politician. It's a habit. I try to learn all about everyone I deal with. It helps me in what I do. It's not personal."

Linda shrugged. "It just feels eerie. I guess that's modern life. Everyone knows everything about you. Do you know how many children I have and where I live?"

Davenport nodded and said a small, "Yes."

Linda sat back. "Okay. Let's make this even. Tell me who you are besides someone that works for a senator. Are you a good guy or a bad guy?"

Davenport sighed. "Okay, I'm mostly good, but I don't pretend to be perfect. I like people. I like to be around them. I grew up in Kansas and went to Kansas University through law school. I volunteered for Senator McDonald's campaign and worked a lot with his chief of staff, who was then the campaign manager. After I graduated from law school, I contacted him and got a job on the senator's staff here in Washington. That was twenty-three years ago, and I've been here ever since, praying he keeps getting elected so that I don't have to get a real job."

"So, you're a country boy?"

Davenport chuckled. "Everyone here thinks someone from Kansas is a country boy, but I'm from Kansas City, you know, the place where 'everything's up to date.'"

Linda nodded. "As in Rogers and Hammerstein?"

"You got it. But that was long ago. Twenty-three years in DC changes all that, and that's where I am now."

"Married?"

Davenport shook his head. "No. Don't know if a woman would put up with my life."

"Never anyone serious? A good-looking guy like you."

Davenport looked a little embarrassed and uncertain. It was not his favorite subject when talking to a pretty woman. "Some. It's not that I don't like women. There's only so much time available." He wanted to change the subject. "Let's get back to my original question before we went into the personal espionage. Didn't you feel the impact of war when your husband was away?"

Linda felt the guilt she had known since the hospital. "I don't think so. Being in the halls of Walter Reed and meeting Jeanie and Betty made me think more than I ever did when Charlie was away. Those were just assignments. It's like a GEICO commercial. 'That's what you do' when you're in the army. I just knew I had to raise two boys by myself, put together their toys at Christmas, call the plumber to change a washer, manage the bills, and on and on. Frankly, I kind of resented it, maybe felt a little sorry for myself. Charlie never wrote about the danger. For all I knew, he was in some safe compound watching movies and drinking beer at the officer's club. It was only after he came home last time that he talked about riding a Humvee out to check on IED damage to the roads and then going out with repair crews to fix the damage. I asked him if he'd seen the damage the IEDs did to people, and he said he had, had seen the bodies. It sobered me a little."

Davenport was interested. "So, you think you're self-centered?"

Linda thought about that. "Yeah, probably, a little. Army life's not easy, but when you think about it, three years as a single mother is not much these days. I should have taken it better."

Davenport smiled. "Well, I'll forgive you. Not that it's any of my business. You act like you're really interested in this fund-raiser for Jeanie and Betty."

"Oh, I am," Linda asserted. "Even more so now that you've told me more about the two women. I understand how special they are."

Davenport concurred. "Yeah, they are. The senator wants to do all he can to help them."

Linda smiled. "Yvonne DuBois Catering and I will do all we can."

Davenport replied, "I know you will."

He paid the bill, and Linda asked, "So, is that all you wanted, just to know everything was going all right?"

They got up from the table. "Yes. I can call Jeanie and Betty back and tell them everything is okay."

As they went out the door, Linda pursued her question. "And that's it for a free lunch."

Davenport looked at her. "That and getting to know you."

Linda blushed and felt unsure as she got in the car. As Davenport got in, she asked, knowing she was being forward, "And did you get to know me?"

He started the engine. "A little. I found out you're introspective and perhaps a little concerned about your life, since you haven't been completely happy with it and maybe not with your marriage and its responsibilities."

Linda tilted her head back. "God, you make me sound awful, like I've wasted my life. Hell, it hasn't been a bad life. I have a man who loves me when he's not out playing soldier and two great sons I love very much."

Davenport protested. "I'm not judging. I'm not married. Not sure I could handle the responsibilities. I always thought that 'till death do us part' was a little too serious for me."

Linda sighed. She had to get off the subject. "I'm glad you didn't bring the chauffeur."

Davenport looked at her inquiringly. "Because we could talk?"

Linda considered that. "No, because it's too damn conspicuous. But the talking is a good point."

"Yeah, I agree, a chauffeur is conspicuous," Davenport concluded.

Linda got out in front of her building, saying, "Thank you for a lovely lunch, even if you made me think too much."

Davenport smiled up at her. "You're welcome. I had a nice time. We need to do it again some time."

Linda was uncertain. "That would be nice. I'll see you."

As Davenport drove away, Linda thought, *Did I really say that? That another lunch would be nice?*

CHAPTER EIGHTEEN

Bella met her father for lunch at a restaurant in DC. They had lunch together every couple of weeks, depending on their schedules. Robert Elmont Conway, or Bobby, as he was usually called, worked financial aspects of the law relative to the big operators in Washington, hedge fund people and the like. He liked the best restaurants in DC and could afford them.

He was at his table when Bella arrived, and he watched the crowd, men and woman, watch his daughter as she crossed the room. She had slipped off her coat at the door and moved enticingly under a knit dress. Conway stood and held her chair. "Well, sweetheart, you bring life to the room when you sashay in."

"Oh, Daddy. I don't sashay. That's crude. I just stroll with dignity."

Conway sat. "Honey, if that's dignity, I'm a shortstop with the Nats."

Bella smiled. "Hey. I'm my daddy's girl. What can I say?"

Conway laughed. "Good. I'll take all the credit. How've you been?"

"Oh, pretty good. Danny's all involved in a contract proposal. Barely has time for me," Bella lamented. "I'll be glad when it's finished."

Conway grimaced. "You know you could have done better. I've never been thrilled with that guy. He depends on you too much. Don't think he'd make it by himself."

"Daddy, we've been through this before. He has his attributes and I'm sticking with him," Bella remonstrated. "So, let's not ruin lunch by talking about it." "Okay, I give in. Do you want a cocktail?" "Are you having one?" Bella inquired.

"You know the answer. My clients wouldn't appreciate the smell of my breath unless they were having lunch with me. Then it would be fine."

"Then, I'll skip it too. I have my own clients." Bella tried to show her independence, though she still enjoyed her father's generous gifts.

The waiter came and took their order.

"So, what's this proposal Danny's involved with? I assume he's working with Jim Wade."

"That's right," Bella confirmed. "Wade was assigned the proposal."

"By whom, Gunnar Davidson? The guy's a ditz. He was lousy as an Under Secretary of the Navy. Lives off his wife's family money and family name. It'll be a wonder if B-E survives."

Bella chuckled. "Be kind, Daddy. Washington operations are only a small part of B-E. It'll survive."

Conway looked sternly at Bella. "Maybe on the West Coast. And don't get any ideas of you and Danny moving there."

Bella chuckled. "East Coast operations will survive. They've got other work. What I worry about is whether Jim Wade will survive. Evidently, a whole lot is riding on this proposal. Davidson has made it clear that his reputation depends on winning."

Conway observed, "Well, I hope he's not depending on Danny."

"Daddy!"

"Okay. So what's the contract about?"

"It has to do with updating and replacing the Interstate Highway System."

Conway acknowledged the importance of the project. "That sounds like a big one, one that will last forever. It took sixty years to build the system we have now, and Congress isn't doing very well on even maintaining our current infrastructure. That's not much of a priority. You sure this isn't just showmanship on the part of Congress."

Bella looked a little concerned. "I don't know. Danny just needs twenty years or so. Maybe Congress can at least manage that."

Conway smiled. "Let's hope so, for your sake. I'd hate to see you have to support that guy. But with our government, there are no certainties. People just hold their breath at the end of each fiscal year. So, how's your job going?"

"Changing the subject, huh? Job's going well. Lots of people want to create memorials of one type or another, and we help put the proposals together, already knowing the park service will probably not approve them. Setting up shows and conventions is steady and can actually be accomplished. There are always people who want their names in the *Post* or *Washingtonian* magazine as being wonderful, caring citizens. I bet if we went down the list, we'd find you and my firm have some common clients."

"No doubt," Conway responded. "If you look carefully, you'll probably find that I'm on the list, although they probably don't assign you to me."

"That's too bad," Bella observed. "I'd treat you special." Conway smiled. "You always do, darling. You always do."

The lunches arrived, and they settled in to eat.

CHAPTER NINETEEN

"Okay, guys," Charlie announced in the bull pen of office cubicles. "Time for the ten o'clock meeting. Andy and Bennie have some ideas to bat around. Let's go to the team room."

They all picked up their papers and entered the room.

Charlie looked around. "Where's Bennie?"

Andy laughed. "He's grabbing coffee on the way in. Adams-Morgan must have met his liking."

They sat down, and Pelligrini came scurrying in.

Charlie looked around. "Okay, we're here to bat around ideas, find the good ones, and look for problems in all of them. It's not a time for anyone to get his or her feelings hurt. All ideas have merit. But we have to know the problems as well so that we can solve them or discard the ideas." He looked at Wiggins. "I'll get you to go first, Andy. You said you have some thoughts."

Wiggins laid out some drawings on the table. "Here are some ideas. What I picture is a moving highway made up of belts, each about a hundred feet long running end to end, two or three side by side. The vehicles would just sit on them and be carried along with the cars in neutral. That way, if a belt broke down, the vehicle would have enough momentum to role on to the next belt."

Pelligrini interjected, "What if a car had a flat tire. How would it role on?"

Wiggins responded, "Vehicles are not likely to have flat tires if the tires aren't turning. These cars are just sitting still on the belts."

Usher looked puzzled. "How do you get the cars onto and off the belts?"

Wiggins rolled out a drawing. "We'll have a lead-in belt. The car will drive onto that and be put in neutral. Then between the lead-in belt and the highway belt, we'll have an interface that looks like an airport luggage carrier with plates that slide over one another and allow the vehicles to be carried onto the highway. Both the lead-in and the interface will be timed from highway sensors so that the cars will go on the belted highway between cars that are already there."

Charlie considered that. "Seems to me that your system will put the cars on the highway sitting at an angle. Your interface could put them on straight, but that would mean the cars that are already on the highway would have to ride over the interface and get shaken around."

Wiggins nodded. "Yeah, I've thought about that. I think we can make the interface so that it twists the car and slides it on the interface pointed in the right direction."

Pelligrini worried, "Could you do that for both Fiats and big rigs?"

Usher spoke up. "Yeah, Bennie's got a point. Could you do that?"

Wiggins sighed. "That will take some work. I hope it's just a matter of scale. Make it big enough to handle the semis and hope it will work for the little cars as well. It needs work."

The door opened, and Fortiano came in. "Don't let me interrupt you."

Charlie looked at Fortiano as the latter took a seat. "Andy Wiggins was just laying out his ideas of how we might build a highway mechanically with a series of moving belts." Fortiano acknowledged that. "Sounds interesting. Go on."

Wiggins looked uncertain about continuing.

Charlie encouraged him. "Okay, but if you have three belts, or lanes, side by side, how do you get vehicles from one belt to the next?"

Wiggins pulled out another drawing. "Well, you don't. Once in a lane, the vehicle stays in that lane. So, you have to have multiple entrances and exits. The far left belt lanes, at entrance and exit points, will have to be raised or lowered so that vehicles can reach them by going over or under the right belt lanes."

Fortiano spoke up. "I wasn't here earlier, but when a car is to enter the highway, how do you accelerate it to eighty miles an hour so that it enters the highway at the right speed?"

"I talked about that a little. There's an interface like a luggage carousel at an airport and a belt that leads to it, actually a series of belts. A long, slow-moving one where the vehicle makes its entrance and the driver stops and shifts the vehicle to neutral and then a series of short belts of increasing speed that accelerate the vehicle so that it enters the carousel at eighty miles an hour, the accelerations adjusted by the belts so that the car enters the highway in an open space between cars that are already there."

Charlie frowned. "If the car's in neutral, there's no way to accelerate it or turn it on a carousel. It will have to be put in park as the entrance and then shifted to neutral when it's on the highway."

Fortiano grimaced. "So this is not all mechanical. It involves sensors and software to catapult the car onto the highway at the right moment. If something goes wrong, either softwarewise or mechanically at the entrance, there could be a disaster."

Wiggins conceded that. "Yes, there's going to have to be a lot of engineering redundancy and other safety measures in any design we do. When you're traveling at 117 feet a second, there's not much room for error."

Fortiano noted, "Yeah, when you're driving your own car, you don't think about that. Goodness knows there are lots of tailgaters who have no concept. Sorry. Go ahead."

Wiggins stared down at his drawings. "The point's well noted. I don't know any airport carousels or escalators that go eighty miles an hour. It's not as simple as it sounds. This will take some engineering." He contemplated the drawing some more. "You're probably wondering how they get off this thing. It's not so easy, talking about getting catapulted. As I see it, the drive belt at the exit in front of the vehicle will have to tilt up on the far end, either tilting the whole drive motor or just the axle through a differential. That will tilt the vehicle off onto another carousel. It'll be a challenge for an eighteen-wheeler with a sixty-foot trailer. We may have to make the section of the belt longer than one hundred feet. The thing will have to tilt up and back down in about a second, which will take some doing. Car differentials certainly work that fast, but they don't reverse that quickly. There'll definitely be stress."

He looked back up. "Okay, here's the problem. I have a vehicle in neutral sailing along at eighty miles an hour that I have to slow down. The only thing I can think of is to let it coast uphill to a stop and have the driver put it in gear and drive off. The trouble is that we're back to the human being, and if the driver doesn't drive off quickly enough there's liable to be a pileup."

Pelligrini jumped in. "Do you mean that, while in neutral, the engine is running the whole time the car is on the belts? Seems like we ought to be saving gas. The ignition should be off."

Wiggins accepted that. "That would be ideal, but I don't know how to do that and get the vehicles off the highway."

Bahr interjected, "That's a software problem. We need to put the car in neutral at the start and turn off the ignition and then start the car up again when it leaves the highway, without the driver doing anything. We'll have to provide a box to interface with the car and give vocal warnings to the driver. What we can't do is depend on Joe Schmoe to handle things as they should be done. We'll end up with cars in drive on the highway and in park at the top of the hill."

Fortiano interjected, "But you can't do that with older cars."

Bahr protested. "We've already talked about that in these meetings. If software is going to be involved, a lot of vehicles will be excluded. That's one goal we can't meet, and the DOT will have to live with it."

Fortiano shook his head. "I'm not sure we can do that. We'll have to see. It would be best to meet all goals."

Charlie stepped in. "We agree, we would like to do that, but we also have to be realistic. Vehicle technology is going to change faster than we can build this new highway. We have to be able to adapt to self-driving cars or whatever is coming down the line." He looked around the table. "Okay, we have one idea to think about, one you might expect from a mechanical engineer. I'd appreciate everyone thinking about it. See if you can come up with ideas for improving it."

Fortiano stood. "It looks like you guys have some good ideas. Please keep at it." He turned to Charlie. "I think you should give these guys a break for lunch."

Charlie wondered if Fortiano was figuring out a way to get out of the meeting. "Yeah, guys. Let's meet back here at one."

Everyone trailed out, some leaving their paperwork behind. Fortiano waited to talk to Charlie. "Hey, you have some good ideas working. Everyone seems to be participating. Don't forget the deadline, though. You have to pin some things down. And don't forget the criteria in the solicitation. We have to try to meet it all."

Charlie listened and acknowledged what had been said. "Everything is always in mind. We'll be ready."

As Fortiano left, Charlie thought, *Okay, you make the speeches, and we'll come up with the ideas. In the end, you'll have to live with it.*

Charlie followed Fortiano out, went to his desk, and unwrapped his sandwich.

*   *   *

After lunch, everyone but Fortiano reassembled in the team room.

Charlie turned to Pelligrini. "Okay, Bennie. What did you come up with over your gin and tonics?"

"Scotch, man," Pelligrini corrected. "Gin and tonic's not manly."

Charlie hunched his shoulders up and made a face. "Manly, or not, G&Ts taste pretty good on a hot summer day. To each his own. Tell us what the power guy proposes."

Pelligrini opened his own roll of papers. "I propose to let electrical power take care of the whole thing. I propose we borrow from television and use a raster of wiring under a highway that will basically be the same material as that used in existing highways today. What we'll do is have a cart the vehicle drives onto or a wagon that attaches to the front of the vehicle. I like the former for cars because we could develop it so that cars can drive on and off. The frontal wagon would probably work better for trucks because of the size. We'd separate cars and trucks on the highway because of the two different methods or use the wagons for all vehicles. For the cart, we would have the vehicle put in park, but for the wagon the vehicles would be put in neutral—again things we might have to ensure with software. The wagon or cart would then use a motor to take the vehicle out to a highway, being steered by software to where it would latch onto a raster point. The raster would then produce inductive pulses to drive the wagon or cart along and, at the same time, track the location of the vehicle. The wagon or cart would be programmed at entrance to the highway as to where it is to leave the highway so that the electric motor can take over and guide it to the exit."

Usher interrupted. "So, you'd provide all the power from existing power plants? Or would you have to build new plants?"

"Glad you asked." Pelligrini beamed. "The existing electric grid would only be backup. What I picture is an arch over the highway every hundred feet or so in order that the scenic views from the highway will still exist. The arches will be covered with arrays of solar panels to provide the power. That way, we can save gas and meet the worries of environmentalists."

Wiggins volunteered, "Maybe I could use the arches too to drive my belts."

Charlie grinned. "Share and share alike. That's what we need to do."

Pelligrini looked pleased with himself. "Always glad to provide power to help. I'll add my lightning bolts anywhere they're needed."

Bahr interjected, "I suppose you want software to put the vehicles in neutral and such, much the same as in Andy's model, along with the tracking software and the entrance and exit software?"

"Absolutely. I wouldn't want to leave you out. We'll need to control the pulses as well."

Usher looked concerned. "You think the public is going to buy these inductive pulses? Could they produce cancer?"

Pelligrini was disgusted. "You sound like anyone who ever lived near a power line. We'd shield people so that wouldn't be a problem, although I doubt that would be necessary. Anyway, we'll play the game and be ready with the answers."

Charlie pushed to get things back on track. "It seems the entrance and exit processes look simpler than Andy's model. The only problem I see is getting the carts or wagons from the exit side to the entrance side, and, if wagons are used, how do they get attached in a timely and efficient manner and how do we develop a universal way to attach them?"

Pelligrini leaned back and grinned. "Hey, I'm the electrical energy guy. The mechanical business is Andy's job. Now that he's got the right model, I suspect he can work it out."

Wiggins protested, "Who says it's the right model? I like my model." After a moment's consideration he added. "Well, you're lucky you have me. I'll give it some thought."

Charlie interjected, "Andy, that would be great. I suspect that moving a large cart or wagon efficiently between exits and entrances under the time constraints we're talking about is not going to be simple. Additionally, depending on the traffic, we could have an overload or dearth of carts at any one place."

Pelligrini had a quick answer. "That's not a problem. We just track the carts and wagons with software, and if there's a buildup some place, we just put them on the highway by themselves and have them travel to where they are needed."

Usher was pleased. "Sounds like a logistics solution. And with the carts, we don't have to worry about cars having flat tires or breaking down some other way."

Charlie nodded. "But with the wagon, that might still be a problem. Maybe the wagon could make the vehicle rigid so the flat wouldn't sit on the ground. Hopefully, with tractor trailers, there would be enough wheels to compensate for a flat, or we'd have to shove a support under the rear of the trailer. Anyway, think about it."

Wiggins spoke up. "I have the solution. With the carts, we just have the entrance and exit side by side, although probably separated by several hundred yards to allow for cart parking. We'll just shuffle the carts sideways from exit to entrance. The issue is that the carts will have to be designed to run either direction. If we have to rotate them, that's more complexity. The wagons will take more thinking."

Charlie was pleased. "Okay, guys. I appreciate the ideas. Think about details associated with these suggestions and keep thinking up new approaches. We'll meet again tomorrow afternoon at one. That will give you time to think in the morning." He turned to Wiggins. "Before you go, Andy, did you have any luck with road specs?"

"Yeah. Headquarters has all kinds of data they're sending to me. But maybe of more importance, there's a Department of Transportation document," Wiggins responded, looking down at his notes, "called 'The Standard Specifications for Construction of Roads and Bridges on Federal Highway Projects, FP-03.' They're sending it too."

Charlie shook his head. "I should have known. Coming from the army, I know there's a regulation or spec for everything."

CHAPTER TWENTY

Monday evening, Bonnie and Jim Wade were in their car headed for dinner at the Davidsons.

Wade's jaw was set, his face looking like he'd had enough of this world. "The son of a bitch never asked us out when he took over this job. He's only doing it now because he has so much riding on winning this contract. He's just figuring out ways to keep applying the screws."

Bonnie gazed at him with little expression. "Hey. Quit being so sour. This is your job. You and I both enjoy living on the money you make."

Wade glared at her. "Yeah. You keep reminding me of that. I've done just fine in this company, gotten ahead, taken the responsibility, and make good money. I earn it."

Bonnie turned her head away. "Yeah, and you've always enjoyed the house, the cars, and the country club that money pays for. You're accustomed to the image."

Wade put on the brakes hard at a stop sign. "Hey, what is this shit? You've certainly never complained about it."

She continued to not look at him. "No, but you've never been the shit you've been since you got assigned this project." She looked at him. "All you do is bitch about everything. You're not even happy playing golf anymore. I dread your coming home from work and from the club."

He snapped back. "And what do you think you contribute? You're like a lump on a stump most of the time. You don't contribute anything."

Bonnie turned and smiled at him. "So, what am I supposed to be—your charming consort, carrying the social load? I do that, but this is your show, buddy. You need to handle it."

At a stoplight, Wade looked at her, noticed again the tiny dots of her pupils. "Yeah, but we're supposed to be a team. Since you've started on this Prozac, you just go around in a dream. You don't contribute a thing anymore."

Bonnie continued to smile. "Sure I do. I look attractive on your arm. What more do you want?"

They pulled into the curved drive of the Davidsons' house in Potomac. It was a huge new structure of a light-colored brick, with a similar brick wall along the road in the front. They drove in through a gate of brick pillars topped with glowing lanterns.

Bonnie commented, "Well, someone brought money to the table."

Wade frowned. "It's shitting opulent."

They were met at the door by a young Hispanic woman wearing a white apron, who welcomed them and took their coats while smiling. A slightly plump, graying woman in a beige silk dress stepped from behind the younger woman. "Good evening. It's such a pleasure to have you. I'm Sally. Please come in."

The Wades knew she was "Sally," Sarah Bowling Tarleton-Davidson, from southeastern Virginia.

Gunnar Davidson stepped from behind his wife and took Bonnie's hand. "I'm so glad to meet you, Bonnie. I've been looking forward to this so much."

He then shook Jim Wade's hand as the Wades both thought, *So if you've been looking forward to it, why'd you take so long?*

In the two-storied foyer, Bonnie noted the portraits of men and women out of the eighteenth century.

Davidson held his arm wide. "Please come into our living room and have a seat. What may I get you to drink?"

He was looking at Bonnie. "A glass of wine, please?"

"Red or white?"

"White, please."

"And you, Jim?"

Wade was looking at the portrait of an Elizabethan woman over the mantle. "Scotch on the rocks, please."

Sally looked at Wade. "I see you're admiring the portrait above the mantle. It's one of my English ancestors. The cartwheel ruff must have been a pain. At least it kept the head straight." Davidson observed, "Probably worse than a necktie."

Sally sympathized. "At least you poor dears don't have to wear ties all the time now. Lots of men never do. Only the important ones have to."

Davidson went off to get the drinks while Sally and her guests seated themselves in a spacious living room with large glass windows and French doors leading to a vast terrace overlooking an expansive backyard, which was lit professionally. Sally smiled. "It's one of my joys in life to be able to seat my guests in this room. We're so fortunate to have such a lovely view."

Bonnie thought, *And so fortunate to have the money to buy the view.* She returned the smile. "It's absolutely wonderful. I can understand your feeling. Potomac is such a lovely area. I know how much you must enjoy it."

Sally looked pleased. "I agree. It's so nice to have this much space and still be close to Washington with all that the city offers."

Wade interjected, "And you have some great golf courses out this way, too—Avenel and Congressional. I've played Avenel a couple of times."

Sally nodded. "Yes, I understand they're very good. But they're a nuisance when a big tournament is going on. Gunnar doesn't play, but many of our friends do."

Davidson returned with the drinks and passed them around while Sally excused herself and went to the kitchen. He looked at Jim. "I heard you talking about golf, and I've heard from Ralph Evenson about your trips to Hawaii. You must really put yourself into playing the game."

Wade was pleased to be able to talk about golf. "Yes. You have to play regularly to be any good. Hawaii is wonderful, especially during the winter when you can't play around here. I also go down to Pinehurst some in the winter, but Hawaii is the best."

Davidson seemed to consider and assess what Wade had said. "Sounds like it involves a lot of time. Must be a challenge when you're managing a big project."

Wade was suddenly wary. "Oh, I like golf, but work always comes first. If anything of import is going on with a project, it involves me and all my staff with whatever time it takes. It's part of the game."

Bonnie was quick to add, "Sometimes days go by when I hardly see Jim. He's obsessed."

Davidson smiled at Bonnie. "As he should be. A project's success depends on good and ever-present leadership. I expect nothing less than that from my managers. Jim has a good reputation, and that's why I've selected him for the Super Highway project. It's a very critical project for B-E to win. The company is depending on him. You think you're up to it, Jim? Do you have the right people? This is probably the most important project of your career."

Wade felt the pressure and responded, "Oh, I'm absolutely up to it. My team and I will do everything we have to in order to win. This is exciting, and we're all eager." Meanwhile he thought, *What do you mean, 'the most important project of* my *career'? This is the most important project of yours. Nonetheless, I'd better give up golf for a while. I'll be a presence at the office, whether I'm needed or not.*

Sally returned with a tray of cheese and crackers. She passed it to her guests and then to Davidson before she set it on the coffee table in front of the sofa where the Wades sat. "I hope you enjoy this. It's what we have in tidewater. Antipasto's not the thing down there, although I try it sometimes."

Bonnie bubbled, "Oh, it's wonderful. Luscious-looking cheeses. And, Gunnar, the wine is lovely. It couldn't be nicer."

Davidson smiled and acknowledged what had been said. "I'm delighted you like it. I usually just have wine, although I've found that life in government circles often requires something stronger, just to keep up. Fortunately, for Sally, she can usually get by with her CocaCola, as she still calls it. *Coke* has the wrong connotation these days."

Bonnie chuckled. "My relatives from Georgia have always said Coca-Cola. I think it's a Southern tradition."

Davidson smiled. "Well, that's good to know. Sally's not odd man out after all."

Bonnie protested, "Oh, she's definitely not. Most up to date."

Wade sipped his scotch. "I guess I'd fit right in with the government types tonight."

Davidson waved his hand. "Oh, a good drink now and then is fine."

Somehow Wade felt he was the odd man out, almost a real boozer. He drank slowly.

Davidson returned to his subject. "You know, the West Coast wanted to bid on this contract. They thought it was too big for us in the Washington area. I really had to work on them to convince them that our proximity to the Department of Transportation was important and that we had the wherewithal to do it. I told them about you, Jim, and your broad experience in winning proposals. They finally gave in and told me we had better produce. It should make you feel important, Jim, to have your name out there like that. We're all depending on you."

Wade forced himself to speak firmly. "We have a good team, Gunnar. B-E can count on us. We're well into it, and things look good." He wished he felt that way. *Shit, this is a hell of a situation to be in.*

Just then, a woman wearing an apron came to the door. "Mrs. Davidson, dinner is ready."

Thank God, Wade thought.

CHAPTER TWENTY-ONE

Wade called his staff together at eight thirty Tuesday morning.

He looked at Fortiano. "Where the hell have you been, Danny? I wanted to hold this meeting at eight o'clock, but we couldn't find you."

Danny snapped to attention. "I work out at the gym every morning. Sometimes I get held up in traffic after that."

Wade glared. "I understand all those muscles take work, but do it on your own time. I want everyone here by eight and no later." He turned and looked at his managers. "I had a cometo-Jesus meeting with Davidson last night. He made it clear that our futures are riding on this proposal. You'll be here from eight in the morning until six at night. I don't want Davidson or Evenson coming here and not finding us working. Does everyone understand?" He looked around and got nods and earnest stares. "That having been said, how about giving me an update?" Wade turned to Davies. "Sid, where do we stand?"

Davies looked like he was caught a little off guard. "Well, Jim, as you know the creative teams have had several sessions brainstorming ideas. Those that they have looked at are being fleshed out into more detail with illustrations and so forth. I'll let Danny speak to them in more detail."

Fortiano spoke up eagerly, hoping to redeem himself and show he was in charge. "The creative teams have made good progress. I've sat in on many of the meetings and have been able to give a lot of input, to help drive them forward. Let me outline some of the ideas we're working on."

Fortiano opened a file of input the teams had given him and took out a pile of papers, some typed, some handwritten, all with notes scribbled in the margins.

"Hendricks's team is working on a couple of ideas. One is based on a grid of wire, a raster, under the road that will drive vehicles along with magnetic pulses. It will require a drive attachment, a cart or wagon to be attached to each vehicle to receive the pulse. Through the grid, we'll also be able to track the vehicles, ensure their safe separation, move them from lane to lane, and control their exit. Basically it uses the same road surfaces that are in existence today, upgraded for eighty-mile-an-hour traffic and with the grid implanted." He turned to another paper. "Their second idea is heavily mechanical. It proposes the use of short drive belts on which the vehicles will simply sit while they move along. The belts will be short enough such that, if any single belt fails, the vehicles will be able to simply roll over them. That requires the vehicles to be in neutral, something that will have to be ensured through software. The system would require a mechanical system like an airport baggage carousel to load the vehicles on and take them off the belts and requires each highway lane of belts to have separate entrances and exits. A major issue is the exiting of vehicles traveling at eighty miles an hour in neutral. Since the team's initial meeting, their software and logistics people have come up with a third idea, a modification of the first proposal. In this proposal, they'll have the vehicles drive onto a cart or have a wagon attached that would then do the driving for the vehicles, using internal, battery powered motors rather than magnetic pulses. With the carts, the vehicles would be in park, but with the wagons, they would have to be in neutral. Again, software would have to be used to ensure the vehicle transmissions would be in the correct gear. In all these systems, the automobile ignitions could be turned off while traveling on the highways, thus saving gasoline. Again, software would have to be used to ensure the ignitions are off. There is, further, the problem of lost time in restarting the vehicles after arrival at the destination.

"Manny Brown's team offers different ideas. One is the landlocked ferryboat approach. This will use ferryboat-like assemblies. Many vehicles would be loaded onto the ferry, which would then follow electric tracks buried under the roads and run on tracks using railroad-like wheels. This would eliminate any need for software to interact with vehicles and save on gasoline, and on long trips, it would allow vehicle passengers to leave their cars and go to rest rooms, cafeterias, and the like. The two major issues are that there would have to be a separate ferry for each exit, and the time required to load and unload may be prohibitive. As a second proposal, they are considering a trolley car approach, in which an electric drive wagon with an electrical wand interacting with an overhead power cable would be attached to the vehicle with different-sized wagons for different-sized vehicles. As in some of Hendricks's models, software would have to ensure the cars are in neutral, and the cars would have to restart when they leave the system."

"For power, most of these ideas use fields of solar panels along the roads, solar panels on arches over the roads, or wind turbines on towers along the roads, supplemented by the power grid. They emphasize the use of clean energy in driving the vehicles down the highway.

"The third team, Gabriel Winnick's, has still other ideas. One is more software driven. It would attach a solar -powered box to the roof of the vehicles. The box would have software controlled by a master station that would interact with the vehicle's internal software to take control of the vehicle and drive it along. The big difficulty is that not all vehicles have software with which to interact, and much of the software is not uniform from vehicle brand to vehicle brand. The idea is simpler than some others proposed but excludes a lot of vehicles currently on the road. It also fails to use renewable energy. Gabriel's team has also proposed a swamp boat model with a fan cart or wagon attached to each vehicle to drive it forward. Again, the vehicle would have to be in neutral. The wagon or cart would have its own solar panels and could have its power upgraded each time it is returned to an exit. I suspect that could be done to many of these systems.

"Nearly all these systems will have to be controlled by a master software system to ensure speed and separation are maintained, especially on entrance to and exit from the system. It's going to be a big challenge."

Wade waited a moment. "That's it? Sounds like the Wild West— all these carts and wagons whizzing around from exit to entrance, being detached and reattached, and being charged along the way. It's hard to imagine that we can do it fast enough, especially with all the plastic bumpers cars use these days. I can just see them being torn apart. And having to restart engines at exits, depending on human response times to prevent pileups. It makes me cringe. Make sure you address these things and assure me that they can be done."

Wade thought a moment. "As a side thought, I hate this wagon and cart nomenclature. With a wagon, I picture a child pulling something by a handle. It's a lousy image. We need a different name. *Tug* won't do because it sounds like something moving at two or three miles an hour. *Tow* won't do because we might push. Let's call them *guide vehicles* or *drive carts*. I like the latter best. Let's go with that."

Wade turned to Beverly Byrnes. "So, Bev, what do you think?"

Byrnes hesitated. "'Drive carts sounds fine. Is that what you're asking about?"

"No, no. I'm asking about the ideas for the proposal."

Bev looked a little concerned. "I think there's a lot to do. I just wish I knew what plan to work with. Seems like we're going to do a lot of controlling. Right now, I'm trying to learn as much as I can about the software in today's vehicles. Unfortunately, a lot of it is proprietary. If we do this, I may need government help to get the information from the vehicle manufacturers. As far as the design is concerned, I'm going to need a lot of engineering help with antennas and such to help track these vehicles along the way. Grids or rasters may help, but it's going to be a challenge."

Lionel Haverford was next. "Lionel, what are the logistic concerns?"

"The biggest is all these carts and things. We're going to have to have them built. We don't have a team member to do that. We'll have to find someone, and they're going to have to ramp up. It's no small thing. We're going to have to build more than the number of vehicles that will be on the highway at maximum traffic. Don't have any idea how many to build for this twenty-mile test case, and there's no way to start early. We have to win the first phase before we do much more than feel out some manufacturers. The earlier I can figure what we're talking about specifically, the better off we'll be."

Next, Wade addressed Matt Somers. "You think there's enough systems engineering here, Matt?"

"Lord yes," exclaimed Somers. "I just don't know what we'll be bringing together. There are going to be changes in the current highways or additions of overhead or underground third rails, construction of power systems, insertion of underground wires, strange entrance and exit systems, hardware to move around, carts or wagons or ferry boats, manufacture and delivery of those things, toll gates, and I don't know what. And it will all have to come together at the right time. This is going to be wild."

Finally, Wade looked at David Swenson. "Dave, I know the proposal has lots of blanks. What are you doing while you wait?"

"There's always a lot to do. There's lots of boilerplate the government requires, and I have that coming along pretty well. I've got the skeleton for the proposal. I'm waiting to fill in the blanks."

Wade leaned back and sighed. "This is a real mess. We have a lot of wild ideas that need to be refined and made realistic. Matt, I want you and Danny to work with our guys and make sense out of what is happening. I'd like this all narrowed down to two plans by Monday noon of next week. Our plans have to be on Davidson's desk by next Tuesday. The burden's on you two."

CHAPTER TWENTY-TWO

Wade parked in his driveway. He sat and fumed. Finally, he opened the door and got out. The morning's newspaper was still lying in the front yard, double wrapped in thin plastic bags. He picked it up and angrily threw it at the front steps. He needed to beat up on something. The newspaper was as good as anything. He picked it up again and unlocked the front door. He dreaded having to talk to anyone.

In the entrance hall, he listened for noise that would lead him to Bonnie. He heard the television sound coming from the kitchen. He headed that way. Bonnie was watching the news on the small television on the kitchen counter. Wade set the newspaper on the island, took off his suit coat, placed it over the back of the bar stool, leaned on the stool, and made his pronouncement. "Another shitty day!"

Bonnie had watched him the whole time, trying to judge his mood. She finally decided it was the same as it had been ever since the proposal work began. "And hello to you, too. I gather things are getting no better. You've been extra miserable to live with since the Davidson dinner Monday."

"Hell, you heard him put the screws to me. The rich asshole. He has everyone afraid to leave our office building. He wants to win this thing like there's some magic solution out there. The whole proposal is DOT's wet dream of the future. What time is it, anyway?"

Bonnie was leery about responding. "It's a little after seven. I've kept dinner warm."

"That's great. Work's gone to shit, and I have to eat warmed-over food."

"Hey, it's only been half an hour since it was ready. It's fine. I'll start planning to have dinner a little later."

Wade pulled out the stool and sat at the island. "Might as well eat here. Get it over with."

Bonnie sighed. "The mood you're in, you're probably not going to taste it anyway."

"You'd be in a 'mood' too if you had to listen to the wild ideas my so-called engineers are coming up with. Fancy software driven tugboats pushing four-person ships across America. I told Davies they were proposing everything but pneumatic tubes. He said they had thought of that but couldn't figure out how to send more than one car at a time. Bank teller mentality." Bonnie had no patience. "Damn, Jim, you're the leader. Why don't you come up with ideas and guide them?"

Wade wheeled toward her. "So, it's my failure."

"Didn't say that. But you're the boss. The old 'the buck stops here.'"

"Not a buck. A handful of loose change thrown into the air. A nebulous problem with many dubious solutions. A real mess."

Bonnie gave up. "Let me make you a scotch and you can sit in the den. I'll leave you alone." *And, hopefully, you'll leave me alone.*

Wade took his scotch to the den. Bonnie went upstairs and took a pill.

* * *

Charlie arrived home to find both Linda's and Ralph's cars were already in the driveway. He parked behind Ralph's car so that his car wouldn't stick out in the road. Linda had no sense about where to park.

He entered the house to find the boys in the living room watching television, Ralph stretched out on the sofa and Ed slouched in a chair. Ralph's cleaned dinner plate sat on the coffee table.

Charlie thought, *Everybody's home but me.*

He looked around. "Everything okay with you guys? Football practice go okay?"

The boys didn't take their eyes off the television. "Yeah. Everything's good."

Charlie made his way to the kitchen. Linda looked up when he came in. "You didn't tell me you were going to play handball?"

Charlie kissed he cheek. "I didn't play handball. New rules at work. We have to work at least till six, no matter what. Has to look like we're working hard and looking creative in case the big boss walks in."

Linda shook her head. "Do you get paid overtime for that?"

"No such thing for managers. Only the worker bees get that."

"You're not a worker bee?"

"I guess I'm a high-level worker bee. It's a privilege for folks like us to work late. I think you'd better plan on it for the near future."

Linda made a dinner plate for Charlie. "That's going to mean the boys are going to be alone more than I had hoped, but I'm not going to give up my job. I've waited too long for it."

Charlie was irritated. "No one is asking you to give up your job. The boys are old enough. They'll adapt."

Linda put Charlie's plate on the kitchen table. "They're going to have to. I have dreams too."

Charlie hated being defensive. "I know you do. What are you working on now?"

Linda knew Charlie was trying to change the subject and the mood. She sat down opposite him. "Okay. I'm sorry about sounding off. I guess I'm feeling a little guilty about the boys. It's a mother thing." She swallowed and looked thoughtful. "I guess we're both in new worlds, and it's going to take getting used to. Yvonne's got a job at the State Department Friday night. Reception for some foreign dignitary. The job's hard work, but it's exciting to work on this level, seeing all the important people, serving them, hearing them talk, getting to look at all the beautiful dresses. Feels like I'm flying at a high altitude. Way above anything I've ever known, even if it's only as an observer."

Charlie held his fork in the air. "I'm sorry."

Linda was startled. "Sorry for what?"

Charlie put the fork down. "For not giving you the life you deserve. All I've given you is parties at officer's clubs with all the guys I work with, backyard barbecues, dinner out at Chili's, not a lot of excitement."

"Charlie. Don't be silly. I didn't grow up in a world of glamour. We've managed all right. It's just that I'm doing the catering I love and seeing all the glamour from just outside the fishbowl. It's fun. I'm fine with it."

"Good. I'm happy for you."

Linda accepted that. "Are you happy, Charlie? You were comfortable in the army, but I never knew if you were happy. Is this new job working out?"

Charlie thought about it. "I think so. It's always hard being new. In the military, it always seemed like everything was a continuing process. There were people around you who had done the same things before. In the engineering district, there were civilians who had been there for years. Dredging the harbors was nothing new. In Afghanistan, we built roads, patched roads, built airfields, and the like. It had all been done before. At Bedford-Ewings, I initially had a very boring job, and now I've volunteered for this proposal, thinking it would fit into my engineering background. Instead, I'm beginning to feel I'm in over my head, working on a problem that may have no answer, with my job depending on it. I feel like we're all going to be fired if we don't win, but we don't seem to have a winning strategy. The leaders don't seem to have direction, and the little guys are just dreaming big. But the dreams seem untenable."

Linda thought she'd never heard Charlie talk so much or so hopelessly. "Charlie, there must be a bunch of companies working on the same proposal, a bunch of people feeling the same pressure. Everyone is not going to be fired. Companies lose proposals all the time."

Charlie was beginning to feel the pressure he had been denying. "Yeah, but this would be like Lockheed Martin losing a fighter contract to Northrop Grumman. The impact of winning is so important. The loss is devastating."

Linda put her hand on Charlie's. "Charlie, all you can do is your best. You're not the one losing millions. Life will go on."

Charlie smiled wanly. "I think it's billions. It's a figure I don't understand anyway."

Linda smiled. "There's only so much the little guy can do. Eat your dinner, and let's go in with the boys."

*   *   *

Sid Davies sat at a bar in Rosslyn nursing a bourbon and water. His condominium overlooking the Marine Memorial had grown lonely since his wife, Anne, had passed away. The horror of her long fight against breast cancer and her rapid decline to death in the end still weighed on him. He had felt so helpless. He recalled the surgery and the long hours of sitting in chairs while Anne was filled with chemicals, a process that seemed to go on for months as if it would never end. But it did end. Precipitously. A rapid descent into helplessness and then death.

Davies wondered why he didn't just pack up. The children were in Alabama and California. If they were in one place, he would move to be near them; but with their separation, he couldn't make a decision. He'd just stay.

He didn't really enjoy his job. He was sorry he hadn't just stayed with the government relations office in Rosslyn. He could walk to work. Now, he was driving every day to a job where he really didn't have a job. He was just using his army rank to give some kind of panache to the position of deputy. Getting his one star was an achievement, but it wasn't like having three or four stars and becoming a corporate VP or advisor to a president.

He glanced at the gentleman sitting next to him. "By yourself?"

The man didn't look up. "Yeah. My wife left me."

Davies was sorry he had asked and didn't know if he should commiserate. "I'm sorry to hear that."

"Oh, it's not her fault. I can't blame her. My work hours were too long. We couldn't have children. She was lonely. Moved in with another woman. Needed companionship. Hell, I understand. Still, I miss her."

Davies felt for the man. "So, why the long hours?"

"I work for Congress. Oversee the work drafting the bills, trying to resolve issues. Often goes long. All those guys have their agendas. Iterate and iterate. Never ending."

"Doesn't sound like it makes you happy."

The man lifted his head and stretched his neck. "Hell, it was exciting in the beginning, when I was young—interacting with all the congressional staffs and sometimes the big boys themselves. But it got old. Wish I could have given it up fifteen or twenty years ago. Done something else. But now, I need the paycheck. Waiting to get in my thirty years. How about you? You got sad bar talk too?"

Davies thought, pursed and licked his lips. "Yes. I'm a widower. Lonely too. Work for a government contractor, Bedford-Ewings International. Working on a proposal—the replacement for the Interstate Highway System."

"Yeah. I heard about that. Big bucks. I wish you luck. How you going to do it?"

"Wish I knew. Lots of ideas are being floated. Hope our smart guys can figure it out."

The man looked at Davies. "You're not one of the smart guys?"

Davies chuckled. "No. I manage the smart guys."

The man laughed. "Sounds like a job. Wish I could manage smart guys. My guys are mostly drones."

Davies finished his drink and stood up. He shook the man's hand. "Sid Davies."

The man responded, "Jerry Harlem."

As Davies left, he said, "See you around."

Harlem replied, "I'll be right here."

CHAPTER TWENTY-THREE

Charlie met with his team Wednesday morning. He had given everyone a heads-up after Wade's Tuesday morning meeting. Everyone settled in, looking uncertain. Charlie leaned forward. "I know you guys are working on the details of your plans, but time is running out on us. We have to limit all the plans the various teams are working on down to two by next Monday. There's no way we can do that if we're working on three plans. We have to narrow things in our team, preferably down to one plan. I'll prepare a concept paper by Friday so I can pitch it to Wade.

Hopefully we can make it a strong contender."

Pelligrini clapped his hands and asserted, "Hey. There's clearly only one winner. My electrical system is the best."

Wiggins protested, "Being the loudest doesn't make it the best."

Charlie jumped in. "Settle down, guys. We're going over all the plans."

He walked to the pad of paper on the easel. "Okay, let's start with Andy's system, since it was first out of the gate. Let's list the good points," He wrote:

It requires no gasoline and uses renewable energy.

It doesn't require road maintenance in the traditional sense.

It causes no wear and tear on vehicles.

It requires no movement of drive carts or wagons between exits and entrances.

It requires no mating with drive carts or wagons to cars and trucks.

It would work for vehicles of all ages.

"Anything else?"

Wiggins quickly interjected, "Yes, it's sexy. But what's a 'drive cart'?"

Charlie smiled. "Yeah, it is 'sexy' and will look good when illustrated in *Popular Mechanics.* It's a valid point, but most of these plans fit that bill." He then smiled. "As to your question, Jim Wade doesn't like 'wagons' and 'carts'. He wants them called 'drive carts.' However, for today I need to differentiate between the two kinds, so temporarily I'm going to continue calling them carts and wagons.

Charlie added "sexy" to the list, turned back to the groups and asked, "Anything else?"

Bahr spoke up. "I don't think the 'vehicle of all ages' is true. I'm going to have to communicate with them to keep them in neutral. That's a problem with older vehicles."

Wiggins sighed. "Shit. Software screws up my beautiful system."

Bahr glared at him. "Software is going to have to save your 'beautiful system.' Otherwise, you're going to be dumping cars onto your belts on top of each other."

Charlie had to intercede again. "Okay. The point is valid. Older vehicles are going to be a problem in lots of systems. Even in the newer vehicles, there may be major variations in software in different brands, and that may be a problem. I'm afraid that goes in the negatives. Any more good things?"

Charlie looked around. "All right, let's list negatives. We've already talked about control problems. Let's list them." He wrote:

Difficulty in ensuring vehicle transmissions are in the right gear through software.

Uncertainty in being able to control the mechanical system so that cars are loaded on the belt safely separated.

Wiggins objected. "Hey, that's a software problem."

Charlie shook his head. "Well, I suspect it's both.

"How about this?" Charlie turned back to the list and began writing.

Access for maintenance every hundred feet or so.

"Seems like that's going to require roads parallel to each lane of belts and vehicles that can move some pretty heavy stuff at each belt axle."

Pelligrini agreed. "And how about the exit? Andy said he would figure it out, but it seems to me the vehicles are going to leave the belts like projectiles, little vehicles landing a hundred feet away and semis jackknifed ten feet away. Like flipping pancakes."

Charlie addressed Wiggins. "Have you found a solution?"

Wiggins looked down and sighed. "I'm afraid not."

Charlie wrote it on the board as a negative.

Usher cut in. "With all these maintenance roads and multiple access paths at each entrance, there's going to be a requirement for lots more land and there are big problems with overpasses, underpasses, and tunnels, not to mention bridges. The eminent domain lawsuits are going to tie up the whole thing, not to mention the environmental impact approvals."

Charlie wrote that down.

Pelligrini wanted the final word. "And we have the problem we mentioned in the last meeting. How do you stop all these vehicles with transmissions in neutral when they leave the belts? Are you going to have them go up a ramp? How high do you have to go to stop a multiton tractor trailer?"

Wiggins groaned as that was added to the list.

Charlie scanned the group. "If there is nothing else, let's start beating up on Bennie since he's been so helpful so far. Let's list the good things about his plan. We can start with 'it's sexy,' since that seems to be the appealing thing." He wrote:

It's sexy.

It uses the existing road rights-of-way.

It requires no gasoline and uses renewable energy.

With the cart concept, there would be no wear and tear of the vehicles. With the wagon attachment, only the tire and wheel system suffers wear and tear.

Because of the control by a wagon or cart, entry acceleration and exit deceleration would be handled by the wagon or cart as controlled by software.

The wagon or cart could use sensors to locate itself safely among the wagons and carts, perhaps without continuous control from a base station. Control of the vehicle's transmission might also be controlled from the cart, although this continues to depend on being able to communicate with the vehicle.

Charlie looked around. "Anything else?"

Bahr said, "It almost sounds like it's doable. What are the disadvantages?"

Charlie turned back to the easel. "Well, let's list some." He wrote:

The lead time and expense of building wagons or carts.

The use of an inductive drive system that probably requires a lot of energy and a raster system, which are unproven technologies.

The psychological response of people being subjected to inductive pulses.

The time issues associated with loading vehicles onto carts or connecting wagons without damage to the vehicles.

The requirement for a huge mechanical system to move wagons or carts from exits to entrances and being able to store them during lulls between peaks in traffic.

The space that would be required for the aforementioned mechanical system. This would probably preclude exits and entrances in urban areas. Again there would be the eminent domain and environmental impact problems.

Bahr shook her head. "Now it doesn't sound too good."

Charlie acknowledged that. "Yes, none of these proposals is easy. Now, let's look at the idea you and Henry suggested. It seems a little cleaner than the others." He turned back to the easel:

It uses the existing road rights-of-way.

Assuming the wagon or carts would be battery-powered, this would again be a system that would use renewable energy.

Wear and tear of the vehicles would be the same as in the inductive model.

The entrance and exit processes would be controlled by the cart and wagon, as would the vehicle spacing and transmission control just as done in the inductive model.

"It also has many of the same problems as the inductive model":

The lead time and expense of building wagons or carts.

The time issues associated with loading vehicles onto carts or connecting wagons without damage to the vehicles.

The requirement for a huge mechanical system to move wagons or carts from exits to entrances and being able to store them during lulls between peaks in traffic.

The space that would be required for the aforementioned mechanical system. This would probably preclude exits and entrances in urban areas. Again there would be the eminent domain and environmental impact problems.

Limits in the range of wagons and carts using batteries (although we might supplement with solar panels on the wagons or carts).

The requirement to recharge the wagons or carts in the storage area with the associated loss of time.

Charlie turned to his group. "I hope this sums it up. I'm going to make a decision as to what model we'll pursue unless I get violent objections right now. Because of the problems of the mechanical system not having an exit solution and not being adaptable to existing bridges, tunnels, and so forth, I'm rejecting it. I think the inductive system has too much unproven technology. Therefore, I would like to go with the last system. Andy, I think you have plenty of mechanical issues to deal with in the transfer of the wagons and carts from exit to entrance and the connection issue of wagons and carts to vehicles. I'd like you to think, also, about how the wagons and carts can handle the issue of flat tires on the vehicles. Bennie, there are lots of issues for you with the need to charge all these wagons and carts quickly in massive numbers. Perhaps we're going to have to incorporate a third rail of some kind. Joannie, you have to worry about this software on the wagons and carts and whether it can communicate with the vehicles. Henry, you need to explore sources for constructing carts or wagons; find out capabilities and response times. And, finally, I want you all to look into what happens at the exits. Drivers need to restart their vehicles and drive off. Otherwise, we'll have pileups. I'd like to meet again on Thursday morning at ten. Please have ideas, drawings, and whatever you can bring to the table. Any questions?"

He looked around. Everyone looked a little stunned.

He got gathered his papers and got up. "See you Thursday."

CHAPTER TWENTY-FOUR

Fortiano knocked on Wade's door frame.

Wade looked up, looking slightly annoyed. "Hi, Danny. Come in." He looked back down at whatever he was studying.

Fortiano went in, took a seat, and waited.

Wade looked at him. "What's up?"

Fortiano launched into his practiced pitch. "I'm becoming worried, especially about this guy Hendricks. His ideas seem too complicated. I don't know that he's providing good leadership."

Wade's eyes became hooded. He knew he had to listen to Fortiano, but he didn't trust him. "How so? His team seems to have more ideas than the other teams, and everyone's ideas seem to be from the Syfy Network. I'm worried, too, but not about the leadership. I'm worried about the rationality of the whole thing. What about Hendricks worries you?"

Fortiano continued. "He's a civil engineer. I think he's in over his head in the technical world involved in this proposal. Besides that, he's new in the company. He doesn't have the experience needed."

Wade nodded. "Okay. Say you're right. What do you propose that we do about it?"

Fortiano struggled for an answer. He hadn't thought ahead. "I would like to be more directly involved in his team."

Wade hesitated. It would be singling out Hendricks's team, showing a lack of faith in the man. "Tell you what. He has his next meeting scheduled on Thursday. Why don't you sit in for the whole meeting? See if you can guide the group in the direction you think is appropriate."

"That sounds fine. I just wanted you to know there may be a weak link in Hendricks."

* * *

Wade phoned Davies and asked him to come to his office.

When Davies came, he hesitated to sit, unlike Fortiano. "Have a seat, Sid," Wade directed.

Davies pulled up a chair. "How do you think things are going?"

Wade leaned back. "I'm not sure. In fact, I'm a little worried. All these plans seem too complex. If I had better ideas, I'd push them. What's your feeling?"

"I agree with you. They're all very complex and, I think, superexpensive. Plus, procurement of all these drive carts is going to have a long lead time. I think they're more significant than a subcontract. We're going to need another partner. Something that can drag a tractor trailer along at eighty miles an hour, running on batteries, is going to take a monumental design and manufacturing effort. Just the development costs are going to be enormous. I'm worried about meeting timelines and I'm afraid that, if our competition comes up with a simpler idea, we'll be dead in the water."

Wade mulled that over. "Not a very encouraging assessment, but I'm afraid that I agree with you. I'm worried about giving Davidson a heads-up on this. Don't want to blindside him later, but I'm concerned about getting relieved or fired now."

Davies was startled. "You think he'd react that strongly?"

Wade sighed. "I think he might. He's putting so much import into this proposal. Like his life is depending on it."

Davies considered that. "Then let's think a little longer. Maybe the guys will come up with some other ideas."

"God, I hope so." Wade leaned back. "Different subject. What do you think about this guy Hendricks? You worked with him before."

Davies thought he needed to be careful. "He's a good man. Maybe too honest and caring. Obviously, he has little experience in the territory where he's now working, but he has plenty of support, and I've heard no complaints from the bull pen. Why do you ask?"

Wade wondered if he shouldn't put Danny on the spot, but decided, *What the heck?*

Danny was no friend. "Danny has some reservations about him. Thinks he is too inexperienced. Wants to step in and provide more leadership."

Davies became wary. He didn't want to overstep himself. "Well, Danny might be right, but I haven't been very impressed with *him* either. You put the burden on him and Matt. Hope he's not trying to pass the buck to someone else. Obviously, you know him and have confidence in him."

Wade replied cautiously. "Let's just say that I owe him. But I also watch him." He rose from his desk and shook Davies's hand. "I appreciate you being straight with me. I need someone I can talk to confidentially."

Davies nodded. The message was clear, and he liked being a confidant.

CHAPTER TWENTY-FIVE

Linda was at Goshen Towers working on the Walter Reed Hostel fund-raiser when her cell phone rang.

She answered and a voice said, "Hi. It's Stephen."

Linda's mind raced. *Stephen? Stephen who? Stephen Davenport.* "Oh, hi, Stephen. We were just talking about you."

"We?"

"Yes. I'm at Goshen Towers going over the fund-raiser with Betty, Jeanie and Ben Swaim. It's a nice facility. We'll have a good layout of tables, and I know what flowers we'll need. It's coming along." She moved away from the others. "The kitchen is a little small, but we'll make do. Probably have to do some prework somewhere else. No problem. We've done it before."

"That sounds great. I'd like to talk to you some about it so I can give an update to the senator."

"Do you want to come by the office?"

"No. What I'd like to ask is a favor."

"A favor. What's that?"

"I have to go to a fund-raiser at the Willard for the Kennedy Center on Friday night.

Black-tie affair. When I go to these things by myself, I always feel I'm a wallflower."

Linda remembered him talking to the young blond. "Seriously, I doubt that."

Davenport protested. "You'd be surprised. Sometimes it makes me feel like I should get married."

Linda laughed. "That would be a drastic move. More than parties go with marriage."

Davenport agreed. "I know. That's why I save myself each time."

Linda needed to get back to her group. "I can't help you there, so what can I do for you?"

"You can be my escort."

Linda almost gagged. "I'm married. And besides, Yvonne has an event that night."

"Are you in charge of the event?"

"No, just helping."

"Then let the others run it. As for being married, that doesn't matter. I'm not asking you for marriage. I just want an attractive woman by my side so that we can have a pleasant evening. There'll be a lot of glamour. You'll enjoy it. And these donors are people you don't see every day. All the dresses and the whirl will be wonderful. There will even be a few celebrities there. Please say you'll do it?"

Linda's mind whirled. *Charlie will never know about it. The attendees will be people he'll never meet.* She would just have to say she was catering a function. "Well, okay. That would be fun."

"It's at seven. May I pick you up at the office about quarter of?"

Again, Linda thoughts scrambled. "No. People are going to start asking questions." Especially if she got dressed at work in an evening dress and went out the door.

"Okay. What do you want to do?"

"I'll have to get dressed at the hotel and meet you there."

Davenport laughed. "I can just see you doing that in the lobby ladies room."

"I'll do it if I have to and then change back before I go home."

"That sounds awkward as hell to me. Tell you what. I'll get a hotel room. Have the key at the front desk in your name. I'll phone you in the room when I get to the hotel."

Linda thought, *What the hell am I doing?* "Okay, I'll be there waiting for your call."

"Wonderful. We're going to have a great time."

After he hung up, Linda thought, *I'm going to have to get an evening dress. Haven't had one in years. And a purse and shoes. What will I do with them after the party? No way to hide them or justify them at home. Maybe I'll just leave them at the hotel, but they might phone me about them since they'll have my name. I'll have to figure something out. Hate to waste the money, but what can I do?*

CHAPTER TWENTY-SIX

As Charlie entered the conference room, he was surprised to find Danny Fortiano there waiting Fortiano was sitting at the head of the table, Charlie's usual place. He smiled at Charlie and said, "I thought I would sit in so I can be up to date."

Charlie had always heard about the Cheshire cat and wondered what its smile looked like. "Sure. Glad to have you. I hope we're getting close."

The rest of the team filtered in, eyeing Fortiano sideways and wondering what he was all about.

Charlie sat in the middle of the side of the table facing the door. It was kind of an alternate position of authority and not too close to Fortiano.

Everyone sat. Charlie looked around and said, "All right. I'd like to go around the room and see where everyone stands."

Fortiano interrupted and pronounced. "I'd like to remind everyone that we need to have a package on Wade's desk Monday noon. I expect full-time work until then."

Everyone looked uncomfortable.

Charlie frowned. "I'm afraid to say it, but I'm going to need everyone's input by five Saturday afternoon. I'll need Sunday to put things together and will need you all on standby. Hope you didn't have anything planned."

He turned to Wiggins. "Andy, you have a lot to do. I'll need sketches of possible wagons and carts, along with specs. I'll also need sketches of a system for moving carts or wagons from exit to entrance and for storing them. Where do you stand and can you be ready?"

Wiggins gave Charlie a tired look. "Since you didn't buy my system, I was a little behind. I've been working till ten o'clock the last two nights. I need to ask, will we have graphic and typing support this weekend?"

Charlie looked at Fortiano while the others followed his look.

Fortiano thought, *These guys are the ones who are supposed to be answering questions, not me.* But he had to act with authority. "Of course you'll have that support. I'll make sure of it."

Andy looked pleased. "Then I can do it. However, I would like to only use wagons, not carts, probably three sizes of them. For most vehicles, the wagons will come from behind. They'll have padded arms that will clamp to the sides of the vehicles for guidance and a soft bumper that will contact the vehicles from behind. Tractor trailers will have to be pulled by large wagons. They'll again have arms, but these will reach behind the cab to clamp and pull. I recommend that tractor trailers use a different entrance and exit from the other vehicles, and I've designed the transfer and storage areas to support this concept. When the wagons release from the vehicles, they will maneuver using internal software guidance to move to parking spots until required at the entrance. It'll be first in, first out. We'll have to do a study of the traffic load for each geographical site using data from the interstate system. That will determine the size of our parking sites, although we may have to modify that based on the charging time for batteries, which Bennie will discuss. We'll have to get some mathematicians in to do a queuing study. The internal software will also control the wagons on the highway."

Charlie nodded. "That sounds good. It segues to the software."

Fortiano spoke up. "We need to deal with what Google and the automobile industry have already done with self-driving vehicles."

Joannie Bahr joined in. "Of course, that's right. We already planned to do that. We can do a lot internally, but I suspect we may have to partner with one of those outfits. I would think their systems are proprietary. We plan to also interact with the software through central control rooms to monitor the systems and ensure they are working correctly, that proper spacing and speed are being maintained, and so on. We'll also monitor for vehicle breakdown that will need servicing, such as flat tires. That includes vehicles and wagons. The internal software will monitor these things and take action to interact with other wagons to permit the damaged vehicles to move to the highway shoulder. I'm well on the way to specifying the requirements, but obviously the software development will have to wait for a development phase, which I suggest would happen during actual construction."

Fortiano cautioned. "We obviously need to have a system defined to the greatest extent possible when we make the bid. The government will want to know what it's going to get."

Bahr responded. "Yes. That's obvious. I'm the only one working software now, but once we decide on the model for the proposal, we'll have more people. This proposal is a three-month process. We'll do what we can, but complete software won't come that quickly."

Fortiano glared at her. "Well, be warned. You don't want to be the broken cog."

Charlie ignored Fortiano. "Bennie, what's happening with power?"

Pelligrini pouted. "Hell, you cut out a lot of it. We're going to have a lot of charging stations where these carts park. I've talked to Andy. We'll have charging contacts on the wagons that will dock in the parking stations, much like the contacts on our cordless home phones. The batteries and the charging times are unknowns. We'll have to work with a battery company, Tesla or somebody. Another issue will be keeping the contacts clean. We're planning to have the docks covered and doors on the wagons that will close when not charging. Obviously, we'll also have to have power for the control center and for any antenna sites for use by the software in interacting with the carts. We'll assume that the control centers will be colocated with the parking lots so that they and the docking stations can be run from wind turbines that will also be located at the parking lots. The antennas would be run off the existing power grid."

Fortiano queried, "Aren't wind turbines expensive?"

Pelligrini looked irritated. "Yeah. As is everything else in this proposal. If you wish, I'll look at putting a field of solar panels over the parking lot, but I can't do that by Monday."

Fortiano gave Bennie a stern look. "We just want to make sure we're competitive in cost.

Go on."

Charlie fumbled with his notes. "Okay, last but not least. Henry, what do you have?"

Usher smiled. "I thought you'd forgotten me."

Charlie smiled back. "With a name like yours, we expect a song and dance."

Usher looked at his notes. "And you will get it, but without music. Obviously, there will have to be a lot of major procurement. Wagons, docking stations, control centers, batteries, antennas, or is it antennae?"

Bennie piped up. "It depends on if they're feminine." He looked at Fortiano, who did not smile.

Usher continued. "Some of these things we can procure. We know how to put together control rooms, and wind towers and turbines are available. Probably the antennae are available. B-E has people on the West Coast who can help us there. The wagons, batteries, and some of the software are going to require contracts with other companies. We may have to bring some folks in as partners, although subcontracting may be possible. I think the wagons are the biggest problem. There are going to be lots of them. They will require major manufacturing plants, probably from the automotive industry, although General Dynamics or Boeing or someone like them might be interested. I figure the new highway will take years to complete, and a long-term manufacturing contract might be lucrative. The additional thing I see is the requirement to address vehicle breakdowns. We may be able to subcontract towing companies, but we're going to have to have shops for cart breakdown. They may not be part of this demonstration build in Georgia, but we'll need them eventually."

Charlie commented, "From a civil engineering standpoint, I'm fortunate that this system just requires old-fashioned highways. For the Georgia demonstration, we just need to subcontract road construction that meets an eighty-mile-an-hour standard. As a final comment, from now on, we'll cease to use the word *wagon'* and start calling the units *drive carts* as Jim Wade wishes. Are there any questions?"

He looked around. "Okay, I'm available any time for questions. I'll finalize the proposal for this concept with Jim Wade tomorrow. I feel certain that he'll buy in, so keep working and I'll look forward to your input by five Saturday afternoon."

Fortiano stood up. "And I'd like to see it as soon as it comes in. Make extra copies."

CHAPTER TWENTY-SEVEN

Charlie felt tired and inadequate. Additionally, he was annoyed with Fortiano. The musclebound ass had gotten to him.

He decided to get out of the office and go to the cafeteria for a soda and some potato chips.

He found Pelligrini sitting there by himself with a cup of coffee and decided to join him. "You look kind of melancholy for our team party guy."

Pelligrini smiled ruefully. "I miss my wife and kids. The guys and I have to do something to kill the evenings on the road, so we go to the bars and watch the girls. I make a lot of noise, but it gets old."

Charlie was surprised and tried to console him. "Hey, I know it's tough. It will only be a couple more months. Do they let you go home on weekends?"

"Yeah, if I don't have to work. But so far, I've worked every weekend."

"Well, I hope that will ease a bit." Charlie had a feeling that it wouldn't. "Do you often have to leave home for work?"

"Yeah. That's part of being with a power company. You go where disasters and weather take you. You never know where the work will be next. The pay's good, but it's like being in the army. I even spent time in Africa. Don't know whether I can stick with it or not."

Charlie nodded. "Yeah, I can commiserate. I've been to Iraq and Afghanistan. Not exotic worlds. How do you think this proposal is going?"

Pelligrini looked Charlie in the eye. "You really want to know? I think it's too complicated. I keep struggling with ideas, looking for some simple solution, but all this mechanical work just stays complicated. My company can do the electrical design, but I think the costs of everything proposed will be enormous. I can't imagine the government being happy with that."

Charlie sighed. "Yeah. I understand. I'm just grateful to have guys like you who can do this kind of work. What kind of things have you done before?"

"Mostly distribution systems for new developments, even theme parks. But mostly small stuff like upgrades to existing systems. And then, as I said, the bosses interrupt my work and send me off to cover the outages."

Charlie gave a doleful response. "At least I'm not the only bad guy. I appreciate what you do."

*   *   *

At home that night, Charlie found Linda humming to herself at the kitchen sink.

He kissed her on the cheek. "You sound happy."

Linda seemed to hesitate. "Yes. Things are exciting at work." She thought to herself, a little guiltily, *More exciting than I had ever really expected.* "How was your day?" It was the polite thing to say, though she had little interest.

"A little rough. As you know, sometimes I feel like I'm in over my head. All these guys I work with know so many things that I only distantly understand—mechanical engineering, software development and the like. I have to ask them to do work that I can't do. Don't know if I can even judge the credibility of what they produce."

Linda rinsed the salad she was tossing over the sink. "Uh-huh. Isn't that what managers always have to do?"

Charlie sat at the kitchen table. "I suppose so, but in the army I knew how to build the roads I worked on; knew how to use the equipment, even if I didn't run it; and knew what materials I needed and how to get them through the system. This is all new. Seems so much more complex."

Linda put the salad on plates and added small tomatoes and bread crumbs. "Umm, I understand. I can make a lot of the food we serve, but turning out the volume is complex; and I'm only so-so at flower arrangements. That's why we hire experts. My job is to plan, to coordinate, and to bring things together."

Charlie thought, *Yeah, there's an analogy, but the complexities don't compare.* "Yeah, but at least you can personally do those things. I wouldn't even know where to start."

Linda set the salads on the table. "Hey, you're just starting. You'll learn with time. You're a smart guy."

Charlie got up and got the eating utensils and napkins. "I hope you're right. What are you up to at work?"

Linda's mind raced. "We have a diplomatic reception Friday. It will probably go late."

Charlie was sad but reconciled. "This job is really eating your time. You're going to miss another football game. Hope you're going to be here this weekend. This proposal is going to work me both days, probably Saturday night and Sunday night too. I have to have the initial draft of what we want to do on Wade's desk Monday."

Linda wished she had something going on over the weekend, but she didn't. It would be lonely. "No problem. I'll be home all weekend."

Charlie was relieved. "That's great. I'm sorry. Seems like we're passing in the night."

Linda pulled a pork roast from the oven and began slicing. "It's a lot better than Iraq and Afghanistan. Still, I hope you reach nine to five sometime in your new job. It was nice before you got involved in this proposal."

Charlie acknowledged her thoughts. "I know. I'd liked that too. This proposal is really complicated, almost overwhelming in complexity. Lots of creativity involved. Software, batteries, renewable energy, almost anything you can think of."

Linda served the plates—pork, small potatoes, and salad. "You mean windmills and solar panels?"

Charlie corrected. "Yeah, wind turbines. Trying to get away from gasoline and diesel. Way of the future."

Linda was vague as she put the plates on the table. "That sounds interesting. Will you call the boys?"

CHAPTER TWENTY-EIGHT

Fortiano sat down heavily in a dining room side chair. Bella had been sitting at the table with papers spread out in front of her.

"Whatcha working on, gorgeous?"

"I'm doing the layout for a gun show at Dulles Expo. Coming up in mid-January. I'm making sure we don't double book space." She looked at Fortiano. "You look like shit. What's going on?"

"Looks like I'm going to be at work all weekend. Not really much I can do, but the other guys will be working, and I've got to be a presence. I'll get some input late Saturday and will have to make sure it's worked up into a decent package for Wade on Monday."

"Shit. I was hoping we might go to a show at the Kennedy Center Saturday night. Fortunately, it will still be on next weekend. Does the proposal have problems?"

"Well, it's complicated. And this guy Hendricks is annoying me. I think he has Wade's eye. He's running one of the teams, and they seem to be coming up with the best ideas."

Bella moved behind Fortiano's chair and pulled his head back against her breasts. "Just means you have to move in on him. Co-opt the ideas."

Fortiano stretched his neck back against Bella. "Already am. I ran his meeting today. Took over. The work will be delivered to me Saturday night. I'll get it put together and take the credit."

Bella rubbed Fortiano's shoulders. "Sounds like you're getting it under control." She walked around and looked at him. He had relaxed some. "I'm sorry about this weekend. I always love to spend my time with you. And I'm afraid my father has compounded the problem. He wants to have me as his escort at a fund-raiser Friday night. Mother's sick. I really think she's trying to avoid the whole thing, so I'm stuck. Life depends on keeping Bobby C happy, as you well know."

Fortiano frowned. "I know." He reached up and took her hands and pulled her onto his lap. "I guess we better make the most of tonight."

CHAPTER TWENTY-NINE

Linda had felt silly carrying her dress over her arm across the Willard Hotel's lobby. She had on her business clothes and was carrying her cosmetics, shoes, and evening purse in her briefcase. Only the dress seemed out of place. And there should have been a suitcase for someone staying overnight. She felt conspicuous, or was it guilt?

She had used the valet parking at the door. She hadn't been able to picture herself carrying the dress through an underground parking lot. Fortunately, it was in an opaque plastic bag, and that helped.

She gave her name to the man behind the reception desk and he brought up a computer window. "Oh, yes. Room 634. And it's paid for." He processed the door key card and put it in an envelope, writing the room number on the outside. He gave her a knowing smile as he handed her the key.

She took it and glared. She thought, *You don't know anything.*

She took the elevator up to her room, set the briefcase on the hall floor, and struggled with her dress as she passed the key card into the slot, getting a red light, trying again, and finally getting a green light and opening the door.

She picked up her briefcase and entered. It was a nice room, bathroom to the left in front, a single king bed, and a view overlooking part the Ellipse and the National Mall. Her mind staggered. *Davenport must have paid a fortune to get this view.* She wished she could see the White House, but the Department of the Treasury was in the way. Still she stood at the window mesmerized, watching the traffic along Constitution Avenue and looking at the World War II Memorial and the tip of the Washington Monument. She finally brought herself back to the moment and reluctantly drew the draperies closed. She stripped off her suit and hung it in the closet, took her things out of the briefcase, putting the shoes on the floor and the evening purse on the bed. She took her cosmetics to the bathroom and applied her makeup, grateful that the lighting was better than what she had at home. She stood back and looked at herself until she was finally satisfied. In the bedroom, she took her dress out of the plastic bag, admired the blue, and slipped it on. She had a terrible time with the zipper. She remembered similar struggles as a teenager.

When was the last time I had on a long dress? She pondered the question. *Maybe ten years ago, New Year's Eve at the Fort Belvoir Officer's Club, maybe only two or three times since college.* She pulled up at the bodice. *I don't remember it being cut so low when I tried it on.* Still, the exposed skin was clear. She thought she looked good.

She checked the clock by the bed. Six thirty. She had a few minutes to wait. She had never done that in high school. She had always been running late. *Mom and Dad would be downstairs to entertain my dates, making them nervous so that they were relieved and excited when I had finally come downstairs.* Now she had to wait.

She was afraid to sit and wrinkle her dress. She opened the draperies again and looked out at the National Mall. She wondered if people could see her at the window. She wondered if they thought she was a fairy princess, all dressed up for the ball.

Finally, there was a knock at the door. She wondered who it could be. Davenport was supposed to phone. She went to the door. "Yes, who's there?"

"It's Prince Charming, come to escort you to the ball."

She opened the door. Davenport was standing there with a corsage. She hadn't had one since college. "You were supposed to phone."

Davenport smiled and handed her the corsage. "Don't you think it would be awkward to have a lovely woman wandering around the lobby in an evening dress looking for her date?"

The word *date* startled Linda. It was different from *escort*, for helping out a friend. "Come in. The corsage is lovely. Let me put it on."

Davenport took it back from her hand, opened the plastic box, took out the corsage, and withdrew the pin. "Here, let me put it on."

Linda felt him pull the fabric loose at her breast. It felt very personal. She was afraid she was blushing.

Davenport seemed not to notice. He smiled and held his arm out for her to take. "May I escort you, Miss Hendricks?"

No Mrs. Thoughts whirled through Linda's mind.

Davenport led her to the elevators. The door opened. Four people were already on the elevator. They all moved awkwardly to give her room for her skirt.

As they entered the lobby, Linda was relieved to see other evening dresses and gentleman in tuxedos. Most looked older than her, but not everyone. They were all headed for the ballroom. Davenport guided her to a table. "I checked the table number and its location before I came upstairs. We're with Senator McDonald's party."

He introduced her to the people sitting near her. "This is Linda Henderson, my lovely date."

Linda looked at him, questioningly, thinking, *So I'm Henderson tonight. Not even a real person. A clandestine "date."* She felt uncomfortable. She shook hands with the man next to her. "Pleased to meet you."

Then she reached past him to shake hands with his wife, who said, "Well, Stephen's done very well tonight. You're lovely."

Linda pulled back and looked at Davenport, who was talking to the woman to his left and thought, *Looks like you've been with these same people in the past with different "dates." At least it sounds like I pass the test.* Then she thought, *Why am I being testy? Of course he's had other "dates." He's been going to these things for twenty-odd years. What did I expect?* Still she didn't like being a "date."

Finally, Senator McDonald arrived and was introduced, and they all sat. The senator seemed to appraise her without subtlety from across the table. She hoped she passed.

People kept coming to the table throughout the dinner, talking to the senator, who often had to stand for ladies. She wondered how he ate. *Maybe he is experienced enough that he ate before he came.*

People spoke to Davenport as well. He repeatedly introduced her a Linda Henderson, the daughter of an old friend from Iowa who was in town visiting. She was glad to know who she was. She talked to the man next to her and told him she was a family friend who hadn't seen Stephen for years. She told him how exciting it was to be able to see Stephen again in such glamorous circumstances.

Finally, when dinner was over and speeches were made about the Kennedy Center, the dance floor was opened, and the band began playing. She felt someone standing by her chair and looked up to see Senator McDonald.

"May I have this dance?"

Linda was startled and blurted, "Shouldn't you dance with your wife first?"

The senator laughed. "She hates to dance and knows I like beautiful women."

As McDonald led her to the dance floor, Linda was blushing. It was nice to be called "beautiful" by a United Stated Senator, although she suspected it was just for show.

As they danced, the senator looked down at her. "So you're from Iowa. What part?"

Linda thought, *If I lie, I'm just going to bury myself.* "You know I'm not from Iowa. How many dates has Stephen had from Iowa?"

The senator chuckled. "A few, but you're up there with the best. I assume from your answer you're an honest woman."

She gulped at the question. "I am. Aren't they all?"

He smiled. "Oh, yes. Absolutely. Every one."

He pulled her close and danced without talking.

After the dance, he led her back to Davenport. "You're a lucky man, Stephen. She's a delightful dancing partner. Thank you, Miss, uh, Henderson is it?"

"Yes. Thank you, Senator."

Davenport took her arm. "And now, may I have a dance? Hate to be second, but my boss is a little pushy."

As they moved past other tables toward the dance floor, a gray-haired man stood up from a table and intercepted them. "Stephen. It's great to see you."

As the two men greeted each other, a woman stood up from the table beside him. She took Davenport by the shoulders and kissed him on the lips. "How's my handsome friend from Capitol Hill doing these days?"

Davenport awkwardly pulled away. "I'm great, Bella. Let me introduce my friend. This is Linda Henderson, an old friend from Iowa. Linda, this is Robert Conway of the law firm of Conway and Harrington, and his daughter, Belinda."

Bella took Linda's hand in hers. "Bobby and Bella. Stephen's very formal." She then leaned forward, her mouth near Linda's ear. "Watch yourself with this beautiful man."

Davenport looked nervous. "Don't believe a thing she says."

Conway laughed. "And Stephen knows."

Linda thought, as they moved on, *That's one of the most gorgeous women I've ever seen.*

Definitely what is meant by the word woman. She asked Davenport, "Who the hell was that?"

"Oh, Conway is a very successful lawyer."

Linda punched him in the arm. "No, not Conway. You know whom I'm talking about." Davenport smirked at her. "You mean Bella?"

"Yes, I mean Bella."

"Well, Bella's Bella. What can I say? She's Bobby's daughter, and he loves to show her off at these things."

Linda whistled. "Well, she's something. Looks like she would have no trouble holding up that dress, even without the straps."

Davenport laughed, as he took Linda in his arms to dance. "You, noticed, huh?"

"And you didn't?"

Davenport looked at her in the eye. "I've known Bella a long time. I keep her at arm's length."

"Short arms, I'd guess from that kiss."

"Hell, it's just her way of saying hello."

"And I bet you didn't notice how she smells."

He chuckled, "She smells good, but so do you."

Linda grimaced. "My smell is supposed to be subtle."

Davenport looked at Linda seriously. "I have a sensitive nose and an eye for beautiful women. I'm with one now and don't need to think about anyone else. We're on a dance floor, under crystal chandeliers in a beautiful ballroom, and I don't want to talk about anyone else. Just you."

With that, he pulled her tightly to him and danced easily around the room. He was a beautiful dancer. She had been afraid that she had forgotten how to dance, but with Davenport, it seemed she was floating. She whirled around the room, the colors of beautiful dresses and the lights of the chandlers a kaleidoscope in her mind. He put his cheek to hers, and it felt natural. It was a life she had missed. She hadn't felt this way since college. She was young again.

"I'm sorry." Davenport's voice came out of a dream. "The party's breaking up, and we need to say good-bye to the others at our table."

They returned to the table and said good-bye. Everyone expressed his or her pleasure to have met her and wished Davenport had shared her more. Senator McDonald beamed and waved to her across the table. "Good-bye beautiful. I hope I see you again." His wife looked indulgent and took his arm to lead him away.

Linda felt Davenport's hand on her back. "All good things must end. We need to take you back to your room so you can change."

He led her through the lobby. She followed obediently, her mind in a fog as the world swirled around her. At the door to her room, Davenport asked for the key card.

Oh, yeah. It's in my purse. She fumbled with the clasp and finally got it open.

Davenport took the key card and opened the door. He took her hand and led her in as the door swung closed behind them.

He lightly kissed her lips and gently turned her around.

She felt him pull down her zipper. She wouldn't have to fumble with it this time.

CHAPTER THIRTY

Charlie and his son Ed were at the football game. The wooden stands only had eight rows. and they were in the fifth, right on the aisle. Ed had brought his iPad and was playing a game on it while the football game went on.

Charlie elbowed him after the opposing team had scored. "Hey. Ralph's going in to receive the kick."

They watched as the kick only carried down to the ten-yard line, where a player caught it and headed straight up the middle, cutting to the right at the twenty-five-yard line to try to avoid the group of tacklers and blockers who had come together in the middle of the field. His cut was too late, and he found a pile of players on top of him. They got up. Ralph had been in the middle of the pile. As the other players left, Ralph continued to lie on the field, holding his right arm with his left, and rocking back and forth.

The crowd hushed, and Charlie rose to his feet and rushed down the aisle with Ed shouting behind him, "What happened? Where are you going?"

Charlie sprinted past the line of players on the sideline and out to where two coaches and a medic were gathered around Ralph, helping him sit up. "Ralph. What happened?"

It was a stupid question. What happened was obvious. A bone stuck out through the skin and blood of Ralph's right arm. It was a compound fracture.

Ralph, in all his pain, looked at Charlie, appalled. "Dad. What are you doing out here? You're not supposed to be on the field."

Charlie exclaimed, "You're hurt!"

Ralph shook his head and looked down at the bleeding arm. "Coach'll take care of me. You aren't supposed to be here."

Charlie looked to end of the field. An ambulance was driving toward them. No carts for high school games.

Charlie felt awkward and out of place. He was embarrassing a son in pain. He backed up.

The medics helped Ralph into the back of the ambulance.

Charlie went to the sideline where Ed was waiting. Mollie had joined him. "Dad. What were you doing out there? Ralph's not a baby. You ran out in front of a couple of thousand people."

Charlie looked at Ed. "I'm his father. I don't care about all these people."

Ed shook his head. "Yeah, but Ralph cares."

Mollie looked alarmed, as if thinking Ed and Charlie were going to have a fight.

She asked, "Are you going to the hospital?"

Charlie broke out of a daze. "Yes, what hospital do I go to? Let me ask a coach."

Ed reached over to stop him, placing his hand on Charlie's arm. "I know where they're taking him."

Charlie looked at his son, who was suddenly acting mature. "Okay, let's go to the car."

As they started off, Mollie asked, "May I go too?"

Charlie looked back at her. "Of course, but phone your parents and make sure it's all right. I don't want them worried too."

As they approached the car, Mollie finished her call, and Ed said, "Dad, get in the passenger's seat. Mollie's going to drive."

Charlie protested, "But I'm all right."

"Dad, both Mollie and I would prefer that she drives."

Mollie looked embarrassed but took the keys that Charlie handed to her.

At the hospital, they all parked in the parking lot. Ed had said that Mollie couldn't drop them off and then have to walk in alone.

Charlie went to the desk in the emergency room and told the staff who he was and that his son had just been brought in. He was told he could go back, but the others would have to wait.

He found Ralph in a curtained alcove with a nurse giving him a shot. "This will help with the pain. The doctor will be here in a minute, but we're going to need the on-call orthopedic surgeon. We've phoned him, but he'll probably be half an hour getting here."

Charlie asked, "How fast will the shot work? That's a long time to wait."

"Should help in ten or fifteen minutes. The doctor coming in will want him alert, so I can only give him a minor shot. We may have to put him under for the arm repair. Are you the guardian?"

Charlie nodded as his face went pale. "Put him under? It's that serious?"

The nurse looked at her clip board. "Mr. Hendricks, is it? Yes, it's a bad break but the kind the doctors often take care of. It should be all right."

Ralph gritted his teeth. "It will be all right, Dad. You don't need to panic. That was awful, you coming out on the field. Made me feel like a fifth-grader."

"I wanted to help."

"There was nothing you could do."

"I'm sorry if I embarrassed you. I felt helpless."

Ralph looked down. "Dad, I'm sixteen."

"I know. I'll be quiet and just sit with you."

Ralph looked at his father. "Is Mollie here?"

"Out in the waiting room."

Ralph looked uncertain. "If you don't mind, could she come in and wait with me?"

Charlie felt thoroughly chastised. "Sure, I'll go get her."

Without looking at his son, Charlie rose and brushed out through the privacy curtain and headed for the waiting room, walking quickly, as if he were trying to avoid being seen.

"Mollie, he wants you to sit with him. We're waiting for an orthopedic surgeon to arrive. They may have to operate on the arm."

Mollie looked alarmed. "Not just a plaster cast? It's more serious than that?"

Charlie sighed. "Yeah. It looks that way, but the nurse said it's not unusual."

123

Mollie stood up. "Okay, if it's all right with you, Colonel Hendricks, I'll go stay with him?"

Charlie looked at her, "Thanks, Mollie." He pointed. "You go through that door, and he's behind the curtain in number five on the right. And, if you would please, will you let us know, now and then, what's going on?"

Charlie sat down in the plastic chair, his hand in his pockets.

Ed turned his iPad back on. "You're in the doghouse, huh?"

"Yeah."

"Dad, you just have to remember. Mollie's prettier than you."

*   *   *

It was almost one o'clock when the surgery team finished the operation and brought Ralph out in a wheelchair.

While they had waited, the nurses had had Charlie sign lots of papers as the guardian. He had done it quickly, not reading them as he should. He wanted the doctors to get on with it.

He phoned Linda's cell phone repeatedly. There was no answer. He kept leaving messages.

When Mollie came out, as they took Ralph to an operating room, Charlie asked her to call home again. He didn't want to be in the doghouse with Mollie's parents too. They apparently offered to come get her, but she declined.

After the operation, when Ralph was ready, Charlie went out to the car and drove it to the emergency room entrance. Ed and Mollie helped Ralph into the front seat.

As Ed got into the back seat next to Mollie, he said. "Okay. Let's take a vote. You think it's all right for Dad to drive?"

Charlie tried to hit him but was afraid of hurting Ralph. "I'm fine. Play with your iPad."

"I would if I could, but my brother keeps me up too late."

Ralph said, "Dad. Will you hit him again?"

Charlie smiled and drove off.

When they stopped at Mollie's house, Ralph tried to get out and walk her to the door.

Mollie had gotten out of the car quickly and held Ralph's door so he couldn't open it all the way. "What do you think you're doing? You fall on that arm, and we'll all be back at the hospital. We need our sleep, Ralph. Just sit here and watch me to the door."

Ralph pulled his hand back, wincing as he did so.

Mollie closed the car door and walked to the house, waved to them, and went inside as they all watched.

Charlie put the car in gear. "You have a nice girl there, Ralph."

"Uh-huh, I know."

At home, Charlie held Ralph's good arm loosely as they walked to the front door. He didn't want to be shaken off but wanted to be ready if he were needed.

Ed unlocked the door and held it open. He bowed his head and made a gallant sweep of his hand toward the inside. "I welcome the weary travelers to the inn."

Ralph looked for a place to put his hand on the door frame for balance, but Ed was in the way, so he put his hand on the top of Ed's head, pushing down as he walked into the house, and smirked. "Thanks, bro."

He sat in a dining room chair. He was still wearing hospital pajamas, a bath robe, and a blanket he had wrapped around this shoulders. "How am I going to get on my pajamas?"

Charlie took the blanket and said, "I think you're going to sleep in what you have on. We'll figure out clothes in the morning. Maybe cut an arm out of a shirt and pin a sweater around you. Right now, you and Ed need to get to bed. I have some pills if you need them during the night, but we're supposed to wait six hours from when you had surgery, so that's about 6:00 a.m. Just shout and I'll come to you."

Ralph rose to head for his bedroom. "Where's Mom?" "I assume she's working late on whatever she's catering."

Ralph said, "I guess so," and headed for the steps.

Charlie followed him up the stairs, ready in case he should fall. "You need any help getting to bed?"

"Nah. I'm fine."

Charlie didn't want to push it. "Okay. Shout if you need me."

Charlie went back downstairs, got a glass of water, and sat in a living room wing chair where he could watch the front of the house. *Yeah. Where the hell is Mom?*

CHAPTER THIRTY-ONE

Linda awoke in alarm and shook Davenport. "My God, what time is it?"

She reached over him and grabbed the clock from the bedside table. It was almost 2:00 a.m.

She leaped from the bed and ran to the bathroom. She threw cold water in her face, dried it, and began desperately repairing her makeup and brushing her hair.

Davenport was standing in the door. "It's not too late. I'll drive you home."

She closed the door in his face and used the toilet, opened the door and got her suit from the closet and her underwear from the floor, and returned to the bathroom and got dressed.

She opened the bathroom door, holding her cosmetics, and found Stephen dressed in his tuxedo shirt and pants, trying to get his shoes on. He used the bathroom while she grabbed the rest of their clothes. He phoned the desk and asked for his car to be brought to hotel the entrance.

They hurried out the door, letting it close behind them. They exited the elevator, hurried across the lobby, feeling guilty and trying to ignore the looks of the few people, mostly workers, who were there.

Linda threw all the clothes into the trunk of the car and hurried to the passenger's seat. She suddenly wondered why they were taking Stephen's car. She had been in too much of a hurry to question it.

She leaned back and sighed. "Lord, what am I going to tell my husband?"

Davenport responded, seemingly under control. "Just tell him you were catering and the party went late. By the time your team finished cleaning up, it was after two. You've got the perfect cover."

Linda thought, *How many times have I lied to Charlie, maybe a half dozen, and always for a good reason?* "Christ, you make it sound easy. Sounds like you've been here before."

"Oh, come on, Linda. This is no big deal."

Linda breathed deeply and stared ahead, not seeing anything but lights whirling past. *Easy for you to say. You just have an empty house to go home to, if it is a house. Maybe an apartment.*

Davenport tried to change the subject. "How's your husband's proposal going?"

Linda's mind raced. *When did I tell him about that? How can he talk about my husband so casually?* "I don't know. He's sweating it. Creating a highway system and using renewable energy to try to be on the cutting edge."

Davenport guffawed. "Renewable energy? Like wind and solar? That's crazy. The petroleum lobby won't allow it. Texas senators will kill it."

Linda was shocked. "How do you know that?"

"Darling, I work for a senator. I know a lot."

Linda was suddenly appalled and guilty. "Stephen, I'm not your darling."

"Hey. Don't act resentful. I think you enjoyed tonight. You didn't give me any reason to think differently."

Linda didn't respond. She felt that anything she said would be wrong. "Here. Take this exit at Van Dorn, and I'll give you directions."

Davenport decided that silence was the best route to follow.

As they approached Linda's home, she said. "Let me out at the corner."

"I can take you to the door."

"No. At the corner."

"We need to get your clothes out of the trunk."

"No. Throw them out. Burn them. Just save the briefcase."

"But the dress must be worth a lot."

Linda glared at Davenport. "Yes, it is, but I have enough to lie about without trying to explain the dress. The corner's right here."

Davenport stopped the car and went around to hold the door for Linda, who was out of the car by the time he got there. "I'll stand here and watch you until you're inside."

As Linda started down the sidewalk, she turned her head back. "No. You need to be gone."

Stephen sighed and returned to his car.

Linda hurried home. She was grateful that Charlie had turned on the outside lights for her. Then she noted that the living room lights were on too. She wouldn't have to enter a dark house. She stopped at the door and dug in her purse for her keys. As she started to insert the house key, the door opened. Charlie held it as she entered. "Where have you been? I've been calling and calling you."

Linda was startled by his exasperated tone. She took off her suit jacket and replied, "I had the phone off while I was working. What's going on?" She wondered where her briefcase was. *Oh, no. It's in Stephen's car trunk.*

Charlie watched her as she hung her jacket over a chair and seemed to be thinking about other things. "Ralph broke his arm in the football game."

Linda looked up at Charlie, her mind going from a defensive mode to motherly concern. "Is he all right?"

Charlie nodded. "He will be. It was a compound fracture. They had to operate on him to put the bones back together. We didn't get home until a little after one. He was still a little hung over from the anesthesia and went to bed. I checked him a couple of times. He finally went to sleep."

"My, God, Charlie. I should have been home."

"Hey, I know you can't do this catering job and be home every night. Thank goodness I was there. It worked out."

Linda went to him and held him. "Thank you. I'm so grateful."

Her mind spun. *What the hell have I done? I have a family, and they need me. I should have been here.*

She stood back. "I need to go see him."

Charlie shook his head. "There's nothing you can do. Just be prepared to help him if he wakes up."

"Do we have pain medicine?"

"Yeah, but we can't give it to him until six. I have a prescription for more. I'll get it filled in the morning."

"Okay, but I still have to go see him."

"All right, but be quiet." As she turned, Charlie stopped her with a worried look. "Do you have to work this weekend?"

She gave him an understanding smile. "No. Are you concerned?"

"I'm sorry to say I have to work. I put the burden on everyone to have input on my desk by five o'clock tomorrow—uh—today. I have to put it all together by Monday."

Linda nodded. "Don't worry. I'll have everything under control."

She climbed the stairs thinking, *Only one lie—at least, so far. Maybe, poor Ralph saved me.*

She tiptoed into Ralph's room and looked down at him. She wanted to kiss him but was afraid of waking him up. Tears came to her eyes as she thought, *I'm sorry. I should have been here.*

She went into the master bedroom, entered the bathroom, locked the door, sat on the toilet, and sobbed. *What the hell have I done?*

CHAPTER THIRTY-TWO

Charlie awoke before everyone else. He made coffee and sat with a cup thinking about all that happened last night. It had been awfully rough on Ralph. But he was young and would survive. The boy had even cracked that he was lucky and wouldn't have to warm the bench the rest of the season.

After all the trauma had cleared, Charlie worried about Linda. He had come upstairs slightly after her and found her locked in the bathroom. He's waited for her to come out. When she didn't, he went to the door and asked if she was all right. She said yes, but it sounded like she struggled to get the word out. When she came out, she was holding a washcloth to her eyes and tried to hurry to the bed. He knew she had been crying. He'd tried to ease her worries. "Linda, you've no reason to be upset. Ed and I were here, and Mollie helped. She was a jewel. There's really nothing you could have done. Everything was fine. Don't be upset."

Linda had taken a deep breath. "I know you took care of things, and I thank God for you. But I should have been here."

She'd climbed in bed and burrowed under the covers.

Charlie hadn't known what else to say. He decided to let her sleep in the morning.

About five thirty, he heard Ralph call and wondered how long the boy had been awake. Charlie gave him pain pills, although it was a half hour early. Fortunately, Ralph went back to sleep.

Linda came down at ten thirty. "I thought you needed to go to work?"

Charlie got up to get her a cup of coffee. "I wanted to make sure you were all right."

Linda smiled wanly. "I'm fine. I can take charge now. I'll be here all weekend, longer if I need to be. The job can wait. You've done your duty."

"Hell, it's not 'duty.' It's just being a father, although I admit I'm relieved to now have his mother with me."

He picked up the bottles of Ralph's pills and explained them to Linda. "He has enough for today. I'll get the prescription for more filled on my way to work."

Charlie got up and put on his suit jacket.

Linda asked, "Aren't you going to be cold?"

"No. I have to drive these days, so I'll use the heater in the car. Should be fine."

He headed for the door. "Do I need to move your car?"

Linda's eyes widened. "Uh, no. A friend drove me home last night. I was so tired." *Lie number two.*

Charlie smiled. "Thank heaven for friends. Call me if you need me. I love you."

He left before she could struggle to respond.

*   *   *

Charlie didn't get to the office until early afternoon. Everyone was working hard in the bull pen. He knew they were watching him, and he felt guilty. He thought he would sound weak if he made excuses, although he certainly had one.

He went into his cubicle and fired up his computer. He had already developed an outline of what he wanted to present to his bosses. He began filling in the introduction. He had been over it enough that he pretty well knew what he would need to say, although he knew he would have to make some tweaks based on the team's inputs. What worried him was whether he would need to do major editing of the others' work. Engineers could be lousy writers. He hadn't observed them in the corporate world, but he expected they were all the same. He had given them each a format to follow. He hoped the various inputs would come together in what looked like a carefully coordinated process.

Inputs began being delivered at ten minutes to five. Everyone had used all the time allotted. With each delivery, he told the team member to go home and get some rest but to please be here at ten in the morning.

Sending them home made him feel a little less guilty about being late.

He spread the inputs out on his desk. The team members had obviously tried to follow the format, but some had a single sentence under some topics and others had two pages. He'd need to work on them to create more uniformity.

He stacked them and sighed. He was exhausted. He'd go home tonight and try to be in by seven and have questions for his team by the time they came in at ten.

Just then, the phone rang. He picked it up with trepidation. It was Danny Fortiano asking Charlie to come to his office.

As he picked up his papers, Charlie thought, *Oh, shit. This is all I need.*

Charlie knocked on Fortiano's door frame.

Fortiano had been looking at the door expectantly. "Come on in and have a seat."

Copies of Charlie's team's inputs were lying across Fortiano's desk. Fortiano tapped them with his fingers. "There's some good stuff here, but it's ragged. What do you plan to do with it?"

Charlie gave Fortiano a slightly defiant look. "I'm going to edit it and get some uniformity. I'll mark it up and go over it with my guys in the morning. I've already got an introduction drafted."

"Okay. I have to go home. My wife was out partying with her father last night and kept me up late. Sounds like you ought to have a rough cut by noon. I'd like to meet with you then."

Charlie responded, "That sounds good." He didn't want to call Fortiano "boss" or "sir." He didn't want to call him anything.

Fortiano rose. "I hope you have a good night. See you at noon."

He walked out of his office in front of Charlie, who thought, *So, that's why he gets paid the big money. At least he won't see me leave too.*

CHAPTER THIRTY-THREE

Linda had Charlie drop her off at the Metro Monday morning. He offered to take her to the Orange Line's Vienna Station so that they could visit in the car, but she had him drop her at the Blue Line's Van Dorn Station because she told him she was more familiar with that station. In reality, she wasn't ready for a long conversation.

In DC, she got off at Metro Center and walked to the Willard Hotel. She gave the ticket for her car to the doorman. She was glad she didn't have to go inside. She was afraid someone might remember her. She knew that she must have been a sight.

When she got to work, she went straight to her office. Although she knew no one at work was aware of her Friday escort service, she still couldn't look her colleagues in the eye.

She took out the package on the Walter Reed Hostel fund-raiser. It had been a joy to work on, but now she wished she could pass it to someone else. She wasn't ready to see Stephen Davenport.

She carefully reviewed the package to see if she had missed anything. Then, she phoned the florist to ensure herself that the selected flowers would be available for the arrangements.

About midmorning, Margie stuck her head in the door and told Linda she had a call from Mr. Davenport.

Linda bit her lip. She looked at Margie. "I haven't quite gotten everything ready to discuss with him. Will you tell him I'm in a meeting and will get back to him?"

Margie nodded, uncertainly. "Sure. Do you know when you'll call back?"

Linda didn't want to be questioned and said, curtly, "Just tell him I'll call him back."

Margie looked chagrined and left, saying, "Okay."

Linda was annoyed at herself for snapping at Margie. She was a good woman.

She knew that eventually she'd have to talk to Davenport and began planning what she was going to say. The words went over and over in her mind and consumed much of the day.

A little before three in the afternoon, Margie cautiously knocked on Linda's door frame.

"There's a call from someone who wants to talk to you about the Walter Reed fund-raiser."

"Man or woman?"

"Man."

"Same man as this morning?"

Margie was reluctant, afraid of the backlash. "I think so."

Linda made a face. "Thanks Margie. I'll take care of it."

She picked up the phone. "Stephen?"

"Hey. Are you avoiding me?"

"So, what do you want to know about the fund-raiser?"

"You know that's not the reason I phoned you?"

"Well, it's under control. You don't have to worry."

Davenport became exasperated. "Linda, cut it out. Are you trying to tell me you didn't have a great time Friday? Lord knows, I did. You're a fantastic woman, Linda. Really, fantastic."

Linda grimaced. "Look, Stephen. Friday was something that should never have happened. I'm married. I'm a mother and not a *fantastic* one. My son broke his arm playing football Friday night, and no one could contact me because I was off shacking up with someone I hardly know. It's not going to happen again."

There was silence on the phone. Then Davenport said. "Gosh, Linda, I'm sorry about your son, but he'll get well. You need to think about yourself."

Linda shook her head. "No I don't. I've been doing too much of that lately."

Davenport persevered. "Linda. You're a beautiful, vibrant woman. You're locking yourself away from a world you enjoy. You know you like it."

"Yeah. I did a lot of cockeyed dreaming. It's out of my system."

"Hey, we'll talk about it some more at the fund-raiser."

135

"I'll be working at the fund-raiser, Stephen—doing what I'm supposed to do."

"Okay, but we'll find time to talk. You're special, Linda. Don't close me out."

"Good-bye, Stephen."

"See you at the fund-raiser."

Linda hung up and thought, *How am I going to get rid of him?*

But she couldn't help thinking, *"Fantastic woman." "Special." I haven't heard words like that in years. How much of it is a line? It would be nice if it were real.*

CHAPTER THIRTY-FOUR

After letting Linda off at the Metro, Charlie arrived at his office early on Monday morning. He gathered his papers, went down the hallway, and entered Jim Wade's outer office.

Daphne O'Leary looked up from her desk. "Good morning, Charlie Hendricks."

"Good morning, Daphne. I have the package for Mr. Wade to review."

Daphne smiled. "You're the first in, Charlie. Jim will be pleased to start early. Just stack it on the credenza, and I'll take it to him in a minute. He's on the phone right now.

Charlie was a little disappointed. He wanted to give the package to Wade himself. He thought it was pretty well done, although he had been startled by the acreage required for transferring the drive carts. There were good illustrations of the entire transfer area, with wind turbines interspersed, drawings of the drive carts, the charging stations, the transfer tracks and the control center, along with verbal descriptions. Additionally, the software concept was laid out in fair detail. Charlie would have been happier if he had more time to edit the description, but he had summarized the overall plan and was pleased with the result.

His competition was Manny Brown's trolley car proposal. Although, it didn't have the problem of developing batteries in the way Charlie's proposal did, it basically had the same problems of multiple drive carts, mechanical movement of the drive carts, and a large storage area.

Charlie returned to his desk and began cleaning up the mess he had made assembling the package.

Suddenly, Fortiano appeared, standing behind Charlie's chair. "Do you have the package ready for me to review?"

Charlie swung his chair around to face Fortiano. "I can put one together for you. It'll take twenty minutes or so."

Fortiano looked incredulous. "You mean you haven't put it together yet? It's due this morning."

Charlie looked baffled. "Oh, I delivered that to Wade a while ago."

Fortiano's eyes flashed. "You did what? I haven't seen it yet."

Charlie became defensive. "Hey, after I gave you my notes at noon yesterday, I waited for your input while I finalized things. Late in the afternoon, I went looking for you, but no one knew where you were. So I had Sid Davies look it over. It needed to be finalized so that I could get it in this morning. I had to meet a deadline. Sid said to go ahead."

"What the hell does Sid Davies know? He's never worked on anything like this before. I should have looked at it."

"Look, it's only a concept paper. You attended the meetings. You know it's going to have to be turned into a proposal. You'll have plenty of time to provide input and guidance."

"That may be, but I'm in charge of the engineering. I should have had a say. You screwed me, Charlie. I should have given it to Jim."

Charlie realized what was bugging Fortiano. "Don't worry. I didn't give it to Wade. Daphne did. She's the one in charge."

Fortiano snapped, "Don't be a smart-ass. You were in the army. You know what a chain of command is. I'm your boss. Don't forget it. Don't screw with me."

With that, Fortiano turned to leave.

Charlie asked, "Do you still want a copy of the package?"

Fortiano stopped and glared at Charlie. "You're damned right I do."

Charlie nodded. "I'll put packages together now for you, Haverford, Byrnes, Somers, Swanson, and Davies. I'm sure everyone will have input."

Charlie turned back to his desk. *Thank goodness I had Davies look at the package.*

But he knew he had better watch his back.

CHAPTER THIRTY-FIVE

Jim Wade had studied the two packages and was disconcerted. He didn't like either one. Both were complex as hell. Further, he had been having nightmares about attaching drive carts to vehicles. He could picture things going wrong and tearing up some fancy cars. The packages before him did nothing to ease his concerns.

He called Daphne. "I'm going to lunch. Get Sid Davies and tell him to come with me. I'll meet him in the lobby in a few minutes."

He left his suit coat, grabbed a light jacket, and swept past Daphne as she was phoning Davies.

They drove to the restaurant in silence. Davies thought Wade should take the lead, so he said nothing.

At the restaurant, they settled into a booth. Wade put his utensils on a bread plate, picked up his napkin, shoved it into his lap, and said, "Shit."

With some trepidation, Davies opened the conversation. "I guess the proposal packages are not making you happy."

Wade retorted, "You're damned right they aren't. Too complex. I have to have them into Davidson tomorrow. Can't do anything about it. I don't think he's going to be happy. We can no doubt build what we are proposing and make a lot of money, but I'm not sure the DOT is thinking about big money, at least not this big. And the requirement for land for drive cart parking lots is an enormous negative in the way it limits highway access points to the wide, open spaces well away from metropolitan areas."

"But don't you think most plans are going to require that kind of space?"

"Probably. But I still wish we had a plan that I really liked. I don't like messing with everyone's vehicles. Clamping things onto them. There just seems to be so much that can go wrong, especially with all the vehicle sizes and shapes out there."

"Well, I think the guys are planning on all kinds of padding and such. Still I understand your worries about all the shapes and sizes. Do you want me to have these guys go back to the drawing board and see what else they can come up with?"

Wade waved over the waitress. "Get me a Manhattan. You want anything, Sid?"

"No, thanks. Maybe an iced tea."

Wade pondered things, tapping his fingers on the table. "No. I think they've thought of everything. Just ask them to see if they can make things simpler, less mechanical."

"Okay, but I think that means software, with all its inherent problems with crashes, lapses in communication, and hacking. I'll see what we can do."

Wade drank half his Manhattan. "God, I wish life was easy. Flying to the moon seemed so much simpler. No interactions with real people and their personal property. If you didn't have to deal with people, life would be so much easier."

CHAPTER THIRTY-SIX

Wade arrived home and found Bonnie in the kitchen.

She turned toward him uncertainly, not knowing his mood but suspecting a bad one. "Dinner will be ready in ten minutes."

"Don't worry about it. I'm not hungry."

Bonnie watched him get a glass and fill it with ice. "I'm going to the den."

He left the kitchen, and Bonnie heard him open the liquor closet, close it, and move on to the den.

She sighed. She would eat alone and then maybe watch a little television. It was better than being snapped at.

When she was ready, she'd take a pill and go to bed.

CHAPTER THIRTY-SEVEN

Fortiano parked in the garage and sat there, seething. First, that bastard Hendricks had cut him out of taking the package to Wade, and then Wade had gone off to lunch without him, taking only Davies. He was being cut out on all fronts. What the hell was happening? He was supposed to be Wade's fair-haired boy.

He got out of the car and took the elevator to his apartment's floor level. Bella was sitting near the door, drinking a glass of wine and obviously dressed to go out for dinner.

"Shit, Bella. Can I just have a drink and order something in?"

Bella sighed. "Yes, I suppose so. You have a bad day?"

He told her about Hendricks cutting him out and about Wade's lunch."

"This Hendricks really bothers you, doesn't he?"

"The dumb shit isn't showing me any respect. And he's never even done a proposal before. He acts like I'm not important. Additionally, he's Sid Davies's boy, and Davies seems to be getting in tight with Wade."

"Well, maybe Wade needs a little encouragement and a reminder of who his man is. I think I can take care of that."

Fortiano stripped off his tie and unbuttoned the top button of his shirt.

Bella looked at him with disapproval. "Your chest hair is showing above your T-shirt. You need to shave lower."

Fortiano retorted, "Hell, no one sees it."

Bella tried to be patient. "I do. You need to look polished. You don't always wear a tie. You need to look clean and neat all the time. You never know when you might have to remove your tie."

Fortiano shook his head. "Jesus Christ, I have to deal with all these asses at work, and then you get on me when I come home."

Bella kissed him on the cheek and then on the mouth. She leaned back and smiled. "I just want you to be beautiful all the time. I like working my hands in your chest hair, but it's mine.

The rest of the world can do without."

She went to the phone and ordered Chinese.

Returning to Fortiano, she took his head in her hands and kissed his forehead. "I'll just have to think about what to do with Wade and this guy Hendricks. You'll have to introduce Hendricks to me at the Christmas party.

CHAPTER THIRTY-EIGHT

As Charlie turned into his driveway, he was happy to see both Linda's and Ralph's cars already parked. He parked behind Ralph to ensure he didn't stick out in the road.

In the house, he cut through the television room, where he found Ralph stretched out on the sofa and Ed playing a game on his iPad, sitting in a club chair with his legs stretched over the arm.

He asked Ralph, "How're you feeling?"

"Not so hot. Arm kind of throbs. Feel worn out."

Charlie nodded. "The adrenalin's worn off. You do okay in school?"

"Felt finished by noon. Mollie drove me home as soon as school was over. Then she called Mom."

"Mollie called Mom? She's really taking care of you, isn't she?"

Linda was standing in the doorway. "And I'm grateful. I should have stayed home. I'll do it tomorrow, in case Ralph needs to come home."

Charlie acknowledged her words. "That would be great. Really, he should just stay home if he's feeling bad. The break in his arm isn't trivial. He needs to take care of it."

Ralph protested, "Ah, Dad, I'm all right. I don't want to look like a weenie."

"Weenie or not, you don't want to end up back in the hospital."

"Why would that happen?"

Charlie gave an exasperated sigh. "I don't know. You just have to take care of it."

Linda remonstrated, "He has his father's stubbornness. We'll just have to watch him."

Charlie followed Linda into the kitchen. "How's your day been?"

Linda opened the refrigerator door. "You want a beer or a glass of wine?"

"Beer, I guess."

She took one out, breaking it out of the carton and popping the top as she gave it to Charlie. "Kind of unexciting. Mostly worked on the fund-raiser coming up Friday night. Hope you can be home."

Charlie sat at the kitchen table and took a sip of beer. "As far as I know, I should be home. I turned in the proposal package today. Wade will probably give the packages to Davidson tomorrow. Hopefully, it won't hit the fan."

Linda looked at Charlie. "You look tired."

"Hell, I feel tired. Heck of a weekend, and I'm not happy with the proposal."

Linda stopped working and tried to concentrate on what Charlie had to say. She had decided she needed to do better. "What do you think the problem is?"

Charlie was glad to talk. "I think things are just too complicated."

"Do you know why that is?"

"I thought about that driving home this evening. Sometimes I think I do my best thinking at stoplights. I think the problem is trying to use renewable energy. Trying to figure out a way to address all vehicles—gasoline, diesel, electric, whatever. One of the other teams suggested putting a control box on top of the vehicle, basically ignoring what type of fuel it used."

"So, why don't you do that?"

"Well, everyone seems to want renewable energy these days."

Linda thought a moment, trying to figure out how to say it. "Charlie, at a party we were catering the other day, I heard some congressional types talking about the Super Highway. That's what you're working on, right?"

"Yeah."

"Well, they said the petroleum industry, lobby, or whatever, would never let the system be built if gasoline wasn't still being used to run the cars. Are you sure you have to use renewable energy? Do the government papers say that?"

"The RFP?"

"The RF what?"

"The request for proposal. No, come to think of it, I don't think it does."

"So, there you go."

"Only problem is, we still have to deal with old cars that don't have built-in software.

We're supposed to be able to handle them."

"So, is this thing going to be built tomorrow? How long have they been building the Interstate Highway System? Fifty, sixty years? This isn't China, where they make a decision to build a road, hire fifty thousand coolies, and have it built in two or three years—while our Congress is still arguing about how many miles to build and which state it will be built in. Forget the old cars. They won't be around by the time we build a few hundred miles of the new highway."

"Shit, Linda, you're a cynic, but you ought to be an engineer."

Linda grinned. "They couldn't pay me enough for my unconstrained thoughts."

Charlie sat nursing his beer and pondering the situation.

Linda asked, "What's worrying you now?"

"I'm wondering if this is what they call 'insider information' and what the FAR has to say about it."

"The FAR? You and your acronyms."

"The Federal Acquisition Regulations. Hundreds of pages that control the acquisition process."

"Yeah. Does that address words heard at a party? Do you have to turn yourself into Big Brother or somebody? Hell, Charlie, you said yourself that the RFP, or whatever, doesn't preclude gasoline. Just go with it as your idea."

Charlie shook his head. "That would be simple and probably safe, but I have to convince people at work, and the overheard words are the only way to do it."

Linda acquiesced. "Well, Charlie, I've been a free consultant and done the best I can. From now on, it's your problem."

Charlie had become a little disconsolate. "Yeah, and I appreciate it. I need to think. I'll see if the FAR is online."

"Okay, but let's have a nice dinner before you descend into gloom."

CHAPTER THIRTY-NINE

Tuesday afternoon everyone working on the proposal was called to meet in one of the team discussion rooms. There wasn't enough space for everyone, but it was the only room they had. Except for the senior staff, it was standing room only.

Wade waited for everyone to settle down. He looked gloomy and beaten down. "I passed our two proposals to Davidson. I'm afraid he's not happy. He thinks everything is too complicated and too expensive. He wants us to go back to the drawing board. He needs new input by next Wednesday. That's the day before Thanksgiving, if we get to have it this year. So, by Monday noon, I want new ideas on by desk. I know you've worked hard to get where we are, but I really need for you to do some original thinking. There's nothing more to say, so get to work."

Charlie gathered his group in a corner of the big office. "Guys, you heard the boss. Work up anything you can. I'll schedule the conference room for some time Thursday afternoon, and we'll meet. Bring any ideas you can come up with, and we'll beat them around."

Wiggins started to complain. "Charlie, we've done the best we can." He noted Charlie glaring art him. "I know. Do better than best, and the sooner the better, or it's another weekend down the tubes."

Charlie nodded. "You said it right, Andy. I'll see you all Thursday."

*   *   *

Charlie watched everyone walk away despondently. He sympathized.

He wasn't sure who he should talk to or if he should talk to anyone. He decided on Sidney Davies.

He knocked on Davies's door frame.

Davies looked up and waved Charlie in. "If you're looking for ideas, I wish I had some."

Charlie looked serious. "No, I need to talk to someone."

"That sounds sinister. Have a seat." Charlie closed the door and sat down.

Davies looked apprehensive.

Charlie tried to pull his thoughts together. "I've been reading the FAR. Under the definition of 'organizational conflicts of interests,' it states that one exists if 'because of other activities or relationships with other persons …a person has an unfair competitive advantage.' That's kind of vague. I tried to do a search of the FAR to define the meaning better, but mostly came up with information on 'personal conflicts of interest,' none of which seems to cover what I'm talking about. I think it means you know something about the selection process that you shouldn't because of contacts with other people."

Davies felt hesitant. "Should I be stopping you here, Charlie?"

Charlie took a deep breath. "I really don't know. I think I'm all right, but it's my opinion, and I don't want to ask a lawyer."

Davies looked alarmed. "I guess the worst that can happen is that you and I would have to excuse ourselves from working on the contract. I hope it's as simple as that."

Charlie gave Davies a moment for second thoughts. "Well, you know that most of the proposals we've come up with are based on renewable energy, and that has made us look for ways to build the Super Highway without gasoline cars using gasoline."

"Yeah. Seemed like the way to go."

"Well, here's my problem. You may or may not know that my wife works for a catering company in DC that puts on all kinds of high-powered functions."

"No, I didn't know that, but go on."

"Well, at one of these affairs, she heard some congressional staffers talking about this project. What they said is that there is no way the petroleum lobby will ever allow a system that is independent of the use of gasoline. I don't know whether or not the lobby is really that powerful, but it makes me wonder if we're going in the wrong direction. What worries me is that this information might result in one of those 'organizational conflicts of interest.'"

Davies leaned back and stared at some spot on the ceiling. "You know, I can't imagine that overhearing something at a party fits that bill. Seems like it would involve unauthorized access to procurement documentation or input from DOT procurement personnel. And if I remember correctly, the solicitation doesn't say not to use gasoline. I think we just made an assumption. If we came up with a proposal using petroleum products, I don't think any ethical questions could possibly arise. But, like you, I don't know."

Charlie hesitated. "So what do you think we should do?"

Davies bit his lip. "Eventually, if we go this direction, Wade is going to have to buy into the idea of using gasoline, and I'm going to have to use your information to justify it. However, I don't want to put him on the spot until I do a couple of things. I'll let you know."

Charlie left, feeling better now that he had dumped the burden on Davies.

CHAPTER FORTY

Davies wanted to verify Charlie's rumor. He thought about his old office, the Government Relations Office of Bedford-Ewings. The office certainly had contacts with congressional types and could probably talk to the petroleum lobbyists, but Davies worried there might be an underground of talk if B-E started asking those questions. Right now, only he and Hendricks knew anything.

Davies went to his usual bar and ordered a Reuben for dinner. As he sat there mulling over his options, he noticed Jerry Harlem sitting at the bar. Davies picked up his sandwich and bourbon and walked over. "Evening, Jerry. Is this stool taken?"

Jerry looked at Davies, clearly trying to remember who he was. Then he pointed his finger at Davies, "Oh, yeah. The Super Highway guy."

Davies acknowledged that was who he was and stuck out his hand. "Sid Davies. You said I could always find you here."

Harlem patted the stool. "And here I am. Have a seat. How's the highway coming?"

Davies sat. "Oh, it's coming."

"You got some whiz-bang ideas? Something out of a *Jetsons* cartoon?"

Davies chuckled. "No. We're not there yet. Still trying to figure out whether to use wind turbines or let the cars run on gasoline."

"Well, you better run on gasoline. When that project was being funded, the staff was talking about that. The lobby's running that show."

Davies wanted to diffuse the talk. "Well, we'll probably offer some options. We don't know which way the proposal reviewers are leaning."

Harlem smirked. "Hell, I know exactly which way they're leaning. They've been told."

Davies finished his bourbon. "Well, we'll do the best we can. May I buy you another drink? It's nice to have someone to talk to on a lonely night."

Davies signaled the bartender and thought, *Well, army intelligence wouldn't consider Jerry Harlem a great source, but two sources agreeing is worth something."*

CHAPTER FORTY-ONE

Davies made an appointment with Ralph Evenson, Davidson's deputy, on Thursday morning. If they were violating some ethical standard, he wasn't ready to involve Wade or Davidson. They would have to sign off on the proposal, and he wanted them to stay honest.

Evenson was elderly, maybe sixty; balding; and wore old-fashioned spectacles. He was what Davies pictured as an accountant bending over a desk in some Dickens novel. He had always been quiet, behind the scenes.

Davies closed the door behind him. That always raised eyebrows. *Are we firing someone? Has somewhat passed secrets to the enemy? Are you quitting?* All kinds of things go through the office owner's mind.

Davies sat down. "I know a little of how Davidson feels about the Super Highway proposal. He thinks it's too complicated, too expensive, and wants it revised. With our current mind-set, that's not going to happen."

Evenson looked like he'd been slapped across the face. "What do you mean 'our current mind-set'? What needs to change?"

Davies leaned forward and looked Evenson in the eye. "Our mind-set is to use renewable energy, produced externally to the cars, to provide power to a cart or something that moves the cars on the highway. What we need to do, instead, is let the cars use their own power—gasoline, diesel, battery, hydrogen, whatever."

Evenson shook his head. "But isn't that regressive? Won't the government expect us to look like we're moving forward?"

Davies felt a little frustrated. He didn't want to use Hendricks's hearsay. "The RFP doesn't say anything about using renewable energy. If we can use the vehicles' own drive systems, we can simplify the whole proposal."

Evenson frowned. "How are we going to convince Davidson of that? You've given him a mind-set with your existing proposals."

Davies hesitated. "I'm talking to you because I have information that I'm not prepared to give to Wade or Davidson. I'm not ready for them to be involved."

"My God, man, you're making this sound like a spy novel. Do I want to be involved?"

Davies sat back and tried to decide whether or not to proceed. "I think you have to be. Otherwise, we're going to lose this bid."

He told Evenson about what Linda Hendricks had heard and what Jerry Harlem had told him. "I don't know whether that's insider information or not, but it seems to be common talk among congressional staffers. They're not worried about what they say. I think it best not to discuss where our motivation comes from. I think we just need to proceed down a new path."

Evenson studied Davies over his frameless glasses. "I don't know whether that's insider information or not or even if it should be given credence. Let's not ask the lawyers and let's pretend it might be true. We can proceed along the new line, like it's natural, considering the lack of limitations in the solicitation. For now, let's do it as an alternative. Unfortunately, if we're to use that approach, I suspect we're going to have to make Wade and Davidson aware of your 'intelligence' and ask them to buy into it. We don't want to do that too soon, and we need to do it in private. Keep the information to limited distribution and keep me informed."

*　　*　　*

Davies returned to the proposal office. He stayed in his office, working over papers for half an hour before phoning Charlie to come in. He didn't want his conversation to be connected to his time missing from the office. When Charlie arrived and started to close the door, Davies told him to leave it open. He wanted to limit any kind of speculation about his relationship with Charlie.

Davies spoke sotto voce, "Go ahead with your suggestion, but don't talk about what your wife heard."

Charlie started to ask a question but thought better of it. "Yes, sir. Will do."

*   *   *

Charlie asked Joannie Bahr to come with him and have a cup of coffee in the cafeteria. The place was almost empty, and Charlie led Bahr to a table well away from all ears. He spoke quietly. "I'd like to keep this low-key for a day or so. I'm going to postpone my meeting this afternoon. In the meantime, I'd like you to do some thinking about an alternate plan. I'd like you to think, from a software point of view, what we would need to do if we were to let vehicles on the Super Highway run on their own power, be that gasoline, diesel, or whatever, but control them to run at a steady speed of eighty miles an hour, safely separated from one another, positioning them in different lanes to limit congestion, and responding to emergencies by safely moving them to the shoulder of the highway. That is, take control away from the driver. Do it all ourselves with software."

Joannie whispered back. "You're talking in a low voice, so I'm assuming this is a secret. Is it for real?"

Charlie looked her in the eye. "It's for real. I wouldn't say it's a secret, but I want it thought through before I go further with it."

*   *   *

Next, Charlie invited Gabriel Winnick into a team discussion room, and again spoke in a low voice. "Gabriel, remember that proposal you had about attaching a box to the roof of vehicles and controlling everything with software?"

CHAPTER FORTY-TWO

Late Friday afternoon, Linda and her team were in the Goshen Towers Ballroom setting up the for the hostel fund-raiser. Commander Alspach came in briefly, as if to see if everyone was there, and then vanished. Ben Swaim was in periodically, checking to see if anything was needed. The tables were set up, the tablecloths on, the centerpieces in place, the silverware arranged, and the glasses and napkins in place. Linda had checked that the bars were set up and the bartenders ready. Jeanie Carville and Betty Gaskins had arrived early and helped arrange things. As a result, Linda was going around correcting any errors, ensuring that every setup was the same. The women followed her, constantly talking. She wished they would go somewhere else, but this was one of the hazards of the catering trade. The people you were working for seemed to think they had something to say about the setup and always needed to be involved.

A half hour before the fund-raiser was scheduled to begin, Stephen Davenport walked in.

He tried to join Linda but ended up with Jeanie and Betty as part of an entourage following Linda around. "Everything looks beautiful. I always admire the work Yvonne DuBois does."

Betty gushed, "Oh, isn't everything wonderful. Linda has done such a festive job."

Jeanie joined in. "I can't imagine anything more elegant and beautiful. Stephen, will you thank Senator McDonald over and over again for all his help and your help too?" She gave Davenport a winning smile as if looking for some kind of reaction.

Davenport gave a very charming, professional smile back. "The senator is so pleased to be able to help. Your cause is near and dear to his heart. I hope that I have been able to represent him well."

Betty looked please. "Oh, you've been a dear to work with. Thank goodness for you and Linda."

Davenport smiled at Linda, who had hardly acknowledged him. "Oh, I know Linda must be wonderful to work with—an industrious and lovely lady. I look forward to working with her often in the future."

Linda looked down at a table and straightened a knife. "Stephen. That would be very nice. Yvonne is always happy to work with Senator McDonald's office." She had thought of calling him Mr. Davenport, but that seemed too pointed, and she was afraid Betty and Jeanie would notice.

She started to head for the kitchen, and as soon as she separated from the women, Stephen came after her. "Linda, wait. We need to talk."

Linda turned and glared at him and then backed off, afraid the women would notice. "I don't think we have anything we need to say. I have work to do."

Davenport stood his ground. "You're going to brush me off, just like that."

Linda nodded. "Just like that."

"You're going to pretend you didn't have a good time?"

"I'm going to pretend it didn't happen. Stephen, I'm married. I have a family—a wonderful family. Please let up."

"But you were so beautiful that night, just as you are now. You danced like Cinderella, the belle of the ball. You glowed. You were so wonderful to be with."

Linda sighed. "Unfortunately, when Cinderella got home, the glass slipper didn't fit."

CHAPTER FORTY-THREE

By Monday, no one had come up with any new ideas, and Wade was discouraged. He complained to Davies who, frustratingly, seemed unconcerned. Davies told Wade the guys were still working and not to give up.

Early in the morning on the Tuesday before Thanksgiving, Wade was called to Evenson's office, where he was briefed by Evenson and Davies. He had his doubts, but the others seemed very convinced.

Upon his return to the proposal office, Wade set up a meeting in a team discussion room for Wednesday morning. He wanted Hendricks to brief the senior staff—Davies, Fortiano, Somers, Byrnes, Haverford, and Swenson. As they all settled in the room, looking apprehensive, Hendricks entered, followed by Joannie Bahr and Gabriel Winnick. Evenson followed and took a seat against the wall.

Wade looked up. "What's Gabriel doing here?"

Charlie set down his papers. "It was originally her idea, so I think she ought to brief it." Gabriel gave them all a how's-that-for-an-answer look.

Joannie and Gabriel sat down while Charlie stood at the end of the table. "Because of the complications associated with all the plans that have been presented for the Super Highway, Gabriel, Joannie, and I have been looking at another approach. We've abandoned the idea of using renewable energy to move the vehicles on the highway and are now proposing we let vehicles run under their own power, but under the control of the highway system's software. That eliminates all the wagons, carts, and ferries, with all their complications, and allows us to use all the existing highway entrances and exits. I have some things I want to add, but for the time being, I'd like to turn it over to Gabriel.

Winnick moved to the head of the table. "The other day when we were going over all the proposals, I suggested that we attach a box to the roofs of cars. The box would be powered by solar panels attached to the top and would contain electronics that would interact with the electronics in the vehicles in order to control those vehicles. After meeting with Charlie and Joannie, I've modified that concept. There's always been a concern about damaging vehicles by attaching mechanisms to them. We now propose to use a box that will be powered by plugging into the vehicle's cigarette lighter. Should the vehicle not have a cigarette lighter or similar source of power, we propose having a number of rechargeable, battery-powered units. These units would be passed in the passenger window when the vehicle arrives at the highway entrance gate."

Fortiano interrupted. "Look. The proposal doesn't permit us to only address vehicles that have internal software. We're supposed to address all vehicles. And you're ignoring renewable energy."

Charlie glared at Fortiano. "Yes, there are some gives and takes. Let Gabriel finish, and I'll address those issues."

Wade waved at Gabriel to continue.

Gabriel gathered her thoughts. "The issue is not only that some vehicles don't have internal software, but also that different brands have different software, and the software in each brand may differ from one model to the next. Further, much of the software is proprietary. The major issues in creating our box is that the vehicle's manufacturers are going to have to pony up their software, and we're going to have to adapt our boxes to work with all brands. Our concept will evolve. First, we will interact with all the manufacturers to create standards for their software, kind of like the IEEE does in electronics. In turn, we will create a standard design for our box so that the manufacturers can incorporate it in their vehicles and eliminate the passing of boxes through vehicle windows. The boxes will not only control the vehicles but will also serve as the equivalent of an E-ZPass. As we conceive this system, we will use the raster approach, creating a grid under the highway to locate and control the vehicles' speed, spacing, highway ingress and egress, and movement to a maintenance lane. We will use the safety systems built into the vehicles as supplements to our system."

She looked around briefly. "Now, Charlie's planning to address the issue of vehicles without internal software and cars with limited internal software, but I'm going to beat him to it. We're going to pretend that the DOT will review our proposal using common sense. This new highway is not going to appear overnight. We've been working on the current interstate system for sixty years. The new system may take as long. The automobile and trucking industries are incorporating their own software systems in a rapid fashion. By the time this new highway construction is implemented, the vehicles with no software are going to be few and far between. To design a system based on vehicles that will be antiquated makes no sense, especially when considering the costs involved. Our proposal needs to make that point."

Gabriel looked at Charlie. "Does that cover it?"

Charlie got up. "I think so."

He replaced Winnick. "Danny asked one other question, about not using renewable energy. We tried to do that because it's the modern thing to do, but we found out that the problems it created with all our carts and wagons, attaching them onto vehicles and pushing those vehicles down the road, were just enormous. We needed huge parking lots for the carts and wagons and mechanical systems for moving them around, all of which precluded use of many of the entrance and exit points of the current interstate system."

Fortiano shook his head. "But this is a dull system. It has no interest."

Charlie concurred, "I agree. It looks like the current system, but even less interesting. With all the vehicles evenly spaced and no one weaving in and out of traffic, it's really dull. All we have to do is install the raster, ensure there is a shoulder for breakdowns, and bring the current highway system up to eighty-mile-an-hour standards. Aside from that, this is a software project that will eventually be provided by the vehicle manufacturers.

"To enliven it a little, I'd like to make an additional proposal. Everything we've proposed ignores the weather—rain and hail and snowstorms. You don't do eighty miles an hour in a snowstorm. I would, therefore, propose that we put a roof over this whole thing and ensure that all precipitation that runs off the roof is drained away from the road. I further propose that a side wall be put up made of tempered glass to prevent blowing of snow, sand, and the like. The side wall would have a space at the top for ventilation, and the roof edges would hang down to overlap this open space to limit dust blowing in. In fact, we might be able to make it aerodynamic such that the roof edge forces wind up and over the roof. If analysis demonstrates the necessity, we might have to add in mechanical ventilation to handle vehicle exhaust. That potential issue, however, I expect to diminish as more and more vehicle manufacturers go to electric cars.

"The roof assembly would have the added advantage that we could build it as an electronic shield to prevent hacking of the system. That would probably mean that we would have to build in commercial radio and cell phone service into our software box, but that might be justified in securing the system from the bad guys."

"That pretty well summarizes what we're proposing to work on. Does anyone have any questions?"

Wade spoke up immediately. "I think we should drop any thought of alternatives. I've bought in. For the last month, I've been feeling like I've been bouncing around in one of those kiddie bounce things they have at fairs. Now I feel like we're getting somewhere. Unfortunately, I have to get to Davidson and get his buy in before our partners or someone else gets to him.

Give me till Monday to do that. We'll kick things off Monday afternoon. Now let's send everyone home and tell them to have a great Thanksgiving."

Wade was relieved. There hadn't been any mention of Hendricks's "intelligence." He had avoided it by simply saying that this was the way we are going to do it.

Evenson joined Wade at the door to his office. "Don't worry. I'll take care of Davidson." Wade entered his office, blowing a sigh of relieve.

Evenson must have decided that the fewer people who knew that Davidson was aware of the "intelligence" the better.

CHAPTER FORTY-FOUR

Wade found Bonnie in the kitchen. "What are we doing for Thanksgiving?"

Bonnie looked startled. "I don't know. We haven't talked about it. I turned my parents down. Told them you were too busy."

"Well, it's too cold to play golf. We need to do something. See if you can make us reservations at a good restaurant."

He turned and went to the den.

Bonnie stood with her mouth open and wondered, *What the hell just happened?*

*   *   *

Fortiano arrived home steaming.

He found Bella in the living room sipping a glass of wine.

"That damned Hendricks has sold Wade a bunch of crap. He wants to build an exhaustfilled tunnel for this super highway, and Jim's bought it. Everything I say is ignored."

Bella was unfazed. "You think it's time to have the Wades over again? It can't be as bad as you seem to think it is."

Fortiano seethed. "Yes, it is that bad. Hendricks is getting all the attention. I might as well not be there."

Bella tried to be patient. "Take it easy. Jim's not going to forget you. The other guy may be having temporary glory, but you know you'll be all right in the long run. Again, do you think we should have them in?"

"Maybe, but I don't know when. This weekend is Thanksgiving, kind of a bad time for a short-notice invitation, and next week is the B-E Christmas party at the Fairview Marriott."

Bella perked up. "Well, there's the answer. I'll work him over at the party. Damned things are dull anyway. That will enliven the evening." She got up. "Let me make you a drink. I have dinner ordered in. Just relax, and try not to think about it. Sleep late in the morning. We don't have to be at my parents' for Thanksgiving until four."

Fortiano collapsed in a club chair. "Oh, shit. I forgot about that. Hope your father is in a good mood. I'm not his favorite."

Bella handed him his drink. "Nobody married to his little girl is going to be his favorite. Bobby's attitude goes with the territory."

*   *   *

Charlie found Linda in the kitchen as usual.

She looked at him. "What's in all the grocery bags?"

"Thanksgiving dinner. I know you haven't had a chance to think about it with Yvonne DuBois Catering volunteering to work the soup kitchen tomorrow."

Linda walked over to him and took a bag as she gave him a brush kiss. "You're a jewel. And let's not call it a soup kitchen. It's a full-course Thanksgiving dinner for the needy at one of the churches—the whole deal."

She started unloading the dinner into the refrigerator. "So, is this our whole meal?"

Charlie was plainly pleased with himself. "You betcha, everything to be finished with vanilla ice cream on pumpkin and pecan pie. I'll have some of each."

Linda started on another bag. "Have you got enough for Mollie?"

"Of course, isn't she a permanent fixture? My guess is that she'll have two dinners tomorrow."

"Don't think so. She's going with the boys and me to help with the serving line. You still coming?"

Charlie grinned. "Of course. I wouldn't miss it for the world."

Linda studied the refrigerator. "You forgot the turkey."

"No I didn't. It's still in the car. It's a load by itself."

He left to get the turkey while Linda checked the roast she had in the oven.

When Charlie returned, he was carrying a huge plastic container that was trying to bend and collapse under the weight of a twenty-pound turkey. "You think this is enough for Mollie?"

Linda smiled. "It will probably do. How'd your big presentation go today?"

Charlie got a beer from the refrigerator. "Blew them out of the water."

Linda laughed. "Doesn't sound like an army expression to me."

"Okay, the caissons went rolling along."

Linda shook her head. "I liked the navy expression better. What the heck is a caisson, anyway?"

"Old army—a wagon for carrying ammunition. But whatever. The presentation went well."

"Did you give me credit?"

Charlie looked guilty. "No, but I shared the credit with one of the other workers, Gabriel Winnick, who had almost the same idea earlier."

Linda shook her head. "Charlie, the good guy. Scout's honor and all that. How are you going to move up in the world?"

CHAPTER FORTY-FIVE

The Hendricks family arrived at the church just after the catering truck arrived.

Linda took charge. She had the caterer's workers unload the food into the kitchen. While they were doing that, she put Charlie and Ed to work setting up the church's folding tables and chairs. Because of Ralph's arm limitation, she had him and Mollie roll plastic tableware in napkins and put them on the tables.

Margie arranged flowers on the tables. They had been offered free by one of the food market chains. They looked a little wilted. Maybe yesterday's flowers, or maybe the day before. But they would do.

Linda worked in the kitchen directing the separation of food into that which would go into warming ovens and that which would go immediately on the serving tables.

Some of the caterer's workers began setting up the serving tables with serving pieces that would hold the large food pans. They opened the Sterno and lit it with a butane lighter.

Linda came out and reviewed the serving table. She directed the workers to get the plates that the church was providing. As she was arranging serving spoons behind the tables for the workers, she heard a voice behind her. "Looks good. What can I do?"

Linda froze. She turned and looked aghast at Stephen Davenport. "You can help me carry food containers from the kitchen."

As they went through the kitchen door, Linda hissed, "What the hell are you doing here?"

"I help Yvonne out every Thanksgiving. Been doing it for years."

Linda tried to reconcile with that. "Okay, but stay out of my hair."

"You know I wouldn't mess your hair up on a day like today."

"Not funny. I don't want you anywhere near me."

Davenport tried to appease. "No problem. Just tell me what to do. Have me dish out the turkey dressing? I have a tendency to let the peas get away from me. Who's the big guy with the short haircut? Your husband? I assume the young man with him is your son."

Linda loaded two serving pans of mashed potatoes into Davenport's arms. "Correct on both accounts."

Davenport nodded in acknowledgement. "Looks like he could beat the hell out of me."

Linda glared. "Don't tempt me."

"You'd have to give him a reason."

"I'll think of something."

"If you had enough guts, it would be easy. Confession might be good for the soul."

"If I did that, you wouldn't survive the day. Come on. Let's get the potatoes in place."

"Glad to help, Linda. I still have your dress in the car, along with the glass slipper."

"Stephen. Get lost."

"Whatever the lady wishes."

"Go back and get the peas."

Ed came over. "Who was that, Mom? You didn't look pleased to see him."

"He's an assistant to a senator. Volunteers to help out each year."

"A US senator? How do you know him?"

"The senator sponsored a fund-raiser I catered a week ago. I worked with him there."

"You must not have gotten along."

"We have our differences."

Davenport came back with the peas, set them in place, and looked at Ed. "And who's this young man?"

Linda reluctantly introduced them. "Stephen Davenport, this is my son Ed."

Davenport smiled, shook Ed's hand, and looked at Linda. "You certainly have a handsome family."

Linda thought, *Oh, shit. I have to be polite.* "Thank you. I'm very lucky."

Davenport smiled winningly. "No luck about it. Ed has his mother's good looks."

Linda wanted the subject changed. "We only have a few minutes to get the food out.

Let's get to work."

She sent Ed and Davenport scurrying off as Charlie finished setting up the last table.

Charlie came over. "Who's the guy with the big smile?"

"Stephen Davenport, a fellow I worked with last week at the fund-raiser. Senator McDonald sponsored it. Davenport works in the senator's office."

"Should have known from the smile that he's a politician. What do you want me to do?"

"Take a break with Ralph. I'll get you guys to hand out the desserts at the end of the line when it's time." *And stay separated from Stephen Davenport.*

* * *

Driving home, Linda stewed over Davenport having been there.

"That guy Davenport certainly gave you a lot of attention," Charlie commented as he glanced at Linda. "You must have made an impression on him. He didn't seem to want to let you go when he said good-bye."

Ed joked. "You need to be jealous, Dad. Mom's good-looking. The guy was hitting on her."

Linda flushed. "Stop joking, Ed. I'm too old a woman to be hit on. It's silly to even think about."

Charlie looked at her in a new light. "Ed's right. I sometimes forget to tell you how goodlooking you are."

Ralph protested. "Hey. Cut out the mush. You're too old for that."

Mollie elbowed him, and he responded. "What's that about?"

"It's about you not knowing how lucky you are."

CHAPTER FORTY-SIX

Bonnie had been hopeful when Wade wanted to go out for dinner for Thanksgiving. She hoped he was coming out of his grouchy funk. She picked a nice restaurant, and he seemed in a fairly pleasant mood as they settled at their table.

As Wade spread his napkin in his lap, he spoke, half to himself, mulling over what had happened on Wednesday. "You know, we finally decided on a direction for this proposal to go, and, initially, I was relieved that a decision had been made. Now I'm not so sure."

Bonnie thought, *Uh-oh. I have to head this discussion off.* "I hear this restaurant has a special corn bread dressing with spinach. I'll be interested to try it out."

Wade looked at the menu. "Yeah, but Thanksgiving dinner's much the same. Good, and I enjoy it, but I'm not sure dressing is going to make a big difference."

"Lord, Jim, you sound like life is just too boring to deal with. Let's enjoy this."

Wade looked up from the menu. "I'll do my best. It's just that the proposal continues to worry me. Davidson wants to win this thing so badly. It just seems that the approach we've decided on may be too simple, and it requires some flexibility on the part of the government—its willingness to accept negotiations with the auto industry and the fact that our plan doesn't address older vehicles."

Bonnie closed her menu and gave up. "So why don't you just push the old cars around?"

Wade made a face. "We looked at that, but it was just too complicated."

Bonnie wanted the subject changed. "Look. You do the best you can do. If it doesn't work out, we'll survive. Davidson's not going to fire everyone over this. Companies just don't work that way."

Wade frowned. "Maybe he'll get fired and take the rest of us with him."

"Christ, Jim, you're talking about doomsday. Like the world is going to end. It isn't going to happen."

Wade reflected. "God, I hope you're right."

CHAPTER FORTY-SEVEN

Early Friday morning, while the boys were sleeping late, Charlie and Linda were in their kitchen finishing cleaning up after their Thanksgiving dinner the night before. As Charlie emptied the dishwasher that had run overnight, Linda rinsed plates for a new load. Charlie leaned over and took Linda's head in his hand and kissed her.

Linda looked startled. "What was that about?"

"I love you and just wanted to kiss you."

"I love you, too. But this doesn't happen very often. Are you guilty of something?"

"Not that I'm aware of. What Ed said in the car on the way home from the church yesterday just made me think of how good-looking you are and how lucky I am."

"Hey. I appreciate the thought, but we're both forty-four, and I think your perspective reflects your age. I bet you think Mollie's mother is good-looking too."

Charlie stood back and looked at her. "She's a nice-looking woman but not fantastic.

You're fantastic."

Linda looked a little astonished. "Where's this coming from?"

"The boys just made me remember how lucky I am. You're beautiful. You've been a wonderful mother and supported me in my army life. I'm grateful. I'm so glad you can now do the catering you've always wanted to do."

Linda shook her head. "Well, this is all a little startling. I guess I should feel special."

"You should. How many women have fourteen-year-old sons who think they're goodlooking and might be getting hit on?"

CHAPTER FORTY-EIGHT

Charlie kicked things off with a meeting of his team Monday morning.

When everyone was settled, he summarized where they stood. "This is that last time we will meet as a team. I very much appreciate all you've done, but as of last Wednesday it has been decided to go in a new direction.

Pelligrini moaned. "You mean all creativity is down the drain."

Wiggins interjected, "Now you know how it feels to have your brilliant idea dismissed."

Charlie tried to appease. "Hey. There's plenty of work to do and opportunities for creativity. We're basically going to follow Gabriel Winnick's concept of having the vehicles move under their own power but controlled by software."

Charlie passed out a package to each team member. "This package outlines the concept that has been selected. Take a minute to read the introduction."

There was a rustling of papers and then quiet as everyone read.

Finally, Pelligrini sighed and shook his head. "Damn. You've killed off all the power work."

"All the mechanical stuff too." Wiggins groaned.

Charlie disagreed. "Not so. There are going to be plenty of opportunities. We're going to have to ventilate this system with exhaust fans or mechanically operated windows all along the highways. That's going to require power, as will the software interfaces. We may even need to light the ceiling of the roof to provide comfort to people in the vehicles. Finally, we may need to have cameras along the highways."

He turned to Pelligrini. "And your company, Bennie, has a huge construction job. The exhaust system, whatever it is, requires a lot of mechanical engineering thought. Nobody's left out. Is everybody happy?"

Wiggins acknowledged Charlie's point. "Yeah, I guess I can sell this to my boss."

Charlie smiled. "Good. As I said, from now on we join up with your corresponding guys from the other teams. I'd like to work with the Futral-Partners people, if I may. I like to think I'm a civil engineer. Matt Somers is going to oversee this thing from the systems point of view with Dave Swenson, making sure we have what we need for a proposal. Beverly Byrnes will direct the software work, Danny Fortiano the engineering, and Lionel Haverford the logistics. They'll all have to get together on developing the interface box and making plans for its procurement. Again, I appreciate all you've done. I know you'll be just as creative for your new managers.

"Finally, I'd like to remind you of B-E's Christmas party next Saturday. I hope all our partners will be able to attend so my wife can see what I have to work with."

He shook the hand of each team member as they left the room.

CHAPTER FORTY-NINE

In order to create a ballroom, the hotel had opened the partitions it normally had in place to create smaller spaces. Long, ten-person tables were arrayed in a neat pattern around the room. Chairs were placed at the ends of the tables to increase the capacity to twelve. They were covered in white tablecloths but with no other decoration. A buffet table was spread out along one end of the room and a head table at the other end. Pay-as-you-go bars were located near the end of the buffet and in the middle of one side of the room. A bandstand and dance floor occupied the middle of the other side. A Christmas tree stood in the corner near the head table. It was the only sign this was a Christmas party.

The room was almost full when Charlie and Linda arrived. Charlie knew Linda was dreading it. She didn't know anyone. Still, she told him she was interested in seeing what the people who populated Charlie's life looked like, the personalities who inhabited the stories he told about his everyday life.

Charlie found the table where his team from work was sitting. He was surprised to see Sid Davies sitting there. Davies stood as the Hendrickses approached. "Sid, I'd like you to meet my wife, Linda. Honey, this is General Sid Davies. He's the deputy on our proposal team and was my boss when I first came to Bedford-Ewings."

Davies smiled. "Happy to meet you, Linda. Charlie and I are the only two around with short haircuts. It's a delight to see someone who might understand that."

Linda felt a kinship with the older man. "It's wonderful to meet someone here who immediately doesn't seem like a stranger. I didn't know if I would have anyone to talk to. Is your wife here?"

Davies smiled sadly and shook his head once. "No. I lost her to cancer."

Linda immediately felt embarrassed. "I'm so sorry. I would have loved to have known her." She thought about asking if he had children, but feared she would make another faux pas.

Charlie changed the subject. "It's an honor to have you at our table. I thought you'd be sitting at Wade's table."

Davies looked over at Wade's table. "I went there but decided I didn't like the feeling of gloom that Jim seems to have brought with him tonight. It's not what I want for my Christmas."

Charlie nodded. "Are your kids coming home for Christmas?"

Davies kind of sighed. "No. I'm going to Alabama for three days and California for three. That's where their homes are. Besides, my one ticket saves everyone money. Better to have it go into Christmas."

Linda was relieved to know more about the man. "Do you have grandchildren?"

Davies looked at her warmly. "Two in Alabama and one in California. They're my joy. Wish they didn't live so far away."

Linda empathized. "I can understand that. My children mean everything. Do you ever plan to move closer to them?"

Davies shook his head. "In this modern, mobilized world, as soon as I moved near one, they'd be transferred somewhere else. I think I'll just keep adding to my airline points … Hey, I'm just making this table as gloomy as Wade's. Let Charlie introduce you to all the young people here."

Charlie put his hand on Linda's back. "Good idea." He led her to the end of the table. "Guys, I'd like to introduce my wife, Linda. Linda, these are folks from companies we're partnering with. Andy Wiggins is a frustrated mechanical engineer from Futral-Partners, our engineering partners. Some of our earlier plans had him doing some exotic things. Now he has to do more mundane things, like ventilation, but his company has all kinds of construction to perform. This other guy is Bennie Pelligrini from our electrical power engineering partner, Florida-Southern. He's the team bad boy. Spends his evenings bar-hopping with his buddies in Georgetown."

Linda shook hands with them both. She addressed Pelligrini. "Are you really bad?"

Pelligrini chuckled and almost looked shy. "Your husband knows better. I spend time with the other guys from Florida-Southern to keep from getting lonely. I have a wife and children in Florida. She's as pretty as you."

Linda blushed. "Younger and pretty, I suspect."

Pelligrini realized he had probably overstepped. "I didn't mean to be offensive. Yes, she's young and pretty."

Linda smiled. "I didn't take offense. I'm flattered. Will you be going home soon?"

"We probably have another month of work on this proposal, but I'm going to run down a few days at Christmas."

Linda looked at Charlie and back at Pelligrini. "Maybe B-E's more tenderhearted than I thought. I'm glad they're letting you off at Christmas."

Charlie looked at Wiggins and Pelligrini. "She has some bad memories of my days in the army. Enjoy yourselves tonight ….and at Christmas."

Charlie led her next to a young couple. "This pretty, young woman, Joannie Bahr, is our software whiz." He turned to the young man with her. "And who's this?"

The man put out his hand. "I'm Terry Slocum, Joannie's date. I didn't know she was a whiz."

Linda thought, *Goodness. They don't look any older than Ralph.* She smiled and shook the young couple's hands. She spoke conspiratorially to Terry. "I know you feel you don't know anyone here, but you're not alone. Half the people here don't know anyone else. Let's stick together."

She turned to Bahr and took her hands. "Charlie's right. You are lovely. Hope the 'whiz' doesn't limit you having fun tonight."

She turned to the last couple. The man looked like he could be the Pillsbury Doughboy if he were dusted with flour. Seemed in his early thirties, older than the others. "I'm Linda. I go with Charlie."

The couple leaned forward. The man shook Linda's hand. "I'm Henry Usher. I work logistics. And this is my wife, Ursula."

The slightly plump woman took Linda's hands in hers. "Don't say anything. I know Ursula Usher is too much. I go by U, or if you're shouting across a room, it's UU. It's something I live with. Maiden name was Ursula Erskine. I've gone by U for a long time."

Linda smiled. "Maybe you should go by Usher and sing a little song. At least it would make people look around."

U shook her head. "The less conspicuous, the better."

Another couple came and sat at the end of the table. They hadn't been able to find room with their coworkers and were odd couple out.

Linda and Charlie sat on the side of the table where they could talk to nearly everyone.

Davies sat farther down, across from the Ushers and next to the extra couple. They seemed to struggle a little to make conversation.

Linda did fine throughout dinner. She enjoyed being with the young people, asking about their lives, and commiserating with Wiggins and Pelligrini about being separated from their families. She knew the feeling all too well.

When they finished their dinners, Charlie whispered to Linda. "We need to go say hello to the big wheels. Then we'll get coffee."

He led her to Wade's table.

Wade saw them coming and stood up, while Bonnie twisted around in her seat.

Charlie led Linda forward to a man who looked unhappy, with heavy bags under his eyes. He looked as if he had a terrific tan that was rapidly fading as winter approached. "Linda, this is my boss, Jim Wade, the man who's running this whole proposal." It was the first time he had called Wade "Jim." "Mr. Wade, my wife, Linda."

Wade didn't smile. He looked like he was fulfilling a requirement. "I'm pleased to meet you." He turned to his wife. "And this is my wife, Bonnie."

Bonnie smiled. "Yes. I've heard about you, Charlie. Jim seems very pleased to have you on his team."

Wade almost smiled. "Yes, Charlie's a good worker. Let me introduce Linda to some of the other people at the table."

Linda turned and found Bella Fortiano turning to look at her. Suddenly, there was a flicker of recognition in Bella's eyes.

Wade continued. "This couple is the Fortianos, Bella and Danny."

Linda nodded to Bella, who didn't take her eyes off Linda's. Linda struggled and finally pulled her eyes away, shaking Danny's hand. She heard Bella saying. "Yes. I've heard a great deal about your husband. Danny says he's a real go-getter. I hope you're having a pleasant evening."

Linda forced herself to look back. "Yes. It's been a lovely evening. So many charming people."

She could feel Charlie looking back and forth at the two women. She took his arm. "Let's get coffee."

"But you haven't met the others."

"I'll do it another time."

"Okay, but they probably think it's funny."

Passing the dance floor, she turned to Charlie. "Dance with me, Charlie."

"Sure."

Charlie took her in his arms and she lay her head on his shoulder, with her eyes closed, not relaxed but closed hard. She remembered dancing with Davenport. She wondered if this would be her last dance.

Finally, she noticed the Fortianos get up and head for the dance floor.

She leaned back and looked at Charlie. "I guess you're right. We should greet the other people."

Charlie looked a little bewildered and followed Linda as she led him back to Wade's table. They met with all the people there while Linda kept a careful eye on the dance floor. When they finished, she headed back to the team table. "Charlie, do you mind getting the coffee. I'd like to sit for a minute."

Charlie held her chair. "Sure. Are you all right?"

Linda looked up at Charlie. "I'm fine." Then she turned to Davies. "Tell me about your career, Sid."

Charlie went to get the coffee, wondering what had come over Linda. It seemed like meeting Bella Fortiano had had some strange impact on his wife. He could understand meeting Bella was like meeting someone from a different world, but the effect it apparently had on Linda seemed a little extreme.

Charlie found himself standing next to Matt Somers in the coffee line.

Somers looked inquisitively at Charlie. "I was afraid we wouldn't get a chance to meet your wife. I'm glad you came back. She's lovely but seemed a little distracted. Is she all right?"

Charlie was a little flustered. "Yeah, I think so. I feel like something's bothering her, but I don't think it's anything significant. She's having a nice conversation with Sid Davies now." Somers seemed to accept that. "Well, I'll look forward to getting to know her better."

He turned and started pouring himself coffee. Charlie followed behind.

When Charlie returned to the table, Davies got up. "Coffee looks good. I think I'll get myself some."

Charlie tried to make conversation with Linda. "Well, what do you think of my management team?"

Linda looked around cautiously and whispered, "Most of them seem very nice, but your boss appears like he has the weight of the world on his back, and his wife looks like she's just hanging on. Is this project really that rough?"

"Well, there is a lot of pressure to win this thing. I guess Wade is worried about his future."

Linda thought about that. "Charlie, are you worried about your future?"

Charlie considered the question for a moment. "Yeah, I guess there's always uncertainty when you involve yourself in a proposal. If you win, you're set for a while. If you lose, you work to get yourself picked up somewhere else."

"How do you know you'll be picked up?"

"I don't guess I do. I'm getting to know all the guys at Wade's table, trying to earn their respect. They all won't get fired. If we lose, I'll try to follow them onto something new."

"Lord, that sounds uncertain. I thought we were settled in life for a while."

Charlie took her hand. "Hey, don't worry. We'll be all right. This is a fluid business. I'll just go onto the next thing."

A voice came from Linda's right. "What are you two lovebirds doing cuddling over here?"

Linda grimaced and turned to find Bella Fortiano sitting in Davies's chair.

Bella gushed, "I'm so glad to finally meet you. Danny has been saying so much about Charlie, how he's really a hustler. I'd really like to get to know you better."

Linda wasn't sure what Bella meant by "hustler." She suspected that it wasn't good. "Well, I've been anxious to meet you too. You all seem so well known throughout the company."

Bella smiled, realizing that Linda was making a mild dig. "Well, Danny has been Jim Wade's most dependable leader for quite a while. Jim really depends on him. No matter who comes along, Danny will always be Jim's man."

Charlie had shied away from looking at Bella but now looked her in the eye, knowing she was sending a message. "I realize that, Bella, and am giving Danny all the support I can." He became a little sarcastic. "I really like to build on all his wonderful ideas."

Bella gave him a hooded look. She got up and leaned past Linda, the bodice of her dress falling away from her body, and straightened Charlie's tie. "It's good we understand each other."

Linda pulled her head back out of Bella's way as Charlie turned his head from the bareness of Bella's breasts.

As Bella straightened up, Linda rose and looked her in the eye. "I think you've demonstrated your point."

Bella smiled conspiratorially. "We really need to get to know each other better. I'll give you a call some time." She looked at

Charlie. "I'm glad to have met you, Charlie. Maybe we'll meet again. Have a drink or something. With Danny, of course."

With that, she left and returned to her table, her rear rotating provocatively.

Charlie looked at Linda. "What was that all about?"

"She was letting us know that we better not mess with Danny's position. She was showing why she has power over Jim Wade."

Charlie concurred. "Yeah, she showed a lot."

Linda glared at Charlie. "Yeah, and maybe you enjoyed it. I only got the side view, but I can imagine."

Charlie blushed. "She doesn't even wear a bra."

Linda wrinkled her mouth in annoyance. "I knew that."

Charlie tried to redirect the conversation. "But why did she involve you in this?"

Linda was afraid of the answer. She avoided what she feared. "Well, I guess she couldn't get to you without me being present."

Charlie pondered that. "But she seemed to be addressing you more than me."

CHAPTER FIFTY

On Monday afternoon after the party, the entire proposal team met in a conference room at B-E's Northern Virginia headquarters, since rooms at the proposal center were too small. Jim Wade, Sid Davies, Matt Somers, Danny Fortiano, Beverly Byrnes, Lionel Haverford, and David Swenson sat at table in the front of the room. The others sat in straight chairs in an auditorium layout.

Wade led the meeting off. "Okay. We have a general idea of where we're going. Davidson hasn't completely bought into our new strategy yet. He feels that it depends too much on DOT accepting our hypothesis that we should stay with vehicles working under their own power and that the automobile industry will work with us in implementing the new highway system. He wishes we had more control over the whole process but has reluctantly accepted the direction that you guys want to take us. We all have our fingers crossed. We have seven weeks until our proposal must be in and need to organize how we go from here. I'd like to turn this meeting over to Matt Somers as systems engineer to provide that direction."

Somers shuffled the papers in front of him. "As I see it, there are three major elements we have to consider. First is the design and construction of the physical system—that is, road construction to include resurfacing, upgrading, adding shoulders, upgrading entrance lanes and exit lanes to accommodate eighty-mile-an-hour traffic, building the integrated raster, upgrading entrance and exits to handle the distribution of interface boxes, building whatever facilities are needed or adapting existing ones, building the overhead cover for the highway, and developing whatever electrical grid will be needed to support the highway system, to name a few. The second is software development. That will include software for tracking traffic to ensure vehicle spacing and speed, control deceleration and movement out of traffic when vehicles leave the highway, and handle similar issues when vehicles enter. This I would expect to use a combination of the raster and the interface box. It will obviously include the development of control centers.

"Clearly, the interface box is critical. I am bringing in engineers from the West Coast to work with our software people to develop this box and design the hardware for the control centers, understanding that the interface box will be conceptual, inasmuch as we do not have knowledge of the proprietary internal software systems of the different vehicles on our highways. Included in this task is the development of a plan to interface with the automobile industry in the future to refine the interface box. Redundancy must play a major role in all designs.

"The third and final element is the logistics concept. That is, we need to look at the procurement of materials, ongoing support of the system, the need for training, and the development of support documentation. Most of this involves a plan. Although we need to consider the procurement of commercial off-the-shelf materials, we also need to consider subcontracting the manufacture of the interface box and perhaps some other internally designed equipment. Of concern will be finding contractors capable of producing the volume of materials needed for a massive construction program that may go on for years. Also included in this area is consideration of how we will physically support the handling of vehicle breakdowns during operations and a long-term maintenance plan.

"For the engineering, I look to Danny to oversee the work. Beverly has the software, and Lionel the logistics. Obviously, the three areas must interface. I wish to ensure this. Therefore, I have scheduled a meeting with the three of you Thursday to go over where you stand and the interface problems you need resolved. We'll meet in a team discussion room at the proposal center at ten in the morning. I'd also like David to be there so that we can consider what he needs for the proposal."

He turned to Fortiano. "Danny, you are going to be working heavily with our partners. How would you like to organize your team?"

Fortiano became alert. "Well, I'd like to put Futral-Partners in charge of the engineering work. I need them to let me know who will be their lead. I'd also like Florida-Southern to designate a lead. I'd like to meet with the two leads tomorrow at 9:00 a.m.

Wade looked around. "Okay. Are there any questions before we go to work?"

Charlie stuck up his hand. "Yes. What do you want me to do?"

Fortiano quickly responded. "Anything Futral-Partners wants you to do."

Charlie nodded. Clearly he was being cut out. He made eye contact with Sid Davies, but there was no obvious response.

*   *   *

Fortiano arrived at his meeting with the Futral-Partners team as planned on Tuesday morning. To his surprise, he found more people in the room than he had expected. Charlie Hendricks was there with the three Futral-Partners personnel who had been on the proposal team since the beginning. The guys from Florida-Southern sat against the back wall. There were three others. Fortiano recognized the man with rolled-up sleeves sitting at the head of the table. It was Bernie O'Hara, whom he hadn't seen since the initial meeting with Futral-Partners.

O'Hara looked at Fortiano. "Come on in, Danny, and let's get down to work."

Danny sat and tried to recover. "Thank you, Bernie. I didn't expect you to be here today. I set up this meeting to kick off the design and—"

O'Hara interrupted. "I appreciate that. My guys have given me a good rundown on what we need to do. I have two more Futral engineers here. They've been looking at how to make the cover for the highway aerodynamic to ensure it doesn't take off in a windstorm. They also propose that the raster grid be put in the roof or cover, whatever you call it, rather than under the pavement. That will make the pavement less likely to break up. I'd appreciate your checking that out with the software people to see if it's a problem. Danny, I'll look to you to be my contact back here and handle the interface with your software and logistics types. I'm moving my guys back to our headquarters in Los Angeles, where we have our own CAD systems to document the design."

Fortiano was taken aback. "Well, we have CAD systems here. I thought we'd be working here."

O'Hara rejected that. "No need. We have all our design capabilities in-house. No need to pay more travel expenses."

Fortiano protested. "What about the guys from Florida-Southern?"

O'Hara gestured to indicate that was no problem. "We have in-house capabilities to handle that." He looked at the Florida-Southern engineers. "We'll coordinate with you guys and look to you to help with the implementation when we win this thing. There's no need to break this up into too many little pieces."

Fortiano struggled for some defense. "Does Jim Wade know about this?"

"Yeah. I talked to him about this last night. He says for you to ensure there is an adequate interface capability in place."

Fortiano, flustered, scanned the room. "Okay. I'd like to send Hendricks out to work with you in Los Angeles."

O'Hara looked at Charlie. "Sure. We'll be glad to have him."

Charlie's mouth gaped.

CHAPTER FIFTY-ONE

Linda sat glumly in her office Wednesday morning. Life was going down the tubes. First Charlie had come home depressed on Monday night, saying he had been shoved aside by Fortiano and didn't have a role anymore. He had really been down. Then he came home last night and said he was being sent to Los Angeles. He couldn't even provide Linda a schedule of where he was going to be when. He thought he would be able to get home for Christmas but wasn't sure. Linda had wanted to scream. She'd thought of all the years she had done all the Christmas shopping, put up the Christmas tree, and handled Christmas Day with the children all by herself were a thing of the past. She had thought that was all over when Charlie left the army. It just seemed to go on and on.

Margie stuck her head in the door. "Linda. You have a phone call."

Linda sighed. "Who is it?"

"Didn't say. Just said she was a friend."

"Okay."

Linda picked up the phone and punched the blinking key. "Hello."

"Hi, Linda. So glad I got you. It's Bella."

"Oh, oh. Yes."

"I so enjoyed meeting you and your husband at the Christmas party. You're such a delightful couple. I'd like to get to know you better."

Linda was wary. "Oh, I enjoyed meeting you too. I'm surprised you know where I work."

"Oh, I have my sources."

Shit, thought Linda. *This is too small a world.* "I guess I'm not trying to hide, Bella. What can I do for you?"

Bella gushed. "You can have lunch with me, just us two girls. Thursday or Friday.

What's best for you?"

Linda didn't know any way out. "Thursday, I guess."

"Thursday, it will be. I'll make reservations for noon at Central Michel Richard. My treat."

Linda was hesitant. "Are you sure you can get reservations this late?"

"Oh, sure. I'm a Conway."

Linda wondered what that meant. *A Conway what?* "All right. I'll look forward to it."

After she hung up, Linda sat and worried. Bella was not the kind to be your Facebook friend or any other kind of buddy. *This can't be good.*

CHAPTER FIFTY-TWO

Charlie had left Dulles late Wednesday afternoon. He'd had to tell Linda good-bye in the morning. He had even missed saying good-bye to the boys after school, leaving home at three in the afternoon to ensure he could make a five o'clock flight. He had arrived at LAX a little after eight in the evening West Coast time. By the time he got to the Hyatt Regency, it was almost ten, and he was exhausted. He didn't look forward to his LA stay. He was by himself.

Before he had left, Charlie had spoken to Sid Davies, who didn't offer any sympathy. "Charlie, with Futral moving its operations to Los Angeles, we really do need someone out there to coordinate, and I can't think of anyone better than you. I know Fortiano has it in for you, but if I had been the one making the decision, it would still have been you."

Charlie had been the good soldier and had refrained from further complaint. He only discussed Christmas and asked to be able to return home for the holidays. Davies had been agreeable, caveating his approval with caution that, if Futral worked over the holidays, Charlie would probably have to stay in LA."

Linda hadn't taken it well. She had been petulant throughout Charlie's last day at home. She had been through it enough times before. Charlie prayed he would make it home for Christmas.

Charlie arrived at the blue glass-faced Futral-Partners's modern headquarters building around seven thirty in the morning. He hadn't transitioned to the West Coast very well and had been up early. He'd had breakfast and three cups of coffee, until the hotel waiter began standing almost next to the table, clearly waiting for Charlie to go.

In the lobby of the Futral-Partners building, he approached the receptionist at the front desk. He asked where he should go for the highway proposal but only got an uncertain look. He then asked for Bernie O'Hara's project.

"Mr. O'Hara is in the management suite, but he's not in yet. Do you want to wait?"

Charlie thought about what to do next. "How about Andy Wiggins? Is he here yet?"

The receptionist took out a phone book and looked through it. "There's an Andrew Wiggins. Is that who you are looking for?"

"I'm sure it is. Would you call him please?"

She lifted her desk phone and dialed. "Hello. Is this Andrew Wiggins?"

She listened for a moment. "Yes. There's a …" She looked at Charlie.

"Charlie Hendricks."

"A Charlie Hendricks here in the lobby asking for you"

She listened for a moment and hung up. "He'll be right down. You can sit over there until he gets here."

Charlie was relieved he had made contact. "Thank you."

It only took a couple of minutes for Wiggins to appear. He put out his hand. "Charlie, welcome to LA. Don't know who is formally supposed to meet you, but I'll do my best."

As he led Charlie to the elevator, Wiggins commented. "I guess you're like me and only beginning to adjust to the change in the clock."

Charlie concurred. "At least I'm able to afford a better hotel than I could in the army. Even have a car to myself."

They got off the elevator on the third floor, went down a hall, and entered a large bay of partitioned desk spaces. Wiggins looked around. "There are a couple of empty desks. I don't know what's planned for you, but we can settle you at one of them until we know more. Would you like a cup of coffee?"

Charlie looked around. "I'm about saturated, but yes. I'd like that. It's been an hour."

"What do you like in it?"

Charlie was a little distracted. It hadn't been a grand welcome. "Uh, just black."

Charlie settled in a chair before an empty desk, opened his briefcase, and took out paper and pens. He didn't know what else to do."

Wiggins returned with the coffee. "I'll let O'Hara's secretary know you're here." He checked the extension of the phone on Charlie's new desk. "Anything else I can do for you? O'Hara's got a meeting scheduled for nine. I expect you should plan to be there. I'll come by and get you."

Charlie looked around at his partition. He wished he had brought some pictures to post and a book to read. He tapped his fingers and swiveled around. People passing kept giving him the eye, wondering who he was and why he was there.

The phone rang. Charlie picked it up. "Charlie Hendricks."

"Welcome, Charlie. This is Bernie. Sorry I wasn't here when you arrived. Did Wiggins get you settled?"

"Yes, thank you. I understand there's a meeting at nine."

"That's right. You're welcome to attend."

"What do you see me doing?"

"You're the liaison guy. Believe me, there will be work for you to do. We need to interact with your people. I see you identifying the right people to answer our questions. You may even have to translate. I think you have a bigger job than you might think. How's your writing?"

Charlie was startled. "It's fine. Had to do a lot of that in the army."

"Good. When you have time, I'd like you to read the input my guys develop. Engineers can't write worth a shit. It's a nuisance to them. They just want to create." "Sure. I'll be glad to help any way I can."

"And, oh, by the way. We're going to be joined by two guys from Florida-Southern. Their CEO got pissed when I took over the electrical design and went to your boss, so they're coming as an appeasement."

"Do you know their names?"

O'Hara was quiet for a moment, perhaps checking his notes. "Let's see. Pelligrini and Nash."

Charlie grinned. "How's the bar scene out here? Pelligrini will want to know."

CHAPTER FIFTY-THREE

Linda took an Uber to the restaurant. The driver was Afghan. He'd been in the States for two years, driving for one. He'd been a translator for the army in Afghanistan. Linda asked if he knew Charlie, but he didn't.

In the restaurant, Linda looked around but didn't see Bella. She asked the maître d' for Mrs. Fortiano's table.

"Oh, yes. Mademoiselle Conway. Right this way."

Linda protested, "No. Fortiano?"

"Yes, Bella Conway. Fortiano? Right."

She was led to a table in the corner. "May I bring you a beverage?"

Linda hesitated. "Iced tea, please."

"Certainly, madam."

He left, and momentarily, a waiter brought the tea and a menu. Linda said she was waiting for someone and asked for a second menu.

She put sugar in her tea, stirred it, and took a sip.

Where the hell is the woman? Linda wondered if Bella was making a point by making her wait.

Finally, Bella came through the door. Linda watched as the maître d' helped her out of her coat. Linda had hers folded beside her. *How come I didn't get that attention?*

Bella came across the room, a fair distance to the corner. She was wearing a conservative business suit. *Work clothes*, Linda thought. Still, Bella's body had a way of moving under the clothes. Men and women looked.

Linda didn't rise to greet her. She put out her hand and Bella took it in both of hers. "I'm thrilled to have this opportunity to get to know you."

Linda was guarded. "Yes. I'm so glad I could make it."

Bella sat down. "Such a wonderful day."

Linda was curious. "The maître d' called you Conway?"

Bella pushed her hair back. "Yes. That's Daddy, Bobby Conway. He has the tab here."

Linda heard the word *tab* and protested. "No, I'll pay my way."

"Don't worry about it, dear. Daddy will be happy to pay. He loves his girl."

Linda probed, "And who is your father?"

Bella radiated. "Bobby Conway! Robert Elmont Conway of the law firm of Conway and Harrington. Works for half the people in DC and knows the other half. Keep your eye on the newspapers, and you'll see his name."

Linda accepted that with uncertainly. "So, how did you become a Fortiano?"

"Because Danny's beautiful. Met him at the gym. Didn't thrill Daddy, but he's a good guy, and we enjoy each other."

Linda thought *enjoy* was a strange way to put it. She wondered if it was equivalent to *love*.

The waiter brought Bella a daiquiri. She spread her napkin in her lap, opened her menu, and said. "And what about you?"

"What about me?"

"Yes. How did you meet Charlie? It is Charlie, isn't it, not Charles? Yes, I know that's right."

You damned well know it's Charlie, thought Linda. "Oh, we met in college."

"Where was that?"

"New York."

"In the city? Columbia?"

Linda tried to withhold her aggravation. "No. CCNY."

Bella smiled condescendingly. "Oh, I'm sure that's a good school. Are you from the city?"

Linda didn't want to say "Mamaroneck," so she said, "Near the Winged Foot Golf Club." She hoped Bella wouldn't know where that was and would be afraid to ask.

"Oh, that sounds very fancy. Charlie from there too?"

"East side Manhattan." *So far east it's in Brooklyn.*

"Must have been exciting, growing up in the city."

"Well, I suspect it was no more exciting than growing up in Washington."

"Oh, Daddy thought he had control issues with me. Boarded me at Madeira School and then shipped me down country to Sweet Briar."

"Doesn't sound too bad to me."

"Oh, it made him feel good. Out of sight and out of mind. He had no idea. I had my ways."

The waiter had been standing by the table afraid to break into the conversation. As if sensing him, Bella handed him her menu and said, "I'm just going to have the club salad. How about you, Linda?"

Linda had been waiting. "That sounds fine. I'll have the same." She would have liked to put a full dinner on Bobby Conway's "tab."

While they waited for their salads, Bella looked Linda in the eye and smiled. "I've been impressed by the way you get around, Linda."

Linda's eyes narrowed. "Oh, what do you mean by that, Bella?"

"Well, obviously the dull B-E Christmas party isn't the only place I've seen you."

Linda waited, apprehensively. "Okay, let's get on with it, Bella."

Bella kept a close-lipped smile and withdrew an envelope from her purse. She took some photographs out and laid them on the table at her place. She seemed to admire them. She picked up one and laid it in front of Linda. "This is a picture of Senator McDonald taken at the Willard Hotel fund-raiser. And look who is sitting at the table over his shoulder. You and Stephen Davenport."

She picked up another. "And if you don't know who Bobby Conway is, here's a picture of him on the dance floor, and look who is next to him with her head snuggled into Stephen's shoulder. Pretty good pictures, huh?"

Linda felt sickened. "Where did you get these?"

Bella smiled. "From a freelance photographer, a friend of mine who covers social events. You have to remember, dear, that if you're going to party with the social elite, you're in the public eye."

Linda waited for the ceiling to fall. "Okay. He's a client. So what?"

Bella pursed her lips and hunched her shoulders. "Oh, I don't know. The two of you look pretty intimate to me. Wonder what Charlie/Charles would have to say about these photos? Bet it would liven up your home life."

Linda felt infuriation, sorrow, and humiliation. "Why do you think that's any business of yours?"

Bella continued her closed-mouth smile of satisfaction. "I think it's my business because I think you're an ordinary human being and that you worry about your marriage."

Linda's anger began to surface. "What's wrong with that?"

"What's wrong with it is that you feel guilty, a hard thing to live with. I can't prove it, but it's not hard to imagine that you fucked Stephen. I did that after one of my Daddy's Christmas parties when I was seventeen, still a minor. I could have put Stephen away and maybe saved you from your pain, but that would probably have made Daddy unhappy. Besides, it wasn't my first time, and it was really no big deal. Stephen's not bad either. The difference between you and me is that I feel no guilt."

"And you're a slut."

"Now, now, let's not be harsh. Are you so pure? Come on, Linda, what did you think of Stephen?"

Linda was appalled. "I didn't think anything. Stephen and I are just friends."

"Sure, I understand. Still, I bet he knows your every dimple."

"Damn it, Bella, what do you want?"

They momentarily became silent while the waiter served their salads and Bella leaned back, thinking. The waiter asked if Linda wanted more tea, and she responded abruptly, "No. No more tea."

When the waiter left, Bella sipped her daiquiri and then leaned forward. "Let me see, what do I want? Oh, nothing big, at least not now. If B-E wins this proposal, someone is going to have to go to Georgia to manage the project. There's no way I want that to be Danny. We're Washington people. I need a volunteer. I think Charlie is the obvious choice. He's ambitious, too. Don't you think he'd like to volunteer?"

"You want me to get him to volunteer?"

"Oh, yes, sweetheart. I want to help with his career."

"You're a bitch, Bella."

"Yes, I am. And I'm proud of it."

Linda closed her eyes and frowned. "If Charlie does this, is that the end of it?"

Bella started eating her salad. "Don't let your salad go to waste, Linda. Or have you lost your appetite?"

Linda clinched her teeth and glared at Bella. "I asked a question. Will that be the end of it?"

Bella chewed her salad thoughtfully and looked blasé as she answered Linda. "They haven't won the contract, so only time will tell. The photographs are live ammunition, and I'll take care of them in a very safe manner."

Linda stood to leave. Bella looked up with mock sympathy. "Oh, are you leaving? Did something ruin your lunch?"

Linda put on her coat. "The last thing I want is lunch from you."

Bella looked up sternly at Linda. "Do we have a deal, lady?"

Linda, angry and frustrated, replied, "Yeah, we have a deal."

She walked out of the restaurant looking straight ahead, feeling that everyone was watching her.

CHAPTER FIFTY-FOUR

Charlie slept in until 9:00 a.m. *Thank God,* he thought, *the boys are teenagers and usually sleep until ten or later. Sleep is now more important to them than Christmas gifts under the tree.*

He had taken the red-eye on Christmas Eve, along with a bunch of other sad-looking people. He'd slept some during the flight, but there was too much on his mind. He felt guilty that he hadn't been at home to buy and set up the Christmas tree and to wrap the presents. In California, he had bought some earrings for Linda and wrapped them, cutting a small corner out of a whole roll of wrapping paper. The package hardly had room for the Scotch tape. It fit easily in the small suitcase he had in the overhead bin. He hadn't carried much. He'd be going back in three days.

When he arrived home, it was almost six in the morning. He had told Linda not to meet him at Dulles, so he had taken a cab. The lights were all on outside the house, and he could see the lit Christmas tree through the front window. He wondered if Linda had left it on to remind him that he hadn't done his duty helping with Christmas or if she was trying to cheer him up. He knew he only felt the former because he was feeling guilty.

Charlie unplugged the Christmas tree and turned out the lights before he tiptoed up the stairs and into the bedroom.

Linda said from the bed, "Welcome home. You don't have to worry about making noise.

I'm awake."

Charlie felt chagrinned. "Did I keep you awake because I arrived so late? I'm sorry."

Linda remonstrated, "Oh, no. Just a lot going through my mind."

Charlie felt a little concerned. "Anything we need to talk about?"

It seemed Linda hesitated a second. "Oh, nothing important. We'll talk sometime."

* * *

Linda's vagueness had concerned Charlie, but his fatigue had taken control and he had fallen asleep.

Earlier in the morning, he had felt Linda get up but hadn't known what time it was. Now he could hear her downstairs in the kitchen and wondered what had concerned her. He washed up, shaved quickly, and got dressed. Downstairs, he found Linda sitting at the kitchen table looking subdued, her hand around a cup of coffee as if trying to draw heat from the cup.

Charlie considered her for a moment. "Merry Christmas."

She looked up and said with a solemn smile, "Merry Christmas. I'm glad your home."

Charlie nodded. "And I'm glad to be home, but you don't look very merry."

Linda sighed. "I know. It's such a hassle getting ready for Christmas. I'll be all right when the boys come down."

Charlie poured himself a cup of coffee. "I'm sorry I couldn't be part of the hassle. I know I've missed it too many times."

Linda looked him in the eye, though her eyes looked watery to Charlie. "You can't help it. You have to earn a living. This house and the bills depend on you."

"Yeah, pragmatic and all, but I know it's not always easy."

Linda nodded. "Pragmatic, huh. Yeah, I guess that's what life's about."

Charlie sat down at the table with his coffee. "Jesus, Linda. You sound like the weight of the world is on your back. What's up?"

Linda protested. "Oh, nothing. Just a little glum. I'll be fine."

Charlie looked at her. "You sure?"

"Oh, yeah. Why don't you go and turn on the tree lights so it will be cheerful when the boys come downstairs?" She got up. "I need to get the cornbread in for the turkey dressing. Got to get life going. Mollie is coming over for dinner. Fortunately, it's late. She's having a noon dinner with her family. Ralph's invited there. I hope they have something other than turkey. Be rough having the bird twice in the same day. And, by the way, would you wake him up? He has to get ready in time."

"Mollie's becoming part of the family. You think this is serious?"

Linda laughed for the first time. "I wouldn't mind. I'd be happy to keep the girl. She organized buying and decorating the Christmas tree and wrapped half the presents. Been a blessing."

Charlie was glad to see some life come into Linda's being. He headed for the living room and turned on the lights on the tree. For a moment, he considered all the packages under the tree and thought of all the work that had gone into their accumulation and wrapping."

Upstairs, he tapped on Ralph's door and heard, "Huh?" come from within.

"Merry Christmas. It's time to get up. Mollie's waiting for you. Hope you have a big appetite because you have a challenge."

The reply came out sounding like a yawn. "Yeah, Dad, uh, Merry Christmas. You getting Ed up, too, so we can get the presents opened?"

"I'll do it as soon as you're out of the bathroom. See you downstairs."

Charlie went back downstairs, opened the front door, went out, and got the paper. In the kitchen, he put the paper on the table and sipped his coffee. He went to the cabinets, took out a cutting board and an onion, and got a knife from the drawer. He set them on the counter and headed for the refrigerator to get celery. "I assume you need an onion and celery chopped up."

Linda was mixing the cornbread batter. "That would be wonderful. I don't think my eyes can take the onion."

Charlie glanced at her and thought, *What's going on? Ever since I've been home, she's looked and sounded like she wants to cry. I'll give her time, but it has to come out.*

* * *

After the presents had been opened, Ralph had gone on his way to Mollie's, and Ed, Linda, and Charlie had eaten brunch. Next, Linda went to the mirror in the hallway and put on the new earrings. She went over and kissed Charlie. "Thank you. They're lovely. Let's take a car ride, you and me. Ed's watching the ball game and the turkey has hours to cook. Maybe we can look at the decorations on all the houses."

Charlie gave her an inquiring look. "Don't know that we'll be able to see much in daylight."

Linda was unconcerned. "That's all right. Mostly, I'd just like to take ride."

They rode around the neighborhood for a while, and at Linda's request, they then headed for Old Town, Alexandria. On one of the side streets off of King Street, Linda said, "Pull over and park here. I need to think."

Charlie held his breath, pulled over, and put the car in park. "Do you want to walk?"

"No, just sit here with the heater on."

Charlie looked around. The trees were bare, and there were few people on the sidewalk. He could see Christmas tree lights through the house windows, and some people had electric candles in the windows. Wreaths were on nearly every door. It all added some warmth to a quiet, peaceful neighborhood.

He waited for Linda.

She didn't look at him. "Charlie, if you win this contract, all the work is going to be in Georgia?"

Suddenly, Charlie thought he knew what was coming. "That's right."

"And, you're going to want to go there because that's where the action will be."

Charlie hesitated. "Yeah. I'd like to." He suddenly found himself trying to defend his statement. "It wouldn't be like Iraq and Afghanistan. If you didn't want to move down there, we could travel and see each other on weekends. There's lots to do down there. Hilton Head, Savannah, and a bunch of island resorts. And it wouldn't be permanent."

Linda looked at Charlie and put her hand on his arm. "Charlie, I've known this since this project began. You've always wanted to be where things were happening." She chuckled.

Charlie was alarmed. "What's funny?"

"It's just that I thought life would settle down after you left the army. These days, civilian life is not all that different from the army. You go where the jobs are, where the opportunities can be found."

The words, almost hopeless sounding, frightened Charlie. "Look. I won't go if it worries you so much. You're more important than the job."

"No, it's not that, but it's almost kind of funny." She drew in a deep breath. "Charlie. I need to talk to you about something far more serious than you going to Georgia." She made herself look at him in the eye. "Charlie, I had an affair. A one-night affair, not that one night is better than more. I don't love the person and have no desire to pursue it. I'm ashamed of it and pray to God that you will forgive me." It was all out without a breath.

Charlie sat, mouth agape, looking stunned. "Was it while I was in Iraq?"

"No, it never dawned on me to do such a thing when you were overseas. I heard of other women doing it, but not much. I didn't ever live in a military community while you were away, so I didn't hear much of that sort of thing. I had children to take care of, responsibilities. I blamed it on the army, but I knew you were where you wanted to be. I understood it but still was angry and frustrated at times. I think all army wives feel that. But I loved you. I loved our family. It was the way it was."

Charlie felt the guilt. He had felt it often, but she was right. He had been where he wanted to be. He fought for the words. "Then when was it?"

Linda bit her lip and looked away. "Last month. The night Ralph broke his arm. A night I should have been with my family."

Charlie was appalled. "Jesus Christ, Linda. Why?"

Linda frowned. "I can tell you what I think, although I suspect some of it is rationalization. None of it is an excuse. There is no excuse. You know I'm working in an atmosphere now that's often pretty sophisticated. I meet some important people and see a lot of glamour. I guess I got caught up in it. Kind of became Cinderella. One of the men I worked with asked me to lunch to discuss a project, but he wasn't really interested in the project. He flattered me, and I met him a couple of more times, again, supposedly about business. Then, one day he asked me to be his date at a fund-raiser at a hotel—not a real date but someone to be his escort so that he wouldn't have to face it alone. I was silly and thought it might be fun, and it was exciting. I met all kinds of important people and felt something like a princess. It turns out that he had rented a room in the hotel. I went there by myself to dress before the fund-raiser and went back there to change after it was over. He followed me to the room. I don't think I need to go further."

Charlie was silent for a moment. "And all this time, I was sitting in a hospital taking care of our son."

Linda burst into tears. "Christ, Charlie. You don't have to make me feel worse!"

"Like hell I don't. What am I supposed to say? That it's all right. You know it's not!" He pounded on the steering wheel, his face red with anger and frustration. "Damn it, you know it's not!"

Linda put her fist against the cold side window and pushed her forehead into it. "God, Charlie, I know it's not. I'm sorry. I'm such a damned fool."

Charlie hesitated. "Was it the guy at Thanksgiving, the guy fawning all over you?"

"Yes." It was a very small yes.

They sat in silence while Charlie breathed heavily and tears continued to flow down Linda's cheeks. They ignored the few people who passed and seemed to question what was going on in the car. Fortunately, most people looked ahead in their own worlds.

After a while, Linda spoke quietly. "What happened later is almost funny."

Charlie looked at her quizzically, afraid to pursue her thought. "What the hell, Linda?

What are you talking about?"

Linda turned to him again. "I need to tell you the whole story, but at least this is not the bad part."

Charlie looked at Linda expectantly as her mind seemed to work on what she wanted to say.

"At this fund-raiser"—she hesitated—"I was introduced to Bella Fortiano, who was there with her father, some kind of important DC lawyer. I didn't make the connection at the time." Now it was coming in a rush. "Then we met again at the Christmas party, and I could tell from her eyes that she knew. Later, she asked me to lunch, which I went to with trepidation. I didn't want to go, but I knew I had to face it. She had some photographs, society photographs, that were taken at the fund-raiser that showed me."

"Photographs that showed you and your date, what's-his-name, Stephen?"

"Yes. Stephen Davenport."

"Have you seen him since?"

"At Thanksgiving and he tried to corner me at a party I was catering, but I avoided him."

"At least you're honest."

"Damn it, Charlie, I'm being honest. How much more honest do you think I can be?"

Charlie sighed, "All right, go on."

"Anyway, she had decided to blackmail me."

"Hell. The Fortianos are something else. What did she want?"

"She wanted me to convince you to go to Georgia so her husband wouldn't have to."

Charlie thought for a moment. "And that's why you started this conversation by making me guiltily admit that I would want to go to Georgia."

Linda nodded and smiled a sad smile. "Yes, confirming what I already knew. I could have met Bella Fortiano's demand without even trying. I didn't have to admit a thing to you. But, I had to. I couldn't live with the guilt. I fell for the glamour, Charlie. A dumb, forty-fouryear-old woman who thought for a moment she was still young and could be foolish, and foolish I was. I'll regret it always. I can't take it back and will have to live with it."

Charlie said, "Shit, shit, shit," and put the car in gear and drove off. He drove past Ronald Reagan Washington National Airport, along the George Washington Memorial Parkway, and onto Interstate 66. He pulled off at the Nutley Street exit and parked in the Metro parking lot.

Linda was uneasy sitting in a lonely spot among the rows of cars. "Why are we parked here?"

"Good a place as any."

"Any? For what."

"For me to say what I need to say. You say you will have to live with what you did. Well, I will too. Don't expect me to forget. I can't. Is it because I'm humiliated, because I feel emasculated, because I'm guilty, because I'm hurt, because I'm sad? Yes, all of those things and more. But I can forgive, not easily, but I can forgive. I'm not innocent. I'm not guilty in a sexual way, but I'm guilty of putting much of my life ahead of yours, of wanting a family and a military life away from my family. They talk about women 'wanting it all.' Well, I wanted it all. I clearly often cut the fun and the glamour short, and for that, I'm sorry. We've only been at this marriage for twenty years. We have a long way to go. We can survive a few bumps. We'll survive this one, but I want you to do something."

"Anything, Charlie."

"I want you to find a fund-raiser that the Fortianos and this guy Davenport will be attending and make reservations for it."

"Charlie, you're not going to do anything bad, are you?"

"Not too bad."

"Okay, I can do that, but it will cost. Fund-raisers in DC aren't inexpensive."

"Just don't bankrupt us."

"I'll do it. What else?"

"I want it to be formal. I want you to wear a red dress, cut low. I want the world to see what a beautiful wife I have and be jealous. I want the world to know what a gorgeous fortyfour-year-old can look like. A woman whom I appreciate without saying it enough."

Linda finally smiled. "You're an incredible man, Charlie Hendricks."

"Yeah, well just keep this in mind. If I ever see your mind wandering while we're making love, I'm going to pinch the hell out of you."

Linda grinned.

* * *

Christmas dinner was warm and happy.

Afterward, Mollie asked Ralph what was going on with his parents.

"I don't know. Seemed like they were in another world."

Mollie smiled. "I'd say they're in love."

Ralph looked at her. "Well, I would hope so."

"No, I don't mean like most couples. I mean 'in love.'"

CHAPTER FIFTY-FIVE

Two days after Christmas, Charlie returned to California. The design was well on its way. After New Year's, everyone would be returning to Virginia to put the final proposal together.

At this stage, the designers were becoming a little wacky. They were figuring out ways to pay for the highway if the government dragged its feet. It was proposed that the highway could be treated like a stadium. For a fee, they could have the Capital One Highway or the Prudential Beltway.

It was also suggested that advertisements could be incorporated, much like the signs inside coliseums that run around the front of the balconies. These would move along the highway at a slightly lower speed than the cars so it looked like they were coming toward the car. There was concern that this would block scenic views, and it was agreed they would only be used in parts of the highway that were clearly not scenic.

Another engineer suggested that the front windshield of vehicles be designed as a television screen, transparent when the television was off but fully active when a show was on. It would be pay-for-view and entertain the driver who had nothing to do as the car whizzed along at eighty miles an hour.

They decided to hold all these things in reserve until the proper time to bring them forward.

Linda phoned Charlie midweek to say they were all set. It was a New Year's Eve fundraiser at Trump's Hotel. He asked if she'd gotten the dress. "Yes, but I'm a little afraid to wear it. I'll get you to make the final decision."

Charlie asked, "Can they see your areola?"

"Not quite."

"I can't wait."

CHAPTER FIFTY-SIX

Ralph and Ed were watching television New Year's Eve after their parents had left.

"How come you and Mollie aren't going out?" Ed inquired.

"Lots of reasons. Finances, leaving you alone, all that. Besides, Mollie's coming over. You're the chaperone."

"Gee, Ralph. You don't have to stay home because of me. You make me feel guilty."

"No, problem, bro. I'm not interested in sharing Mollie with anyone else anyway."

"Sounds like you'd like me to vanish."

"Maybe a while at midnight."

Ed nodded. "No problem. What did you think about Mom and Dad? Never known them to get so gussied up or even go out on New Year's."

Ralph leaned back and shook his head. "Dad's had that dress uniform hanging in his closet forever. Think he bought it as a lieutenant thinking the army was going to be flashier than it is. Pretty fancy with all those rows of little ribbons. Wish I could have seen Mom."

Ed laughed. "Yeah, I know she has on a red dress, and she's all made up with her hair done up to the nth degree. It's strange that she came downstairs with a coat wrapped tightly around her and holding her wrap rather than wearing it."

Ralph's eyes twinkled. "Like she had something to hide. What kind of dress do you think she has on?"

"We'll just have to stay up until they get home. If she goes upstairs in the coat, I guess we'll never know."

*   *   *

When Charlie and Linda arrived in the lobby of the hotel, Linda went straight to the ladies room. After ten minutes, she returned, her wrap tightly wound around her shoulders and her coat folded in her arms held close in front of her.

Charlie held out his hand. "Let me take your coat and check it."

Linda hesitated. "I don't know, Charlie. I think I'll get cold."

"Don't be silly. You have a wrap, and you look beautiful."

"I'm not being silly. You have on three layers of clothing, and all I have is …skin."

Charlie chuckled. "And beautiful it is."

"Charlie, I feel you're showing me off, putting me on display."

Charlie looked into her eyes. "Indeed, I am. I want everyone to know what a lucky man I am. Come on. We're probably going to end up sitting with some losers, so we'll have to entertain ourselves and dance a lot."

They studied the ballroom, looking for a table with some empty seats and with some people near their ages. There weren't many choices, but they found one.

They approached it, and Charlie asked, "Are these seats available?"

A man with an oval, ruddy face smiled and replied, "Been saving them for a handsome couple. Welcome. I'm Ben Jamison and this is my wife, Liz. That other guy is Melvin Johnson Anderson, LLP, and his better half, Abby Anderson."

They shook hands around. Anderson interjected, "Name's Mel. Ben likes to give me a hard time. Where are you assigned, Colonel?"

Charlie corrected. "Please call me Charlie, Charlie Hendricks. And this is my wife, Linda. I still wear the uniform, but I'm recently retired. Still part of the military-industrial complex, though, working for Bedford-Ewings International."

"Jamison grinned. Yeah. Your company is bidding on the Super Highway, and you had better win it. Bought a thousand shares last month on the gamble that you will. You know anything about it?"

Charlie hesitated. "Yes, that's what I'm working on."

"You are? No kidding? Have you got it under control? Tell me about it."

Charlie wished he could hide. "I think we're doing fine. I wish I could talk about it, but I'm afraid I can't."

Liz Jamison interjected. "Don't worry, Charlie. Ben's always sticking his nose into things, but Mel will stop him before everyone gets into trouble. We take Mel with us all the time for protection."

Charlie nodded. "So Mel's your lawyer?"

Liz grinned. "Yes, but he's also a friend. I'm just joking about him protecting Ben."

Abby said, "No, she's not. Mel takes things very seriously."

They all sat down and waiters began filling orders for wine.

Charlie and Linda looked around, wondering about the crowd they had joined. Their tablemates seemed nice and friendly but were clearly of a different financial level. Charlie and Linda were afraid to ask for details about what they did for a living or, especially, where they lived, since they would have to respond, Springfield, rather than McLean or Georgetown or something of that ilk, which they suspected was where the Jamisons and Andersons lived."

Ben leaned across Liz. "Charlie, you sound like you might be from New York? Where did you go to college?"

Charlie felt Linda catch her breath as he said, "CCNY."

Liz's and Ben's faces lit up. "No kidding. We went to NYU. High school sweethearts. Part of the proletariat, unlike this guy over here." He stuck a thumb toward Anderson. "He went to Columbia and his pretty other half did journalism at Syracuse."

Suddenly, Charlie and Linda felt better, and they all spent some time talking about New York City.

After dinner, Charlie stood up. "May I get a coffee refill for anyone?"

Abby held up her cup. "Decaf, please. Thanks, Charlie."

Charlie moved toward the kitchen and found a waiter to ask for the coffee. As he waited for the man to return, he reconnoitered the room. He found the Fortianos sitting at the far side of the dance floor. But they were only part of his target, and he couldn't find Davenport. The waiter handed him the coffee just as Davenport came in from the lobby and joined a young redhead at a table with a bunch of other men with pretty, young women. Davenport's date must have been in her twenties. Charlie wondered how he did it. He thought Davenport was reasonably goodlooking, but he was clearly into the beginning of middle age.

Charlie was satisfied with what he had seen.

He returned the coffee to the table. Abby thanked him but noted that, while he was gone, the waiter had come around with more coffee.

Charlie smiled. "Sometimes I win, and sometimes I lose. I hope you enjoy it just is well."

She smiled. "I'm sure I will. It was a gallant effort."

"Enjoy."

He turned to Linda. "I'll be back in a moment."

Linda caught her breath. "Don't do anything you'll be sorry for." Abby's eyes bugged as she looked up at Charlie.

He smiled and looked at her. "Just going to see an acquaintance."

He strode away with purpose and headed for Davenport. He placed his hand on his nemesis's shoulder. "Good evening, Stephen. Haven't seen you since Thanksgiving."

Davenport turned, a flicker of recognition and fear passing through his face. He stood, turned toward Charlie, and took the offered hand. Charlie squeezed it hard while looking down at the redhead. "Quite a guy, huh. Please excuse us for a minute."

He took Davenport firmly by the arm and led him from the table.

Davenport complained, "Hey, take it easy. What are you doing?"

Charlie smiled. "Just wanted to let you know your girlfriend is here so that you can check her out."

Davenport looked uncertain as Charlie leaned near his ear. "From now on, Stephen, I would advise you to stay away from alleys and lonely walkways. Someone might relieve you of that thing between your legs that leads you through life."

Davenport leaned sway. "Are you threatening me?"

Charlie continued to smile. "Just making an observation."

As Charlie turned to walk away, Davenport had to retaliate. "You know, she's pretty good."

Charlie turned back to Davenport and glared. "You'll never know how good."

As Charlie returned to the table, Linda drew in a deep breath. "At least you're not bloodied."

Charlie looked at her and said, "I wouldn't have been the one bloodied."

He suddenly realized his table was silent, everyone looking at him apprehensively.

He smiled. "Sorry, folks. Just someone I don't like, and I told him so."

They all still appeared uncertain.

Charlie picked up his wine glass. "A toast to a wonderful New Year and to new friends."

Just then, the dance band started to play. He looked at Linda. "May I have this dance?"

Linda stood indecisively, and Charlie whispered in her ear, "Leave the damned wrap on the chair."

He took the wrap, set it down, placed his hand on her bare back and led her to the dance floor.

As he pulled her to him and they began to dance, she pushed her head into his shoulder.

"I feel naked."

Charlie chuckled. "Just because everyone is looking at us."

"Darn it. I'm going to stay pressed against you all evening."

"That's all right with me, but the army ribbons may hurt a little."

"It's worth the pain."

"But, it may leave welts."

"That's a thought." And she backed away and looked up at him.

He smiled. "Tonight, you're my Cinderella."

"And you're my prince."

"I've always wanted to be one."

They put their cheeks together and danced for an hour. About eleven thirty, Charlie broke away from Linda and led her back to the table. "I have something else to do."

"Oh, God. Do you have to, Charlie?"

"I have to."

Linda looked resigned and grabbed for her wrap. As she wrapped it around herself, she realized everyone at the table was looking at her. As she sat in the chair being held by Charlie, she smiled and said, "Goose bumps."

She looked anxiously as Charlie headed back to the dance floor and approached the Fortianos. "May I cut in?"

Fortiano looked surprised. "Oh, hello, Charlie. Didn't know you'd be here tonight."

Charlie smiled. "Sometimes we all have to live the good life. May I, Bella?"

He took Bella's hand and put his hand on her back. As they danced, he said, "You look beautiful tonight, Bella. Lovely dress, but more conservative than at Christmas."

She leaned back, looked him in the eye, and considered. After a moment she said, "You liked that, huh?"

Charlie nodded. "Every man in the room did, Bella. But you knew that. I expect you've been doing it all your life. I think you enjoy it."

She squeezed her mouth, thoughtfully. "Yeah, I do." She gave him a coquettish look.

"What would you like to do about it, Colonel Hendricks?"

"I'm afraid I'm too straight-arrow to do anything."

She smiled. "But I bet you'd like to."

Charlie became serious. "I bet I wouldn't be the first."

Bella made an offended face. "Don't be mean, Charlie. It's unbecoming someone dressed up as pretty as you."

Charlie was quiet for a while. Bella put her cheek against Charlie's and acted as if she were enjoying the dance. As she did so Charlie whispered, "So you want me to go to Georgia?"

Bella jerked back in shock. "What do you mean?"

Charlie looked down at her. "Well, you brought up the subject of being mean, so I thought I'd follow through. I thought, initially, that blackmail didn't fit with a pretty woman, but then I realized it fit well with your kind of beauty."

"What do you mean by 'my kind of beauty'?"

"Do I have to tell you?"

"You bastard."

"Narcissistic. Self-centered. Does that tell you what I think?"

She tried to pull away, but Charlie held her while she shouted, "You, asshole. You have a wife screwing behind your back, and you dare to insult me."

She suddenly realized that everyone around her had stopped dancing and was looking at her. She tried to smile and ignore them. She hissed, "You fucker, let me go."

"Ah, be polite Bella, I need to escort you back to your table."

He took her by the elbow and started walking. "You don't know shit about my wife. It's all conjecture."

"Conjecture, nothing. I know that look."

At the table, he let go of her and pulled out her chair. "I bet you do, Bella. I bet you do."

She turned from the chair and flounced off to the lobby. Fortiano looked after her apprehensively, glared at Charlie, and sat there not knowing what to do.

Charlie smiled at the people at the Fortiano's table, turned, and returned to his table.

Ben smiled at him. "You sure do dance with some of the best-looking women in this room."

Charlie was uncertain about what to say.

Linda smiled. "There's always been something about my husband."

He reached down, pulled her up, and headed back to the dance floor, her wrap falling to the floor, where Abby picked it up.

Linda protested. "Hey. Let me get my feet under me. Did Bella excite you or something?"

"Or something. She's a real bitch."

Linda smiled. "Charlie, watch your language."

Charlie grinned and danced her around to the side of the dance floor where Davenport and Fortiano sat. Just as Bella returned from the lobby, the band began to play: "Should old acquaintance be forgot," and Charlie leaned Linda back and gave her a long, passionate kiss.

*   *   *

As they rode home, Linda tried to cuddle with Charlie but had to undo the seat belt to do it and thought how unromantic the automobile industry was, installing gearshifts and storage bins between the seats. "You kissed me so long I didn't get to toast the New Year with champagne. Just had to chugalug it as we left."

"The kiss was better than any champagne."

"I guess I forgot you could be so romantic."

As they pulled into the driveway, Charlie acknowledged, "I have some making up to do."

They entered the house to find Ralph, Ed, and Mollie waiting up.

"What are you still doing up?" Linda exclaimed.

Ralph grinned. "Just making sure my parents got home safely."

Charlie laughed. "Now you know how it feels."

Linda hit him on the shoulder. "How would you know? You go to sleep and leave the worrying to me."

"Well, I have to work."

"As if I lie around eating bonbons all day."

Mollie interjected. "You look pretty spiffy, Colonel Hendricks."

Charlie smiled. "Thank you. Nice to wear this fancy stuff, but you should see Linda."

Linda hit his shoulder again. "You're embarrassing me."

Ralph interposed. "Ah, come on, Mom. All we can see is the bottom of your skirt."

Linda continued being defensive. "Maybe that's enough"

Mollie spoke up. "Come on, Mrs. Hendricks. I bet you're beautiful."

Linda glared. "Do you want to remain welcome here, Mollie?"

Mollie looked chastened.

Linda said, "Okay," and she flipped her coat open like a flasher, turned, and ran upstairs.

Ralph shouted after her, "Hey, Mom, I was looking down."

Linda shouted over her shoulder, "Ask Mollie."

Charlie looked at the children, flicked his eyebrows up and down a couple of times, and smiled.

CHAPTER FIFTY-SEVEN

Jim Wade was in Gunnar Davidson's office early the first workday after New Year's. The call from Davidson's secretary had come to Wade's office before he even had time to hang up his coat, and his car was still warm from the morning commute as he drove over to the B-E headquarters.

"Have a seat, Jim," Davidson said, gesturing to one of the two chairs in front of his desk.

Wade straightened the chair to face Davidson directly and sat, feeling uncertain and wondering why they weren't sitting in the comfortable chairs in the corner of the office.

Davidson leaned back and templed his fingers. "I've been worried throughout the holidays. I'd always pictured this proposal as having a clean hardware and software solution, and I think that's the way DOT is thinking too. This business of having an open-ended proposal that depends on the auto industry working with us really makes me feel uncomfortable. What do you think?"

Oh, shit, thought Wade, *where were you a month ago?* "Well, we all thought that when we started, but the complexity was just too much. And much of the effort seemed redundant with what the auto industry was already doing. It was like reinventing the wheel. The engineers have pretty well convinced me that this is the only logical way to approach this thing."

Davidson nodded. "It still worries me. We have an awful lot riding on this. Seems to me we have some heavy selling to do. How are we doing that?"

"We're doing it the only way we can—by using the proposal to sell it. We're including a lot of illustrations, even a lot in color. Futral-Partners has some great equipment for doing that. Lot of *Popular Mechanics*-like illustrations, along with real engineering drawings looking like the physical design is well along. We're leading in with a great write-up of the proposal doing a sales job—brief but strong."

Davidson nodded. "That's good. We need to hit it strong and fast and make the point. Who's working on it?"

"Matt Somers; Beverly Byrnes; and this new guy, Charlie Hendricks."

"Hendricks, huh. You think he has the ability?"

"I've been impressed. For an engineer, he writes very well. A blessed talent. He was out in California working with Futral on the illustrations and came back with the document almost finished. We're just refining it now. I feel we're ahead of schedule."

"What about your shadow, Fortiano? Is he working on it?"

Wade didn't want to put down Fortiano but also didn't want to recognize him. "As I said, Hendricks came back from out West with the thing almost done. We're just polishing it from the system engineering and software standpoints."

Davidson pursed his lips as if in deep thought. He knew he couldn't do anything. It was the problem with having your life dependent on your workers. A manager could only do so much. Maybe he hadn't provided enough guidance, but then he wasn't an engineer. "Well, you know how important this thing is. We have an awful lot riding on it." *More me than you*, he reflected to himself. He dismissed Wade with three words: "Make it perfect."

*   *   *

Wade returned to his office and told Daphne to get Somers, Byrnes, and Hendricks into his office right away.

"Will do," she responded. "Should I pull another chair into your office?"

Wade thought a minute. *Should I make them stand?* "Yeah, will you?"

The three assembled in Daphne's office and then knocked on Wade's door.

"Come in and have a seat." He glared at the three. "Just had another 'come-to-Jesus' with Davidson."

Somers frowned and protested. "It's a little late for that."

Wade frowned. "He just wanted to remind us that all our necks are hanging out on this."

Byrnes exclaimed, "He said that! This guy's given us no guidance," she complained. "We're doing this in a vacuum—and doing it damned well."

Wade tried to calm things. "Heck, we've known all along what this means to the company. I'm not telling you you've done a poor job. I think we've done the best we can. I just want to give you guys a final push to do your best."

Charlie tried to bring things into focus and said soberly, "We're doing that, and I think we have a very good product. I don't think you need to worry, sir. You'll be proud of the document."

Wade stared him in the eye. "You talk big, Hendricks. Don't make yours a short career."

Charlie moderated. "I really think we're in good shape." He gestured to Somers and Byrnes. "You put together a good team here. You can be proud of them." Wade responded desolately, "I hope that will be good enough."

* * *

It was a little after 11:00 a.m. when the three left the office. Wade got up and put on his coat. Passing through the outer office, he told Daphne that he was taking an early lunch. *God, I need a drink!*

* * *

Charlie walked down the hall with Somers and Byrnes. "You guys have been through this before. Are things as desperate as Wade implies?"

Somers shook his head. "Maybe for him. We're just worker bees. We'll survive. Just keep making friends. You need a network here in the company, just like anywhere else."

Byrnes interjected, "That's a somber outlook. I think we're doing all right. When we win this thing, there's going to be a lot of fun things to do—a product you can really see. Heck, the world will see it."

Charlie smiled. "Thanks for the bright side, Bev. Let's get back to work."

As Charlie approached his cubicle, Fortiano was waiting for him. "Hendricks, I want to see you in my office."

Charlie looked at Fortiano with mild disdain. "You have anything to say, you can say it here."

Indecision reflected in Fortiano's face, replacing the bravado of his opening salvo. He hissed a whisper. "Stop screwing around with my wife."

Charlie thought of saying, *Everyone else is.* But that was too crude. "Don't worry. I have nothing else to say to her."

He turned back to his desk, dismissing Fortiano, who grabbed him by the arm. Charlie looked him in the eye. "Get your hands off me, you overdeveloped ape."

Fortiano backed up and let go. "We're not done, Hendricks."

"Yes, we are."

CHAPTER FIFTY-EIGHT

Bonnie Wade and Bella Fortiano met for their periodic luncheon, this time at the Fair Oaks Shopping Mall. It was farther from the District than Bella usually liked to go, but Bonnie seemed so highly strung that she gave the other woman a shorter ride.

They skipped the offered small table and took a four-person booth while the hostess frowned. Bella didn't care.

She looked at Bonnie, studying the bags under the woman's eyes. "I guess you'll be glad when this proposal is put to bed."

Bonnie didn't smile. "Let's hope. Jim's almost impossible to live with. Hardly speaks when he comes home. Just grabs a drink and heads for the den. At least it's better than having to listen to complaints and sarcasm."

"Yells at you, huh?"

"No. He never yells. Just suffers and is morose. Mean sometimes." She hesitated. "I really shouldn't be saying that. Should keep my problems at home."

Bella reached across and put her hand soothingly on Bonnie's. "Oh, don't worry. If you can't talk to a friend, who can you talk to? Sometimes we just need to let off some steam."

Bonnie sighed. "Sometimes I hope B-E will just lose the proposal so we can be done with it."

Bella protested. "Don't wish that. This contract has the potential to make a lot of money and get Jim promoted. That would be good for everyone." *And Danny and I will move up, too.*

"I know. I know. And I like the income. Just need to survive."

Bella wanted to change the drift. "So, how does Jim say the proposal is going?"

"He thinks it's going all right, though Davidson would like to see more of a closed package. Jim says this one is little open-ended and will require the government to make some decisions. He's worried they might not like that. Anyway, he says it's coming together. He has Somers, Byrnes, and Hendricks finalizing it."

Bella was horror-struck. "Hendricks? How did that shit head get in the group finalizing the proposal? He's an embarrassment to the company."

Bonnie was struck by the vehemence of Bella's comment. "I know you've said he was pushy and overly sure of himself, but why do you say he's an 'embarrassment'?"

"Haven't you seen the way he acts. And he's rude. At the New Year's Eve party, we went to, he was horrible to me. The man is an abomination. I've never been treated so badly by anyone."

Bonnie was startled. "He went to the same party you went to? Seems a little posh for him?"

"I agree. It was way above him." Bella stopped and sat back. *Oh, shit. I have to be careful. I don't want Bonnie thinking it was above her too. I have to stay on the same level.* "For you and me it was appropriate, but he's ex-army. Didn't work up in the company. Just jumps in, and suddenly he's acting important. It's just not right. And he has all the rough army traits as well. He's hardly civilized."

Bonnie was a little scared by the outburst. "Well, I've hardly met him. Jim seems to think he's all right. I had no idea. What did he do to you?"

Bella thought, *Shit, I can't tell her what's going on.* "He asked me to dance, and while we were on the floor, he made a move on me. Talked dirty. It was humiliating."

Bonnie was dismayed. "He did that, right on the dance floor, while his wife was nearby?"

Bella began to make it good. "Yes. And when I tried to walk away, he grabbed my arm and wouldn't let go."

Bonnie drew a deep breath. "That's awful. I'll talk to Jim about it. I guess I'm not the only one living with stress."

Bella put her hand on Bonnie's again and looked her in the eye. "You will? For me? Oh, thank you, Bonnie. I'd like it taken care of. I told Danny about it, and I'm frightened he might do something. It's so embarrassing."

* * *

During the lunch, Bonnie continued to dwell on the stress she was under. As they left the restaurant and walked across the parking lot, she said, "Thank heaven for the pills you get for me. They help a lot. Sometimes I wish they would just knock me out and that I'd wake up in another world."

Bella commiserated. "I'm glad they help. Are the pills I gave you in December doing the job?"

Bonnie nodded. "Pretty much. Better than before, but when I look in the mirror, I know they're not the complete solution. I'm obviously stressed."

Bella put her hand on Bonnie's shoulder. "Maybe we can do better. Come on and sit in the car with me."

Bonnie looked at Bella hopefully. "Do you have something better?"

"We'll see."

They got in the car and Bella opened a little compartment door under the front of her seat. She looked around to make sure they were alone. Then she took out a bottle of pills, a razor blade, and a mirror. She took out some broken pills, dumped them on the mirror and chopped them into a fine powder, separated it into two lines, and then pulled out a straw from under the seat. "I'll show you," she said and then drew a line of the powder into her nose through a straw. "See how easy it is. Really makes you feel good. If you like it, I can give you more." She gave Bonnie a straw and held out the mirror. "Go ahead."

Bonnie hesitated, and thought, *Should I do this? I guess it's all right. Bella seems okay.* She took the straw and put it in her nose and then drew the powder in—not a continuous single swipe the way Bella had done it, but with a several efforts, she got it all in.

Bonnie sat straight up, staring through the windshield. She could feel Bella staring at her.

She turned, "I think I'm beginning to feel something."

Bella grinned. "You're going to feel good. Forget your worries."

Bonnie looked baffled. "I don't know. It's hard to breath." Her face became panicked. "Bella, I can't brea—" She tried to gasp, and her eyes bugged and rolled in her head.

"Oh, God," Bella screamed. She leaned Bonnie forward and pounded on her back. "Shit, Bonnie! Come out of it!"

But Bonnie didn't come out of it. She fell forward, her head in the corner of the door and the dashboard.

Bella stared in horror. She shook her head. "Oh, damn, damn."

She looked around to ensure she was alone, pushed the car's starter button, and threw it in gear. She backed out of the parking space and headed for the shopping center exit. *Stay calm*, she thought. *Drive carefully, so no one notices. Where's the nearest hospital? I know, out on US 50.* She headed in that direction, pushing Bonnie on the shoulder trying to get a response but getting nothing. She pulled into another outer parking space and tried to feel the pulse in Bonnie's neck but wasn't sure how to do it. She grabbed Bonnie's arm and tried again at her wrist. Nothing. *Shit, shit, shit.* She pulled Bonnie over onto the seat and pulled Bonnie's coat up over her head. *Damn, damn, damn. I can't go to the hospital. They'll turn me in as a dealer. Maybe I can just dump her out near the emergency room.*

She drove out onto US 50, made it through a stoplight, took the ramp onto the Fairfax County Parkway, and followed the signs to Inova Fair Oaks Hospital. She approached the hospital along the edge of the parking lot. There seemed to be people everywhere. She drove around to the back of the hospital and saw construction workers and garbage collectors. She was sure there were security cameras everywhere. She couldn't find anywhere to pull off in a quiet place away from where cameras might be. *Shit. There's no place to dump her.*

She drove back to US 50 and headed west. Every time she came to a stoplight and a car pulled to stop in the lane beside her, she felt panic. She made sure she didn't make eye contact with anyone.

She continued past Chantilly, looking for a quiet area, but everything was built up. *I have to get off this road.*

She turned left at the next intersection. *Pleasant Valley Road. That sounds like it might be quiet.*

Finally, she came to an area where there were woods and some open fields on each side of the road, but she couldn't find any unexposed pull-offs. At the next intersection, she turned right and passed a building on her left, while the woods continued on her right. Up ahead, there was a road going back into the woods. It was unfinished, rutted dirt. Cars were coming from the other direction. She passed the exit for the road into the woods and, in a quarter-mile, found a place to turn around. She went back and turned off onto the dirt road. It rapidly deteriorated but was shortly out of site of the main road. She worried about having to back out. She stopped, got out of the car, opened the passenger door, and pulled Bonnie out. She still thought of her as "Bonnie," not as a body. But as she dragged the woman into the woods, out of site, she realized that the dead weight she held was no longer a living being. She left the body and headed back to her car, smoothing the ground with her foot so that the "dragging" wouldn't be obvious. *God, I hope it rains soon.*

Bella stood by her car and looked back. *Good. I can't see the body, but there are still a couple of spots I need to smooth.* She went back and touched up the spots. Back at the car, she studied the woods again and felt fairly satisfied.

She got back in her car and began to back. She wasn't good at backing and the car went off the path into a deep rut. *Shit!* She shifted to drive and hit the accelerator. The car jumped out of the rut and almost went into a tree. She sat and breathed hard.

She began backing again, more carefully. As she approached the main road, a car was passing. Bella prayed that the driver wasn't paying attention to the side road.

She backed onto the main road. No one else was coming. She slammed the car into drive and roared off with her tires squealing, the car fishtailing as she straightened it out.

Where the hell am I?

At the intersection, she checked the road sign.

Braddock Road. I know Braddock Road. I've seen its exit from the beltway. Maybe it will take me back there.

She continued ahead, returning to civilization, past office buildings, a school, and housing developments. Suddenly the road bent sharply to the left, and she could see another road almost touching hers on the right and a big highway beyond. She came to a stoplight at a highway. *28. Sully Road. Dulles to the left. I don't want to go to Dulles.*

She turned right. There was a sign for Interstate 66. *I'm saved. Shit, a left-hand exit!*

She struggled to get into the left exit lane and turned left down the ramp and onto Interstate 66.

Watch the damn speed limit. Stay calm.

With relief, Bella headed home.

CHAPTER FIFTY-NINE

Bella pulled into her garage parking lot; parked; and sat, breathing hard. She opened the compartment under her seat and took out everything related to drugs. She looked around the car and noticed the mirror, razor blade, straws, and Bonnie's purse. *I didn't think about the purse. At least they'll have a hard time identifying her.*

Bella stuffed everything into Bonnie's purse and carried it with her to her apartment, leaving her own purse in the car. She didn't want to be seen carrying two purses.

In her apartment, she collected all her narcotics and equipment. She put on kitchen gloves. She dumped the pills and powder in the toilet and flushed several times. Everything else she took to the kitchen and began washing all the items with Clorox cleaner. She didn't know if it would remove fingerprints, but she prayed that it would. She wiped down Bonnie's purse and all the drug paraphernalia. She took out Bonnie's car keys from the purse and then stuffed the bottle of cocaine into it. She put the rest of the wiped-down drug items in a paper bag.

She went back to her bedroom and wiped down the bureau drawer where she kept the drugs.

Next, she changed her clothes. She kicked off her high heels and stripped off her dress. She put on jeans, a sweater, and running shoes, followed by a heavy winter coat. Next, she stuffed her hair under a cap. Then she sat and thought for a moment.

She got back up and took off the hat and coat. She found a skirt that looked something like what Bonnie had worn, slipped off her jeans and put the skirt on. Next, she found a beige coat similar to Bonnie's and put it on. She put her hair up. *Bonnie had hers up.*

She picked up Bonnie's purse, the paper bag of drugs, and went back down to her car.

She drove back to Fair Oaks Mall and parked at the edge of the lot a fair distance from the Sears, among cars that probably belonged to the mall's workers. She got out of the car, carrying Bonnie's purse. Staying low, she moved around to the passenger's side, where she opened the door and stood up. She walked into Sears, through the mall, and out the door near the restaurant. She got into Bonnie's car and drove off.

Bella drove to Gainesville, where she bought a heavy, long quilted coat. At another store, she bought a wool cap.

Next, she drove back and parked Bonnie's car in an office complex parking lot off Fair Lakes Parkway. She parked in the middle of the lot and hoped that there were different lessees in the building so that none would be surprised if a car stayed there a while, thinking it belonged to a different building occupant.

She got out of the car and walked toward the mall carrying the new coat in a plastic bag. Halfway to the mall, she moved in among some trees and pulled out the coat and hat from their shopping bag. Quickly, she put them on over the clothes she had on. She tossed Bonnie's car keys in a storm drain. In the mall parking lot, she approached the lane where her car was parked from several lanes over and appeared to go to a car two away from hers. She ducked low and moved between cars until she got to hers and got in. She wriggled out of the heavy coat, feeling like she was going to burn up. She let down her hair and drove off.

At a fast food restaurant, she went through the vehicle order lanes and ordered a meal. She parked in the rear of the restaurant near the trash dumpster, sat in her car, and pretended to eat the meal, while she drank her soda. She stuffed the heavy coat and hat into the bag the coat had come in and got out of the car carrying the plastic bag, the paper bag of drug paraphernalia, her cup, and the fast food bag. She walked across the lot and threw everything into the trash dumpster behind the restaurant.

Finally, she went to a grocery store and bought some Clorox wipes. In her apartment parking lot, she wiped down her car, trying to ensure all signs of drugs were gone.

CHAPTER SIXTY

When Danny Fortiano came home that night, his wife was sitting in a living room chair holding a highball glass in her hand. When she said hello, he immediately realized it wasn't her first drink. He cautiously inquired. "What's up? Looks like you've had a bad day."

She acknowledged that she had. "That, and I'm tired of the job and the winter. I need to get away."

While Fortiano poured himself a drink, he absently asked, "What do you mean? Want to go to a country inn or something?"

"No. I want warmth. Maybe the Cayman Islands."

Fortiano was stunned. "Cayman Islands! Shit, you know I can't leave right now. We're in the middle of a proposal."

Bella mumbled. "Don't need you to go. Just going by myself. Spend a week. Clear my head."

Fortiano looked at Bella with concern and acquiesced. "Okay. I guess that's all right." He knew he couldn't stop her. It was her money. "What's so bad?"

"Just an accumulation of things. Shit at work. That bastard Hendricks embarrassing me. Everything."

Fortiano went to get himself a drink. "Okay. Take a break. I'm sure you deserve it. What are we doing about dinner?"

Bella looked at him with annoyance. "I don't feel like dinner. Can you get yourself something?"

Fortiano was uncertain. "Sure, I guess. I'll go right after I finish this drink. Don't you want me to get you something?"

"Told you I wasn't hungry."

"Yeah. Okay."

After he left, Bella finished her drink and thought about tomorrow. She'd made reservations for Costa Rica. She'd leave her car at Dulles, stay in a quiet hotel, and wait for news from home. *No one needs to know where I am.*

*   *   *

Jim Wade came home in his usual foul mood. Davidson was really getting to him, wanting a miracle, threatening his job and his lifestyle. All he could do was his best and depend on the guys under him.

He entered the house and listened. It seemed more quiet than usual. He inquired in a medium-loud voice, "Bonnie?" There was no answer. He shouted, "Bonnie, where are you?" There was still no answer. He went to the kitchen and found it empty. No lights were on. Bonnie should have been making dinner. He went to their bedroom. He checked the bathroom. He checked the garage and the driveway. Her car was gone. *Where the hell are you?* he thought. *Why aren't you making dinner?*

He went and got himself a drink and sat down. Maybe she would be home soon. About eight thirty, he decided she was doing something that was keeping her out late. He didn't talk to her much about what she was doing each day. *Maybe she had something going on she didn't tell me about, or maybe I've forgotten. She has her own life, but she ought to consider mine. Hell, I'm the one carrying the load around here.*

It finally sank in. *She's not going to make me any dinner.*

Wade finished his drink and went over to the phone. He looked for the phone book in the phone table drawer, but it wasn't there. He went into the kitchen and looked in several drawers. He found the phone book under the dish towels, found the phone number for a local Chinese restaurant, called, and ordered shrimp fried rice and beef and peppers. He asked if the restaurant took credit cards. He didn't carry much cash. They asked for the number over the phone. He didn't think to include a tip.

When he finished his dinner, he put the cartons with leftovers in the refrigerator and thought how empty it was. He didn't go in there very often—mostly just to get ice from the freezer.

He went to the den and turned on the television. He hated the network shows, all the "reality" that wasn't real at all or murders revisited.

He turned on Netflix. They had murders, too, but they weren't "real."

About ten thirty, he started to become concerned. He phoned the Fortianos, woke Danny up, and asked him if he knew where Bonnie might me. Fortiano asked Bella and came back on the phone to say they hadn't seen her. He suggested that maybe she was out with friends. Wade responded that she didn't have any friends but Bella.

Fortiano said, "I'm sorry, but we haven't seen her," and hung up.

Wade stared at the phone. *Sounds like you don't even give a shit.*

He hung the phone up, stood still, and thought for a moment, *Where the hell is she? She never does this.*

He poured himself another drink. He didn't know what else to do. He looked out the front window as if, by doing so, he could make Bonnie drive up. He paced while he drank his scotch.

Finally, at one o'clock in the morning, he phoned the police and reported that Bonnie wasn't home and he didn't know where she was. The policeman asked if she might be staying with a friend or a relative. Wade said, "No." The policeman asked if he and Bonnie had been getting along all right. Did she have any reason to leave home? Wade became incensed at such a suggestion. "Look, my wife and I get along fine. She's missing. You need to do something about it."

The policeman tried to console him. "I'm sorry to upset you, but people go missing like this all the time. They usually show up in the morning. I'll make a note about your call, and we'll phone you back midmorning tomorrow. If she's still not home, we'll put something in motion then. Give me your name, again, and your phone number."

Wade gave the policeman his name and phone number, and the man hung up. Wade thought, *Shit, I should have gotten his name.* He went upstairs, put on his pajamas, and went to bed. He tossed and turned but finally fell into a fitful sleep.

*   *   *

Charlie came home feeling more tired than usual.

He found Linda in the kitchen and kissed her cheek. "Hi. Where are the boys?"

"Hey, you can do better than that," she scolded and kissed his lips while drying her hands on a dish towel. "Ed's upstairs finishing homework so he can play on the Xbox tonight, and Ralph's over at Mollie's. They're studying together."

"Well, that doesn't sound terribly effective. Is he eating over there?"

"Yes. Don't worry. Mollie's parents are home. The kids are studying in their family room."

"Good. Although you must know I think in the highest terms of my son's behavior."

"Of course. I know you were completely above board and open when you were young."

Charlie poured himself a glass of water from the pitcher in the refrigerator. "I was, indeed. I remember well."

"I'm sure you do. How did your day go? Mine was fairly quiet. Everyone is recovering from New Year's Eve."

"Oh, the wheels are fretting again. Davidson called Wade into his office and poured out his concerns. Then Wade called us into his office and did the same. It all flows downhill."

"You and who else?"

"Somers and Byrnes."

Linda pursed her lips and nodded. "Are you a member of the dynamic trio, now?"

"A member of the trio of workers now. Sid Davies wasn't there. He's management."

"How about your buddy, Danny Fortiano?"

"No. Not included. But he cornered me near my desk afterword. Told me to leave his wife alone. I blew him off. Wonder what story she told him?"

"You want to be careful. He's pretty muscular."

"Hey, I'm not going to arm wrestle him."

"What if he corners you?"

"I'll give him a bloody nose before he can do anything. I think marring his beauty will settle him down quickly."

"You sound tough."

"Don't think it will ever happen."

CHAPTER SIXTY-ONE

Wade didn't sleep. He cursed Bonnie for not coming home, wondering if she had left him because of the pressure he was under from the proposal. He knew he had not been easy to live with, but he thought she should have said something—should have threatened to leave, to at least make him aware.

At ten in the morning, he phoned the police again. The person who answered didn't know what he was talking about. Said he needed to check the log. He vanished from the phone. After a few minutes, another voice came on, female. "Mr. Wade?"

Wade tried to be patient. "Yes."

"You reported your wife missing early this morning?"

"That's right. And she still hasn't come home."

"Okay, I guess we need to get some information on her. You want to come down here? Or should I send someone out?"

It all sounded procedural, indifferent to Wade. "For Christ's sake, send someone out. I want to be here if she phones or comes home."

"Okay, stay calm, Mr. Wade. These things usually have a simple explanation. Wives go away all the time."

"Not Bonnie."

"Okay. I'll send someone out. What's your address?"

Wade gave her the information. "And what's your name?"

"Evers, Sergeant Janet Evers."

Wade wanted her to know he had her name. "Okay, Sergeant Evers. Get them to hurry."

Wade sat down and had his fourth cup of coffee for the morning. Soon, he'd finish the whole pot.

Then he got up and paced, looking out the front window every few minutes. "Where the hell are they?"

Finally, a car pulled in the drive, an unmarked, and two plainclothes individuals got out, a man and a woman. The man approached the front door while the woman hung back, her hand resting on the grip of her service weapon. Wade noticed the man was ready, too, as if they were expecting trouble.

Wade opened the door. "Are you going to shoot me?"

The policeman reddened. "Sorry. Just being careful about domestic things."

Wade glared. "What 'domestic thing'? My wife has vanished. Come in."

The policeman relaxed and waved his partner forward. He held the door for her as they both came in. They stood in the foyer. The man pulled out his badge. "Mr. Wade, I'm Detective Bernie Stonecipher," he said and motioned his hand toward the woman. "And this is Detective Hammond."

The woman stuck out her hand. "Maggie Hammond."

Wade shook her hand while Stonecipher growled, "You're not his new friend, Maggie. We're here to do a job." He turned to Wade. "She's new. I'm breaking her in. Where can we sit?"

Wade was alarmed. "You're not new, are you? 'New' scares me."

"Oh, no. I've done a lot of domestic things."

Wade led them to the kitchen table. "I don't like the term 'domestic things.'"

Stonecipher was matter-of-fact. "It's just a general term we use for things that happen in people's houses. I'm sorry if it discomforts you."

They sat at the kitchen table, and the detectives took out folding clipboards and pens.

Stonecipher began. "What is your wife's name, Mr. Wade?"

"Bonnie. Bonnie Wade."

The detectives wrote that down. "And when did you last see her?"

"Yesterday morning, when I left for work."

"And what was her mood?"

"What do you mean?"

"Well, was she unhappy, depressed, angry? Anything unusual? Had you two had a fight, argument, disagreement?"

Wade frowned and glared at the detective.

Hammond interjected. "I'm sorry, Mr. Wade. We have to ask. It's relevant."

Wade nodded and sighed. "No. No arguments, but she looked unhappy, uncertain. I'm under a lot of pressure at work, and I've probably passed a lot of it along to her. But she didn't say anything."

Stonecipher studied Wade. "Well, maybe it got to her more than you realized. Is there any place she might have gone? Parents? Children? Friends?"

"I phoned the children this morning. Worried them to death. They haven't heard from her. Her parents live in Ohio. I was afraid to worry them. Didn't want to scare them, too."

"You're going to have to phone them, Mr. Wade. We have to know where we stand."

"I know."

"You need to do it now. We need to close on that."

"Okay, I'll do it in the den."

"He got up and left the room."

Stonecipher called after him, "You mind if we help ourselves to coffee?"

Wade looked back, a little uncertain. "Oh, sure. Help yourselves."

The mugs were on a tray beside the coffee maker. Stonecipher picked up the carafe and sighed. "Only about a cup left. Split it with you?"

Hammond waved him off. "You take it. I'll get some water."

Stonecipher poured the coffee, felt the cup, and looked around for the microwave. After he heated the coffee, he returned to the table and passed Hammond a mug of water. "Don't know where the glasses are."

They sat in silence until Wade returned. He came in shaking his head. "They haven't heard from her. Upset as hell."

Stonecipher nodded. "Had to do it. What about friends?"

"Only Bella Fortiano. I phoned them last night, and they hadn't heard from Bonnie. Tried again this morning and had to call him at work since no one answered at his apartment. He still knew nothing about Bonnie. Said his wife had gone to the Cayman Islands because she was stressed out."

Stonecipher looked at Hammond and back at Wade. "You guys must have a lot of stress around here."

Wade looked back and forth between the two detectives. "Yes. We're working on a big proposal for future work. There's a lot riding on it."

"Proposal?" asked Hammond.

Wade tried to simplify. "Yeah. When the government wants work done, they ask companies to propose how they will do it and how much it will cost, and the government takes the best offer."

"And this is a big money proposal?"

Wade assented. "Millions, maybe billions."

Hammond made a face as if to say, "Oh."

Stonecipher said, "That would give me stress, too." He looked at his clipboard. "Okay, maybe your wife went to the Cayman Islands too."

Wade shook his head. "She doesn't have a passport. Never been out of the country."

Stonecipher frowned. "I'm running out of ideas. Is her car missing?"

"Yes."

Stonecipher scrunched up his face. "Should have asked earlier. Anything else missing?

Clothing, cosmetics, toothbrush, anything."

"No. I haven't checked the coat closet." He got up and checked the closet in the foyer. He came back. "I think a beige coat is missing. I wouldn't know if a dress was missing upstairs.

Don't know her clothes that well."

"So, you don't know what she was wearing when she left here."

"No. She was still in her robe when I left yesterday morning."

"Okay. I need details about the car and some pictures of your wife. If she has a computer, I'd like to borrow that too."

Wade gathered Bonnie's laptop, the requested information and pictures, and gave them to the detectives, along with the computer password.

The detectives copied the automobile information into their clipboards, gathered the photographs and computer, and stood up. Stonecipher summarized his plans. "We'll get the pictures out to authorities and the public; look for the car; and check the airlines, trains, and so forth. I'll give you a call if anything comes up or at least once a day."

They shook hands, and the detectives left.

The phone rang, and Wade answered it.

"Hey, Jim, it's Barney next door. You okay? Saw the police car."

"Yeah. I'm okay, but Bonnie's missing."

A moment of silence passed. "Oh, shit. Seriously? Anything I can do?"

"No, but I appreciate the offer. I'll let you know."

Wade hung up. *Damn. Everyone is going to know.*

CHAPTER SIXTY-TWO

Sid Davies checked with Daphne O'Leary the next day. Wade hadn't been to the office for two days. He thought it was strange with so much riding on the proposal, but Wade didn't have much role at this stage, so there was no panic. Still, Davies was curious. "Daphne, have you heard anything from him?"

"Just a call yesterday morning. Said he had some issues to take care of and wouldn't be in until the beginning of next week. Haven't heard anything today."

"Do you think I need to phone him, see if anyone here can help in any way?"

"Don't think so. He's pretty private about his own life. Think you better wait for him to contact us." She turned back to her keyboard, and Davies realized he was being dismissed.

Still, Davies thought all the privacy was strange. He decided to find Fortiano and see if he knew anything.

In the hallway, he started to pass Beverly Byrnes, who looked perturbed. "Morning, Bev. Anything up?"

"Did you see the paper? Bonnie Wade's missing. Hasn't been seen for two days. Her picture's in the *Post*."

Davies stopped in his tracks. "No wonder Wade hasn't been in. That's a hell of a thing. Are the police involved?"

"Oh, yeah. Looking for her and her car. Everyone's talking about it."

"Guess I'm the odd man out. Haven't read the paper this morning."

"On the morning news, too. Somebody's bound to know something."

"Let's hope. Awful hard on Jim."

He proceeded to Fortiano's office. "Danny, you hear about Bonnie."

"Yeah. Strange as hell."

"Bella seen her lately? I know they see each other some."

"I don't think so. Know they had lunch together before Christmas, but that seems like a long time ago, and Bella's in the Cayman Islands now. She doesn't even know about this." "Cayman Islands? We should all be so lucky. If you hear from Jim, see if we can do anything to help."

* * *

Wade got a phone call from Stonecipher around ten thirty in the morning. "Your wife's car has been found. A security guy called from an office building near Fair Oaks Mall. We're on our way out there now."

"An office building? That makes no sense. Why would Bonnie's car be there?"

"No idea, Mr. Wade, but at least we've got somewhere to begin. We've had nothing until now."

"Do I need to come out and join you?"

"No, but do you have a key to her car?"

"Yeah, it's on my ring."

"Good. I'll send someone out to get it."

* * *

Wade gave the key to a policeman just before noon and waited, fretfully, until two thirty, when he called Stonecipher's number but got no answer. He next phoned police headquarters and was informed that Stonecipher and Hammond were out working a case. He got the same answer at four o'clock.

Finally, Stonecipher phoned at four thirty. "It's definitely Mrs. Wade's car. Registration's in the glove compartment. We went over it with a fine-tooth comb. Got a bunch of fingerprints. We'll need to get some from your house to compare. I expect most of them belong to you and Mrs. Wade. We'll run them all through the system to see if there are any matches. Unless you, Mrs. Wade, and your friends are criminals, were in the service, or have clearances, there may not be anything there."

Wade's mind scrambled. "I have a clearance, so you'll probably find me in the records."

"Okay. That's good to know. The other thing we have going is the security camera tape from the office building. They have a camera pointed at the lot. We're reviewing the tape now.

I'll let you know if we find anything."

CHAPTER SIXTY-THREE

Charlie came home a little early. He found Linda in the kitchen.

She looked at him questioningly. "You're home early. Anything wrong?" It's what she always thought when the routine was broken.

"No. Just been a day of wheel spinning. Jim Wade's wife is missing, and it's all anyone seems to be able the think and talk about."

Realization struck Linda. "Oh. The woman on the news. I didn't connect the dots. Mr. Wade must be frantic."

"He's not at work. Wouldn't expect him to be. But, yes, I'm sure he's worried to death.

It's a hell of a thing."

"Charlie, what can we do?"

"I'm not sure. His secretary insists he likes his privacy."

"I can understand that, but we need to do something. I'll do what we always did in the army. I'll make some food and take it over. Do you know where he lives?"

"Yeah. I have it on the B-E staff directory in my briefcase."

CHAPTER SIXTY-FOUR

Stonecipher phoned Wade at eight Saturday morning. "Do you have a DVD player? I'd like to show you a copy of the security camera tape from the office building where Mrs. Wade's car was found."

"Does it show Bonnie?"

"A woman parked it there. She's wearing a beige coat, hair up, but it's a distant shot. I'd like to show it to you."

"Yes. I have a DVD player."

"I'll be right over."

Again, Wade was left waiting. He felt that it was all he did lately, but what else could he do to find Bonnie? He wouldn't know where to start.

Stonecipher arrived pretty quickly, after twenty minutes or so. Wade led him to the television in the den and turned it and the DVD player on. Stonecipher inserted the DVD. It showed an asphalt parking lot with many cars. Off to the left, Stonecipher indicated a car, which he identified as Bonnie's. A woman emerged from the car and walked farther to the left out of the picture."

"Does that look like your wife?"

Wade thought hard. "It could be. That's an awful distant shot."

Stonecipher continued showing the tape. The woman reappeared from the left, far in the distance, walking away from the camera and out of sight beyond some trees.

The detective commented. "She's headed for Fair Oaks Mall. At least it looks like that."

The picture blurred and then came back on, the car now magnified. Stonecipher narrated. "This is a repeat of the whole thing, magnified. Does it help?"

Wade shook his head. "I'm sorry. It could be Bonnie, but the coat is real loose and her face is turned away. Besides, it's all blurry. Hardly any detail. All I can say is that it looks like her car."

The detective assented. "Well, that much we know. The next question is where is she going? I have people over at the mall now, gathering up security tapes. From this tape, we know the time, so we know when to look. If we learn anything quickly, I'll get back to you. I'm off tomorrow, but Maggie will be on."

Wade was perplexed. "Maggie?"

"I'm sorry. Detective Hammond. She's off today but will be back tomorrow. If we find anything, she'll contact you."

Stonecipher removed the DVD from the player and put it in its paper sleeve. He looked at Wade. "I wish this were going faster, but believe me, it's faster than many cases. We're working it hard."

Wade escorted the detective to the door. "Thank you. I appreciate what you're doing. It still seems like it's taking forever."

He opened the door to let Stonecipher leave, only to find a woman standing there holding a tray with a bunch of dishes covered in aluminum foil. Stonecipher nodded to her and eased around her while Wade stood holding the door and looking perplexed.

"I'm sorry," the woman exclaimed, disconcerted. "I didn't mean to interrupt anything important."

Wade, startled, caught himself. "Oh, it's all right. The detective is just leaving." There was a moment of silent uncertainty. "May I help you?"

Linda stammered. "Oh. Oh, yes. I'm Linda Hendricks. My husband works for you."

"Oh, yes. Charlie Hendricks. I met you at the Christmas party."

Linda nodded and held out the tray. "We're so upset about your wife and wanted to do something to support you. We thought dinner might help."

Wade felt unsure and a little embarrassed. He took the tray. "Thank you. That's very kind of you." He closed the screen door and noticed Linda still standing on the porch as he closed the main door and thought to himself, *I should have invited her in. Just can't deal with anyone now.*

Can't be polite.

Linda was perplexed. She finally turned and walked back to her car.

Wade watched her out the front window and thought she was a pretty woman and apparently very nice, but life now was just hell.

CHAPTER SIXTY-FIVE

After the detectives obtained the security tapes of the west side of the mall, they settled down to study them. Initially, they matched the time that the office building tapes had shown the woman in the beige coat headed for the mall, but they found nothing. They wondered if she had gone someplace else and studied maps to determine other routes she might have taken and locations of relevant security cameras. While they were doing that, a young policewoman kept going over the tapes, backing one up a couple of hours. As she watched it, she saw a woman in a beige coat walk down a lane of cars toward the mall. "Hey, guys, take a look at this." She backed up the film a little more and saw the woman come from somewhere well out in the lot.

Stonecipher exclaimed, "Damn, Sharon, it looks like her. Back it up further."

The policewoman, Sharon, did. They all saw a car pull into the parking lot and park in the distance. It appeared that the woman got out of the passenger side and then started the walk toward the mall.

Stonecipher exclaimed. "Okay, let's look at the other tapes. See if we can get a close image of her entering the mall. Sharon, you keep watching this tape. See if she comes back and see what happens to the car. Looks like it might be a Mercedes. You think so? A little hard to tell at that distance. Did it have a thingy on the hood? Take a look."

Sharon never saw the woman in the beige coat return to the car. Lots of people walked to and from cars, but only a few were associated with a car far out. After about an hour and forty minutes, the car (Mercedes?) backed out of the parking space and drove off.

Had the driver been sitting there all that time? Where did the beige coat go?

Sharon watched the tapes until they ran out well into the evening.

241

Maybe she went out another door. "Detective Stonecipher, we need tapes from all around the mall! She must have left another way!"

Stonecipher sent a policeman back to the mall to get the balance of the tapes.

The night shift was going to have plenty to do.

CHAPTER SIXTY-SIX

Sunday afternoon, Wade was watching a golf tournament on television. His breakfast plate, with scraps of a bagel and an empty coffee mug, sat on the table beside him. He hadn't had enough energy to make lunch.

The front doorbell rang. He opened the door and found Detective Hammond standing on the porch, another policewoman in uniform behind her. Hammond nervously asked if she might come in. The three sat in the living room, Wade looking expectant.

Hammond hesitated. "Mr. Wade, I hate to tell you this, but your wife's body was found this morning in a park out near Prince William County, south of Dulles Airport."

Wade's face drained, and he stared into space. "Are you sure it's her?"

"Pretty sure. The pictures seem to match, but we'll have to get you to verify that it's her. They took her to the Inova Fair Oaks Hospital, and she's still there, pending the medical examiner's instructions. We'd like to take you out there for the identification, if you're willing to go."

"Did someone murder her? Was she attacked?"

"There appears to be no sign of either, but there will have to be an autopsy. It's required in this kind of death."

"Sure, sure, I understand. How was she found?"

"A couple walking their dog in a wooded park along Braddock Road found her when the dog became upset."

"She was in a park?"

"Yes, a couple of hundred feet from the road, near a dirt road, a road seldom used except by hikers. I'm sorry, Mr. Wade."

Wade shook his head. "Dear God, how could this have happened? What was she doing way out there?"

"I don't know, Mr. Wade. We're still investigating."

*   *   *

After Wade identified Bonnie's body, Detective Hammond and the unknown policewoman drove him back to his home, checked to see if he would be all right, asked if they should call someone to be with him, and left when he refused any help.

He poured himself a drink, sat, took two deep swallows to steel himself, and called his children and Bonnie's parents and then his own parents. The children would be home tomorrow morning. The parents would come when he was ready for them. Bonnie's parents wanted to know where she would be buried. They offered to make arrangements in Ohio. He wasn't ready to talk about it.

CHAPTER SIXTY-SEVEN

The detectives now had a mysterious death to investigate. There was no apparent trauma to Bonnie Wade's body. Stonecipher had no doubt that it was an overdose. He had seen too many. He decided to wait for the autopsy to confirm his belief before he faced Mr. Wade with the information and pursued the implications.

Meanwhile, the detectives continued to go over the security tapes and discs from the Fair Oaks Mall. They traced the woman in the beige coat leaving the side of the mall opposite the side she had entered and saw her get in her car and drive away. Although the license plate was unreadable, the car appeared to be Bonnie Wade's car. The time was about an hour and a half before the car reappeared at the business office building to the west of the mall.

Next, they followed the same security tape back to when Bonnie had first arrived at the parking lot and walked to the mall. Her image was clear in the view of another camera near the mall entrance. After about forty-five minutes, the tape showed her leave the mall with another woman. They only saw the backs of their heads. Following the two women back out into the lot, the detectives watched as the women both passed Bonnie's car and got in a different car. After about ten minutes, the new car backed out and drove off, leaving Wade's car behind. The car looked like a gray Mercedes. It was almost an hour and a half before the car would reappear on the other side of the mall. The detectives went back through the tape and identified the second woman arriving and got a pretty good image of her coming in at the mall entrance. Now they needed to identify her.

Stonecipher went to Bonnie Wade's computer, which they had picked up the morning they had begun a search for the woman. They went to Bonnie's Facebook page. It should have been password protected, but Bonnie Wade had the software save the password so that the page automatically came up. They started working through

Wade's friends and quickly identified a woman who appeared to be the same woman as the one seen at the mall, although the pictures were casual shots. Stonecipher admired the picture of the woman in a bikini but thought it best to print out some of the others.

The woman's name was Bella Fortiano. Somehow that name sounded familiar to him. He checked his notes and found that Jim Wade had said Bella Fortiano was Bonnie Wade's friend. Further, Wade had mentioned phoning the Fortianos but had said they had denied knowing anything about where Bonnie Wade might be. *That's interesting*, he thought. *If this Bella woman was with Bonnie Wade the day the latter disappeared, it seems she would have brought that up.* It further interested him that Wade said Bella Fortiano was in the Cayman Islands.

The detective gathered several police officers around him. He passed out pictures of Bella Fortiano and Bonnie Wade to two of them and sent them off to check restaurants in the mall because the timeline seemed to fit a luncheon. He assigned two others to track down where Bella Fortiano lived; they were to take a look at the place but not to approach it. Finally, he assigned two other officers to check the flight manifests for flights to the Cayman Islands to determine when Bella Fortiano had flown there and when she was due back.

*   *   *

That afternoon, information began to filter back.

Bella had indeed had lunch in the mall. Several waiters identified her. One referred to her as "a real babe." They couldn't say for sure that the woman with her was the one in Bonnie's picture, but they did know there was another woman.

From the airlines, there was no record of a Bella Fortiano or anyone named Fortiano flying to the Cayman Islands. However, a further check of the databases showed a Belinda Fortiano buying a one-way ticket to Costa Rica. That information rang bells and flushed out many questions: Why tell people you're going to the

Cayman Islands when you were going to Costa Rica? When you live in Virginia, why would you buy a one-way ticket? Bella Fortiano was rapidly becoming a person of interest. Identifying her had been the easy part. Now they had to find a link between Bella Fortiano and the death of Bonnie Wade. Stonecipher felt that there was one.

Finally, it was found that Bella Fortiano lived in a high-rise apartment. That didn't make Stonecipher happy. It was hard to track the comings and goings from such a building.

He turned to Hammond. "Find out what kind of car or cars are registered to the Fortianos, either Belinda or Danny or Daniel. Get the plate numbers. Then take a tech with you and survey the Dulles parking lot. When you find the car, see if you can get any prints off the handles or doors.

Hammond noted glumly, "You won't be able to use the prints. You don't have a search warrant. And the lots are huge. It's going to take a long time."

"I know. Maybe we can use the prints, or maybe we can't. We're not breaking into the car. It's a public place. But we need a data point. It may come in handy later."

Hammond nodded sadly. *There goes my evening.*

CHAPTER SIXTY-EIGHT

Stonecipher and Hammond arrived at Wade's house early Tuesday morning. They were met at the door by a young, blond woman, slightly heavy with a wide, round face, bordering on pretty. A young man, looking very much like a sibling, stood behind her. Stonecipher and Hammond showed their badges and introduced themselves. Sally Wade Jennings and Jerry Wade introduced themselves. "Dad's in the den. He's taking all of this very hard."

Stonecipher said he understood.

Sally Jennings asked if anything had been discovered about her mother's death.

Stonecipher tried to be vague. "We're following some leads, and we're waiting for the autopsy report. We're still trying to get more information. We're wondering if we might look around the house, particularly your parents' bedroom, to see if we can find some note, or whatever, that might help us?"

Jerry spoke up. "Gee, that's kind of private. We'll have to ask Dad."

He went off while the daughter and the detectives stood awkwardly in the foyer.

Finally, Sally Jennings offered. "You know this is really weird. Mom was a stay-at-home type. Didn't really get involved in much of anything unless Dad was along."

Hammond nodded. "Yes. That's what we understand. But we have to learn anything we can about what she was involved with outside the house. We need all the information we can get."

Jerry Wade came back. "Dad says all right but would like us to go with you."

They headed for the master bedroom. Stonecipher asked the children to go through the bureau and bedside table drawers and see if there was anything other than clothes. Little was found. They studied a notepad beside the phone and copied down phone numbers. Next they went to the bathroom. Most items were routine cosmetics and toiletries. Of interest, they found, in the medicine cabinet, an unlabeled pill bottle. Stonecipher pulled out a pair of latex gloves and put the bottle in a plastic bag while the children looked appalled. Jerry Wade queried, "What's with the gloves? You think that's a clue?"

Stonecipher tried to deflect the question. "Just an unmarked bottle. I'm wondering what it is and if the pills could have affected Mrs. Wade in any way. We'll take a look at them."

They did similar surveys of the den and kitchen, trying to learn anything they could. Finally, Stonecipher and Hammond asked to talk to Mr. Wade.

They found him in a basement television room talking on the phone. "Thank you, Gunnar. I appreciate that."

He hung up, and Jerry Wade asked, "Who was that, Dad?"

Jim Wade looked at him with a tired, drawn face. "My boss, Gunnar Davidson. Offering his condolences, which somehow doesn't seem like a warm word. Kind of stiff. And offering to help in any way he can, although I can't imagine him doing anything. Said to take off all the time I need."

He turned to the detectives. "Jerry says you haven't made much progress."

Hammond looked at Stonecipher, who proffered, "Well, we've managed to track many of your wife's movements on the day of her death. She had lunch with this woman, Bella Fortiano, whom you mentioned before as being in the Cayman Islands. They went to a restaurant at Fair Oaks Mall midday. After lunch, they got into Fortiano's car, and after about ten minutes, they drove off together. It appears that, later, Fortiano dropped your wife off at the other side of the mall, way out in the lot, which seems kind of strange. Your wife went through the mall and out the other side, got in her car, and drove away. After about an hour and a half, your wife parked in the office building parking lot where her car was found. She got out of the car and started walking in the direction of the mall but was never seen again."

Wade listened blankly to the whole story. "You think someone picked her up on the way to the mall."

Stonecipher shook his head. "We don't know. What we do know and find very strange is that, after Fortiano dropped your wife off, her car stayed parked for a long time before driving off. It doesn't make a whole lot of sense."

Wade's face became more alive. "Well, you have to talk to Bella."

Stonecipher agreed. "Yes, but she's out of town."

Wade acknowledged that. "That's right, she's in the Cayman Islands."

Hammond interjected. "As a matter-of-fact, she's not. She flew to Costa Rica."

Wade looked perplexed. "But Danny said she went to the Cayman Islands."

Stonecipher replied, "Yes. He may think she did. But she didn't."

Wade looked back and forth between the detectives. "This is weird. You need to talk to Danny."

Stonecipher demurred. "We will eventually, but it's Mrs. Fortiano who was the last link to your wife, and we'd like to talk to her first. If we talk to her husband, it might spook her. We hope she comes back."

"Why don't you have her brought back?"

"I wish we could, but we don't really have justification to do so. She's not charged with a crime and may be innocent."

"So we sit and wait," Wade grumbled.

"No. We follow clues and refine what we know. I've made some notes as I've walked around today and would like to discuss them with you."

Wade bowed his head and acquiesced.

Stonecipher went over all the notes he had made, including all the telephone numbers he had copied down. Wade had an explanation for everything. Stonecipher asked if any of the telephone numbers belonged to the Fortianos, but Wade said Bonnie knew the number and wouldn't have had to write it down.

Finally, Stonecipher closed his clipboard and pulled the bag with the bottle of pills from his pocket. "Mr. Wade, we found this bottle of pills in your medicine cabinet. Do you know what they are?"

Wade reached out for them, but Stonecipher held them back. "The bottle's not labeled, which is strange."

Wade nodded and offered. "Well, as I remember, that's the only medicine in the cabinet.

My wife took Prozac for her nerves, and I always assumed that was what was in the bottle."

Stonecipher bit his lip and crossed his fingers. "Well, we'd like to confirm that."

Wade was suddenly wary. He looked at his children and back at the detectives. "You think it's not Prozac?"

Stonecipher was careful. "We have no reason to think otherwise, but if it's very strong, it could have made your wife become disoriented, and we'd like to know." Stonecipher had no idea whether that was correct or not, but he wanted the pills.

The detective's explanation seemed to mollify Wade. "Okay. We'd certainly like to know that."

When the detective got back in their car, Hammond asked, "What's with the pills, Bernie?"

Stonecipher stared ahead and started the car. "Well, Bonnie Wade's body showed no sign of trauma, but something killed her. What's most obvious?"

CHAPTER SIXTY-NINE

In the B-E proposal offices, all the talk was about Bonnie Wade. Progress on the proposal had slowed.

Sid Davies gathered everyone in a team discussion room. "People, this is tragic about Bonnie Wade, but we have a job to do. I want the discussion to stop." He turned to David Swenson. "Dave, we have three days left to get this proposal in. Where do we stand?"

Swenson stepped forward from where he was standing against the back wall. "Fortunately, we have everything. We need to assemble the document, see if we need to add any transition wording between sections, and reproduce the document. I'll work with Byrnes, Somers, and Hendricks. That's enough hands in the pot for the time being. We'll assemble it today. If we need some more writing, I would expect everyone to be available to help if called on."

Fortiano interjected. "What about me?"

Swenson was peeved at being interrupted. "Danny, we'll call you if we need to, just like everyone else. Tomorrow, I expect everyone to be available. We have to reproduce the document. The government wants six copies, and it's about five hundred pages a copy with several foldouts that will require special handling and then incorporation. We have one copying machine here and I've scheduled two more in headquarters. Tomorrow, everyone will be making copies."

*   *   *

The word began to spread in the early afternoon. Lionel Haverford's wife had phoned him. She was following the newswire on the Fairfax County website and noticed a summary of Bonnie Wade's autopsy. She had died of an overdose of cocaine.

Everyone was surprised. Bonnie always seemed like a quiet, upright woman, a good supporter of the company's executive staff.

*   *   *

At three in the afternoon, Ralph Evenson knocked on the door of Jim Wade's house.

Sally Jennings answered. "May I help you?"

Evenson took off his cap and introduced himself. "I'm Ralph Evenson, the deputy to the manager of Bedford-Ewings International here in Northern Virginia. I need to speak to Jim."

Jennings protested. "Right now? He's just received some dreadful news and is very distraught. I'm his daughter and trying to take care of him. Can't this wait?"

"I'm afraid not. I'll be brief."

He walked past Jennings. "Is he in the den? I know the way. I've been here before."

Jennings tried to follow him and slow Evenson down. "Are you sure it can't wait?"

"No. It really can't."

Evenson entered the den to find Wade slumped in a chair, a drink in his hand. He looked up, startled, and stammered, "Ralph, what are you doing here? You didn't have to come. I'm managing."

Evenson stood looking down at Wade. "Gunnar sent me."

"Oh, yeah, he offered to help."

"We're having you transferred to California."

"You're what?"

"Getting you away from here. We don't want narcotics and all the negative publicity reflecting on B-E. You're not to come back to the office. We'll send you information about the transfer and when it will take place. When and if you talk to the press, you're not to say anything about your connection to B-E."

"Christ, Ralph, is that what Gunnar wants?"

"As I said, Gunnar sent me. It's too ugly a business for him to be connected to. Do we have an understanding?"

Wade stood and protested. "Ralph. I didn't do this. I knew nothing about it."

Evenson looked at Wade hard. "You signed up 'for better or worse.' Now you have to live with it." He then turned and walked away past the hatred streaming from Sally Jennings.

*   *   *

The next morning, Sid Davies called the staff together for a briefing. "Jim Wade is indisposed for the near future. Gunnar Davidson has asked me to take his place for the balance of the work on the proposal."

Charlie Hendricks was made Davies's deputy. Danny Fortiano was reassigned to the classified project he had been on before the work on the proposal had begun.

Things happen fast when the house is being cleansed.

CHAPTER SEVENTY

Bella was a nervous wreck. She was pretty much confined to her hotel room, living off room service. She had tried the bar the first couple of nights, but she was hit on too many times. A lone, attractive woman in a bar by herself was an obvious target. Under different circumstances, she could have handled it. She had had practice.

She had left home in a hurry, without getting cash. Fortunately, she had a $50,000 max on her American Express card and $20,000 on each of two others. She could last a while if she needed to, but she was now upset about events at home. Danny e-mailed her every day, sometimes more than once. As yet she hadn't answered, but she fretted over what he'd said: "Bonnie is dead." "Found in the woods." "Died of an overdose." "Wade is gone." "I've been reassigned back to my old project." All of Bella's plans were falling apart.

She finally e-mailed Danny back: "Was there an investigation into Bonnie's death? What had been learned?"

Danny replied that he was sure that there was an investigation but that he was not aware of any details. He said that he wished she would return. They needed to talk about their lives.

She was happy that he didn't know anything about the investigation. That meant no one had questioned him. Maybe it was safe to go home. *I probably never should have left in the first place. Probably looks bad if anyone inquires. Maybe it's okay to go home.*

*   *   *

Customs informed Bernie Stonecipher when Bella returned. His lookout informed him when she drove back into her apartment's parking garage. A half hour later, he and Maggie Hammond knocked on Bella's door.

255

Bella was initially curious as she opened the door. She had few visitors who got by the receptionist in the lobby.

The detectives introduced themselves.

Bella's eyes flicked between them. "What can I do for you?"

"We'd like to come in and ask a few questions."

"What about?"

"A lady named Bonnie Wade."

"Oh, yes. Bonnie's dead. Horrible."

"You had lunch with her the day she died."

Bonnie hesitated. *Damned security cameras.* "Yes, I did. What about it? We were friends. Often had lunch together."

"After lunch, she drove off with you in your car."

"Where's all this leading, Detective?"

"You may have been the last person to see her alive."

"That could be. I don't know what happened to her after I drove her back to the mall."

"We'd like to talk to you about what went on up to that point."

"Detectives. I don't want to be rude, but talking to policemen can lead to misinterpretations, incorrect conclusions. My father has always told me not to do it. You'll have to excuse me. I just got home and need to unpack."

Stonecipher knew he wasn't going to make further progress. "I'm sorry to hear that you think that way. I would have thought you would have wanted to help us learn about your friend's death."

Bella started to close the door. "You'll have to excuse me."

Damn, thought Stonecipher. *I hope I can talk a judge into issuing a subpoena.*

* * *

Danny Fortiano was surprised to find Bella home when he arrived after work. "You should have told me you were coming. I would have met you at the airport."

Bella bristled at him. "I thought you said you didn't know anything about the police investigation."

Fortiano recoiled. "I don't."

"They haven't talked to you?"

"No. Not me. I haven't heard anything about the investigation. I only know what's in the paper and on the news."

"Well, the police were waiting for me this afternoon, knocking at the door as soon as I walked in."

"Jesus, Bella, was it your dope? I know you've been giving stuff to Bonnie."

"I did it to help you out. You wouldn't be getting anywhere at B-E if I didn't help you."

Fortiano protested, "I haven't needed that. I've had Jim Wade in my pocket all along. He depended on me."

"Depended on you nothing. I had things on him too."

Fortiano was startled. "You've been feeding him drugs too?"

"No, Dummy. I have a condom full of his semen in the freezer."

"A condom? How did you get that? ... Oh."

"It's all wasted now."

"Well, I can start over."

"Start over? You didn't start in the first place. I did." She took Fortiano by the chin.

"Danny, you're a good stud, but not much else. I'm the one who has to start over."

"Shit, Bella, you make me sound like a bumbling idiot."

"And I said, you're good for something. We have to think this thing out. So no one has asked you anything?"

"No, but I wouldn't say anything anyway."

"And that's the way it's going to be, because they will come after you. I told them this afternoon that I wouldn't talk to them, wouldn't have them misinterpreting what I might say. The point is, we don't have to answer any questions. We just don't want to be involved. It's our right to say nothing. And that's what we're going to do. Do we have an understanding?"

"Yeah, yeah. But what if they search this place?"

"They won't find anything. It's clean."

"But don't you need stuff for yourself?"

"If I do, I'll go elsewhere to get it. But I'll try to lay off. Don't want them following me. We're just going to go about our routine. You work out as usual and go to work. I'll do my job in DC. Everything's normal. Okay?"

"Okay."

CHAPTER SEVENTY-ONE

Sid Davies had Charlie and David Somers carry the proposal to the Department of Transportation. They drove in Charlie's car because they didn't trust the Metro. They left three hours early because they didn't want to break down or face a demonstration in DC.

Charlie asked Somers what he thought the prospects were.

"Don't have the vaguest. What we're doing seems logical, but that doesn't always work."

"How long do you think we'll have to wait?"

"Depends on how DOT views the whole thing. If they know exactly what they want, it may be a just a few days. If they don't, or if they are uncertain, it may be longer."

"Will they ask for more information?"

"They can, especially if they are uncertain how to respond."

"What should I do while we wait?"

"The truth?"

"Yeah."

"You should have been networking in the company, should have had a new job lined up. For a while, they might pay you out of overhead, but you have to take care of yourself. Stick close to Davies. They'll probably find a job for a senior guy like him. Pray he'll take you along with him. You have to take care of yourself in this world."

That gave Charlie a pause. He suddenly came to the realization that, in the proposal world, you always had to assume you might lose and that you have to have a future lined up.

At the Department of Transportation, they found the visitors' parking spaces and unloaded the proposal on a cart they could pull. They had called ahead and, thus, were able to pass through security. All government buildings were secure now. The guards carefully lifted each copy of the proposal off the cart to make sure a bomb wasn't included.

The B-E staff found the office where they were to deliver the documents and received a receipt.

Somers gave it to Charlie. "Guard this with your life. It's the only thing we have to prove we delivered on time."

Charlie pulled the empty cart back to the car. He almost felt like he had given up a child.

Nothing more they could do now.

CHAPTER SEVENTY-TWO

Bella met her father in the parking lot of the Fairfax County Police Department on Page Avenue in Fairfax City. After she slid into the passenger's seat of her father's Lincoln, he asked, "Is this really as benign a subpoena as you say. I don't want to be surprised."

"It's nothing, Daddy. I had lunch with Bonnie Wade the day she disappeared. Just unlucky timing. Last time I saw her, I dropped her off at Fair Oaks Mall so she could do some shopping and recover her car. When the cops came to my apartment, I was reluctant to talk. Didn't know what they would turn whatever I said into. Felt out of my league and wanted your wisdom with me."

"Okay, let's go in and find out what they want. Let's not respond to them until we find out what direction they're taking this thing."

They went into the building. After being buzzed through, they were met by Detective Hammond, who led them to a small room with a single table and four chairs.

They sat while Hammond left them alone. Eventually she returned with Stonecipher, who introduced himself.

Bella's father extended his hand, "Bobby Conway."

As they shook hands, Stonecipher studied the dapper man. "Detective Stonecipher. Are you Mrs. Fortiano's attorney?"

"I guess so." Conway looked around. "This looks like something from television, like when they interview suspects. Is Mrs. Fortiano a suspect?"

Stonecipher considered the question. "Only a person of interest, Mr. Conway. We're just looking for information."

Conway looked wary. "Well, let's see what you need to know."

Stonecipher contemplated that. "You seem uncomfortable with the environment, Mr. Conway?"

"Yeah, well I've never been in one of these little rooms before. I'm not that kind of attorney."

"Not a criminal lawyer, Mr. Conway?"

"No. And what I understand is that this is not a criminal inquiry."

Stonecipher considered Conway's statement. "No, as I said, your client is only a person of interest. However, we will record this interview. Want to have a good record so that we don't lose any details."

"Well, let's see what it's all about."

Stonecipher turned on a recorder and recorded the date and the names of those present.

He then sat opposite Bella. "As we said in the hallway outside your apartment door the other day, Mrs. Fortiano, we believe that you were the last person to see Mrs. Bonnie Wade before her body was found last Sunday. On Friday, you had lunch with her at Fair Oaks Mall. Is that correct?"

Bella looked down and answered in a small voice, "Yes."

"Do you mind speaking up, Mrs. Fortiano? We're recording this."

Bella looked up and glared at Stonecipher. "Yes."

"Thank you. We know from surveillance tapes at the Fair Oaks Mall that you arrived at the mall at noon, about three minutes after Mrs. Wade arrived. Restaurant employees identified you from a photograph as having had lunch there. We know you left with Mrs. Wade at about quarter to one. You both got in your car, where you apparently sat for about ten minutes." Stonecipher said this while Hammond played the security tapes on the television receiver. "May I ask what you were doing during those ten minutes?"

Bonnie bit her lip. "Just talking, girl talk."

"What were you talking about?"

Conway interrupted. "Hey, this is getting a little personal. What does it matter what they were talking about?"

Stonecipher turned to Conway. "We're just trying to understand Mrs. Wade's mood, whether anything was said that might be related to her later taking drugs." He turned back to Bella. "Did she say anything that might be related? Was there anything unusual about her or what she said?"

"No."

Stonecipher bit his lip and looked down. He signaled Hammond, who turned the security tapes on again. "After the ten minutes, you two drove off. About an hour and a half later, your car appears again on the other side of the mall, fairly far out in the parking lot. It appears that Mrs. Wade got out and walked to the mall while you apparently waited in your car. It appears that you stayed there for about an hour and forty minutes. That seems very strange." He turned back to the television screen. "Here, Mrs. Wade enters Sears. And here, a few minutes later, she leaves the other side of the mall and—"

Hammond stopped the tape and wound it back.

"What are you doing, Maggie?"

"Looking at the skirt. It looks like it has a split up the side."

"So?"

Hammond ran the tapes back to the point Bonnie Wade arrived at the mall. "I don't see a split here. Just looks like a plain skirt."

Stonecipher made a face, while Conway briefly glanced sideways at his daughter.

Stonecipher looked at Bella without saying a word for a while. "Seems like a lot of funny things were going on. We'll save the skirt for later. Right now I'd like to know where you went with Mrs. Wade for an hour and a half and why you sat in the parking lot for over an hour and a half."

Bella looked at her father, who felt her look. "Mrs. Fortiano doesn't have to answer any questions. You seem to be accusing her of something. Simply riding in a car is not a crime. I think Mrs. Fortiano has said all she has to say. She came here cooperatively, not to be treated like a criminal."

Stonecipher stared at Conway for a moment. "I'm sorry to hear that, Mr. Conway. We would have liked to understand what happened to Mrs. Wade and why. We were hoping Mrs. Fortiano could shed some light on an unfortunate incident."

Conway returned the stare. "She's said all she has to say."

Stonecipher shook his head and pulled a plastic bag from his pocket. "Just one more thing for you two to consider." He held up the bag. "The plastic bottle in this bag contains OxyContin. It came from Mrs. Wade's bathroom medicine cabinet."

Conway shrugged. "So, Mrs. Wade was taking drugs."

Stonecipher nodded. "It appears that way. She told her husband it was Prozac."

Again, Conway shrugged. "Yeah. Isn't that what a druggie would do?"

Stonecipher considered the bottle as if he were Hamlet contemplating a skull. "Funny thing is there are two sets of fingerprints on this bottle. One set belongs to Bonnie Wade." He then looked at Bella. "And the other set belongs to you. How's that possible, Mrs. Fortiano?"

Conway scrutinized Stonecipher as the detective turned to him. "Are we going to say anything else, counselor?"

Conway didn't deliberate. "No. Mrs. Fortiano has said all she has to say."

They all stood at the same time.

Stonecipher opened the door and let Bella and her father walk out of the room. As Bella passed, he said, "We'd appreciate you not leaving the area, not going to Costa Rica, the Cayman Islands, or such."

Bella caught her breath. *What the hell else does he know?*

Conway and Bella crossed the parking lot to Conway's car, Conway three steps ahead as if not wanting to be associated with Bella. At the car, he turned to his daughter. "Bella, something smells here, and I don't want anything to do with it. I have a reputation."

"But, Daddy, I didn't—"

"I don't want to know what you did or didn't do. I'll send you the name of an attorney, a criminal attorney—someone who can handle whatever shit is going on."

"But, Daddy—"

"You're on your own, Bella."

* * *

Bella returned to her apartment, angry and annoyed. She poured herself a glass of wine and sat in Danny's chair. She swished the wine around. *Hell, I'm sorry Daddy's upset. Wish I could talk to him, but time will heal the whole thing. He'll come around. He always does. That damned Stonecipher has a pretty good idea what happened, but he can't prove a thing. There were no witnesses, no anything. All I have to do his lay low, keep my mouth shut, and make sure Danny does too.*

CHAPTER SEVENTY-THREE

The B-E team had been invited to the Department of Transportation for a discussion of their proposal. After passing through security, they were met by John Sampson, who introduced himself as a member of the Interstate Highway Upgrade Test Bed Design, Construction, and Implementation Project Government Acquisition Team. They told him they were impressed he could say it all without taking a breath. He smiled and led them to the elevators, which took them to the fourth floor and a conference room where there was a large conference table made of a dark brown metal frame and a surface of beige Formica. Around it sat gray metal straight chairs with gray Naugahyde seats. They were met there by four more members of the acquisition team. Everyone introduced him or herself, and the visitors were offered seats.

One man continued to stand. He introduced himself as Benjamin Moore. "I'm the contracting officer for this project, and unlike my namesake, I don't paint over problems. I'm dead serious about obtaining the best contract I can for the test bed for the highway of the future, or the Super Highway as it's being referred to by industry. Ordinarily, for a proposal, we would not feel a need to meet with potential vendors. However, we have been presented with a large number of very different proposals and have felt a need to discuss them further with several potential contractors. The funding that has been approved for this project contemplated the construction of a road system, twenty miles of highway with required interchanges. We of course visualized software interaction with the moving vehicles. We did not contemplate establishing criteria for the interaction of the software with the entire automobile and truck industry or for establishing standards for such systems in the manner of IEEE. That funding is not currently available, and we are, therefore, uncertain about how to consider your proposal. I'd appreciate your thoughts on this."

The B-E team hesitated. Davies looked at Somers. "Matt, what are your thoughts?"

Somers took a deep breath. "What I might propose is that we modify our proposal so that we deal with only one automobile manufacturer for work on this system—just to prove the concept. That wouldn't require the establishment of standards. That could come in a later contract, once we have proof of concept."

Moore nodded. "In our original thoughts, we conceived some complex interchanges, with associated costs. Except for putting the interface boxes in vehicles, you've virtually returned to the present systems we have for the interstate. As I see it, the funds that we had planned for the interchanges would now go into the roof over your proposed highways, but I think there would still be funds for more."

He looked around.

Charlie raised his hand.

Moore pointed at him.

"Not to be facetious, but have you ever heard of 'end-of-the-year funds.' You find a way to use them. I would suggest if you have funds available, you simply build the highway longer. At eighty miles an hour, you're going to need as much highway as you can get, with several interchanges, in order to prove concepts. It's an area you can build on or cut, but more is better. And I would like to point out that, by the time your IEEE-like standards are enacted, very little of this new highway system will have been built. Further, by the time any significant amount of highway is built, the interface boxes will have become an integral part of vehicles, and interchanges with booths of any kind will have become a thing of the past. Integrated boxes will automatically interface with the highways and charge tolls the way E-ZPass does today. They'll handle the whole thing. In our system, it will handle Wi-Fi and cellular service as well."

Moore sat down, scribbled on a pad of paper, and looked up. "Okay, we'd like you to change your proposal to indicate the interaction with only one vehicle vendor, remove the establishment of interface standards, and permit the construction of various lengths of test facility highway and the number interchanges, justifying why you think more miles and interchanges are advantageous.

"Finally, I'd like to thank you for coming in today. I think what we have done is constructive, but please realize that we are having these meetings with several companies, and we will still make our choice based on what we think is best for the government."

They all stood. Davies shook Moore's hand and thanked him.

As they left the building, Swenson sighed. "Well, we're not dead yet."

CHAPTER SEVENTY-FOUR

The B-E team made changes to their proposal and resubmitted. Then they sat around and waited, although they did make tentative contacts with Ford and General Motors.

Charlie visited the other members of the team, sharing coffee and bagels. It was the beginning of networking. He wished someone would put him in Fortiano's old office, but no one was interested. They were all biding their time.

Charlie thought about volunteering to work on another proposal. He wished that he wasn't still in the learning process.

Finally, the word came.

They had won! So had Northrop Grumman. This was big time. Northrop Grumman had enormous resources. Everyone at B-E cringed. Northrop Grumman probably had stuff sitting on shelves they could throw at the project with little up-cost. No one knew what Northrop Grumman had proposed. The team hoped that B-E's proposal was unique enough and competitive.

They decided to live for the moment and headed for the bar. Charlie sat next to Swenson.

"What do we do now?"

Swenson looked at him. "You eager beaver. Can't you wait until tomorrow?"

"Just curious. I haven't done this before."

"Okay. Our subs will provide us cost inputs. We'll have to put together costs for the software, the design and manufacture of the interface box, and the construction of the software system. We'll also provide the system engineering, make everything come together, and write the specs. All these government guys want B and C specifications—just like they were the Department of Defense. We have experience in that, but we'll probably fight with the subs about who should be writing what. We'll come up with all the labor we need by grade and throw in lots of travel and maybe some relocation. We'll write up sheets for each task, justifying the man-hours needed. A lot of it is seat-of-the-pants—based on experience. The subs will provide the same information. Our contracting guys will plug it all into a software package that incorporates overhead and spits out reams of money data that we'll add to the proposal. Whatever the bottom line turns out to be will probably determine who gets the contract. Government guys don't really like having to justify something that's not the low bid. Subjects them to too much criticism, so we'll try to stay as low as possible without shooting ourselves in the feet."

"But it seems like there are things we don't know much about. How are we going to know how much labor to apply for them? For example, how do we know how many people will be required to write the software?"

Swenson shouted across the table at Byrnes. "Hey, Bev, Hendricks wants to know how you're going to determine how many people you need to write the software."

Byrnes laughed. "I'll do it scientifically. We'll talk to the automobile people and see how many lines of code they wrote for their cars and maybe talk to the E-ZPass people and the cell phone people, extrapolate their numbers, look at what we want to do that all the obtained information doesn't cover, add some more lines of code, and sum it all up. Then I'll spin three times in my chair, and come up with a number. It's called experience, and I'm as good at it as anyone."

Swenson looked at Charlie. "Does that answer your question?"

CHAPTER SEVENTY-FIVE

Four months had passed since Danny had been assigned back to his old project. He knew little of what was happening on the Super Highway proposal and pretended he didn't care. The humiliation of being thrown off that project still infuriated him. What was worse, he felt like he was on the back burner in his old project. Wade's replacement was a West Coast guy named Ted Whittaker who had brought in some of his own guys. "Big Ted" was six foot four and probably weighed 250 pounds. Danny was having a hard time getting to know him.

Bella sat quietly next to him as they drove to the Bedford-Ewings annual picnic. She wasn't anxious to see any of the Super Highway people, especially Sid Davies and Charlie Hendricks. It never occurred to her that she had sabotaged herself. She blamed it all on her husband's old nemesis.

For four months, Bella had been quiet. She had stayed away from all the Washington social events. She had mostly stayed in her apartment. Sometimes, in February, she was convinced, when she did go out, that she was being watched by police detectives. She had to restrain herself from giving them the bird. By March, she had begun to feel that she was no longer being watched and had become convinced that Stonecipher and company had found better things to do. She was glad that Wade wasn't around to push the detectives. Still, she had stayed quiet. It had gotten on her nerves, but she had played it safe. The worst part had been staying away from the drugs, but she had always been able to get them when she had to. She knew she was lucky that way. In late April, she had finally made contact with her old sources, but she bought only a little at a time. She knew the police thought she was a distributor. She had played it safe.

When they arrived at the picnic site, they found that cars were being parked in a large field. Danny ignored the men directing the parking and parked at the end of the field away from the other cars. Bella complained, "Why are you parking here? I'll have to walk forever in these heels."

Danny tried to ignore her. "Hell, whoever heard of wearing heels to a picnic? It might rain later, and I don't want those jalopies splashing mud on my clean car."

Bella threw up her hands. "Fuck that. Drive me over near the picnic and let me out. Then you can park in China for all I care. Besides, they're low heels. I'll be fine on decent ground."

Danny growled, "Shit, all right. I'll take you over."

He again ignored the parking attendants and drove Bella up near the picnic activities. She didn't get out immediately but instead carefully observed the crowd until she located Sid Davies a little behind them. "Pull up fifty feet. I don't want to be near those guys."

Danny grimaced and pulled forward.

Bella got out of the car. "I'll be over where they have the beer kegs."

"But you don't like beer."

Bella glared back through the open car door. "To get through this picnic, I may drink the whole keg."

Danny watched her walk away in her tight white slacks and striped T-shirt. He shook his head. *Shit, she's never going to be all mine.*

He drove quickly and parked, got out, and jogged back to the beer stand. Bella was holding a large, red plastic cup of beer. Seeing Danny, she complained, "They don't even have decent glass mugs."

Danny looked at her in annoyance. "Shit, Bella, it's a picnic."

She whirled toward him. "I don't go to picnics."

"Well, you're at one. It's part of my job. I need to be seen as being interested."

Bella frowned and looked around. "Okay, let's make the best of it. Where's your group?"

Danny studied the crowd. "They're over there. See the big guy. That's my boss, Ted Whittaker."

Bella looked at the man. "That's the guy you call Big Ted?"

"Yeah, that's him."

Bella appraised the man. *Not bad-looking for a fifty-year-old. A little heavy. Bearlike.* Without turning her head, she started walking toward the man with Danny trailing behind. As they walked, Bella proclaimed, "I think it's about time that 'Big Ted' got to know Bella Fortiano."